A House in Pondicherry

LEE LANGLEY

A House in Pondicherry

HEINEMANN : LONDON

'The Sunlight on the Garden' from the
Collected Poems of Louis MacNeice 1925–1948
is reproduced with the kind permission of
Faber and Faber Ltd.

First published in Great Britain 1995
by William Heinemann Ltd
an imprint of Reed International Books Ltd
Michelin House, 81 Fulham Road, London SW3 6RB
and Auckland, Melbourne, Singapore and Toronto

Reprinted 1995

A CIP catalogue record for this title
is available from the British Library
ISBN 0 434 00084 1

Typeset by Deltatype Ltd, Ellesmere Port, Wirral
Printed and bound
by Mackays of Chatham plc

For Harvey Mitchell

PART ONE

Chapter 1

The Grand Hotel de France, Pondicherry, does not appear in *Fodor*. Nor in the *Rough Guide*. The *India Handbook* has never mentioned it. The Hotel de France fails the guidebook test in several categories. Hot water is not always to be had; the service could be described as eccentric. No air-conditioning. No telephone.

The house on the corner of the rue Laval has hosted philosophers and witnessed diplomatic intrigue. It does not, alas, these days command the clientele it once did. Grand no longer, it retains a certain style, but its future is uncertain. The word 'Hotel' itself could be open to question. However, 'de France' it undoubtedly is. The small library for the use of guests contains volumes by the Goncourts, Victor Hugo, Stendhal, Flaubert. The twentieth century is sparsely represented – indeed represented by only one work, complete in its eight parts. For the owner of the Hotel de France, as for the author of *A La Recherche*, the present is less interesting than the past.

Alipore 1909

The Indian in the cage is half-hidden by armed guards. At the back of the courtroom a child about six years old tries to catch a glimpse of him but she is too small to see over the heads of the people in front. She shifts in her seat, her muslin frock catching on a splinter of polished wood. Finally she tucks her thin-soled shoes under her and stands up on the seat, unnoticed by her mother. She stares across the courtroom at the prisoner, the man she has heard described as 'notorious', 'dangerous'. She is so small that even when standing on the seat she is not much above the other observers.

Thin, bearded, dressed in white, hair falling in curls to his shoulders, the young man sits inside his cage, guarded by armed men. Why does he need to be so closely watched? she wonders. He is as securely locked up as her singing bird at home.

'What did he do?' she had whispered to her mother earlier. 'Did he kill a great many people?'

'None, so far as we know.'

'Then why is he locked up?'

'Ssh. Oriane – please!'

Even though they whisper, they are speaking French – regarded here in British-run Bengal as a foreign tongue – which may seem discourteous.

Sunlight slants through a gap in one of the blinds, throwing a narrow beam of light across the room. Dust swirls lazily, specks of gold trapped in the beam; streaming towards the source, vanishing, drawn back to the sunlight like a golden nebula sucked into a blazing furnace.

Overhead the big fan creaks to and fro, pulled by a man squatting beside the doors.

Voices drone on: evidence is offered, testimony heard, witnesses called . . . The trial has lasted six months, there have been two hundred witnesses, four thousand pieces of evidence . . . words are swallowed up in echoes, muffled by coughs, blurred by the noise from the creaking fan. Heat fills the room, pressing against the walls, squeezing air from lungs. Officials ignore it, ignore the perspiration trickling

4

between skin and clothing. The prisoner seems unaware of the temperature.

The girl continues to watch him. Inside the iron cage he sits very still, eyes closed, back straight. Then, surprising her, he opens his eyes and looks across the room, over the heads of the other people, straight at the child. She stares back, and as she watches, the bars of the cage confining him begin to fade. Like threads of smoke, they melt into the air. Now the cage is gone, the man is free, seated like an emperor. No one else seems aware of what has happened. He smiles at her, the dark eyes – darker than his skin – gleaming, and unexpectedly, he pulls a comic face. Her mouth opens in delight and she smiles back, glad the man is free. She feels his eyes on her face, burning like sunlight, and she rises up and floats towards him over the heads of the people, borne on the bright river of his gaze.

She laughs aloud.

Her mother is not pleased: they are here unofficially, privileged visitors, granted admission as a favour and should behave accordingly ('*avec discrétion*'), but in fact the trial is proving very dull and perhaps it is time to leave. Madame de l'Esprit leads the child out, whispering apologies to left and right.

In the courtroom, inside the iron cage, the young man closes his eyes, shutting out the voices, the banging of doors, the noise of horses and wheels from the street. The defence lawyer is inspired to a flight of eloquence, hurled almost tearfully at the somnolent jury: 'Long after he is dead and gone his words will be echoed and re-echoed not only in India but across distant seas and lands. I say that this man is not only standing before the bar of this court but the bar of the High Court of history!'

Judge Beachcroft, who had been surprised to recognise in the prisoner a fellow graduate of King's College, recalls now that this chap Ghose had picked up a Latin prize as well as the prize for Greek verse Beachcroft himself had expected to win. No hard feelings, but even then the chap had been too clever by half, a bit of a firebrand, speeches, pamphlets, that sort of thing. Short of cash too, he rather fancied: the fellow had remarked once that he was living on bread and butter, cups of tea and 'penny Saveloys' – whatever they might be. A fly buzzed loudly, close to the judge's ear. He brought his mind back to the matter in hand.

A routine trial in 1909 in an insignificant Indian town is not the stuff of martyrdom. For lack of evidence, the man in the cage is released. British justice does not include imprisonment without trial. And if the trial fails to prove guilt, well on this occasion at least he must go free. But the word goes out: keep an eye on the chap, up to no good, troublemaker. Pick him up next time he tries something.

Certain actions taken, the small movements of history shift another notch.

Aurobindo Ghose had been named Akroyd by his Anglophile doctor father, and supplied with an English governess to distance him from his Indian roots – 'None of that steamy mysticism,' the doctor ordered. England, St Paul's and Cambridge, were expected to complete the immunisation. Instead, the process was reversed – the student, infected with nationalism, renamed himself, went home, got into trouble . . .

Now Aurobindo needs somewhere he will be safe. The subcontinent has proved surprisingly deficient in hiding places for a wanted man, and the British are thorough in tracking down those they wish to find. He studies the approaching shore-line: palm trees, low-lying houses, a lighthouse. A small town, adequate for what he imagines will be a short stay.

The s.s *Dupleix* heaves in the swell and clumsily comes to rest alongside the pier. He pauses politely to let a family go fiirst: stiff-backed father, mother, cool beneath her parasol, and a small girl who turns to peep at him, hiding behind her mother's sleeve, her blue eyes bright with curiosity. He smiles at her abstractedly and moves off. The child stares after him. Though some time has passed, she remembers the man; she is pleased, and not at all astonished, to see him. Escaped from his cage, he has come here, from Calcutta to Pondi. She notes that he looks happier. Later, when she frees her singing bird, her mother is upset and uncomprehending: *la petite* talks nonsense, babbling of iron cages and men, of freedom and happiness. This must be some native affair she has heard about. She must restrict Oriane's conversations with the servants in the future.

The new arrival is greeted warmly by those who await him in this quiet corner of the Coromandel coast. They lead him from the quayside through the town, point out the Customs House – *Douanes*; the police headquarters in the rue de la Caserne. The policemen wear red képis. The tricolor flutters in the breeze. 'The British cannot touch you here,' he is assured: Pondicherry is, of course, French territory.

There had been many versions of Pondicherry, razed, rebuilt, each model bigger, grander than its predecessors. By the time the fugitive – freed provisionally by the British, but watched, followed, spied on – stepped ashore and looked about him, it was a fine, gleaming town with an imposing Promenade that curved the length of the bay, straight streets lined with trees, houses spilling bougainvillaea down their white walls, gardens filled with flowers and shady fragrance.

Or rather, the European part of the town was all these things. Through the middle ran the canal, dividing the planned from the sprawling, the neat from the messy, black from white. Pondicherry was French territory in name and law from the coast to the limit of what had once been its fortifications. In fact, France ran from the surf-sprayed

Promenade to the east bank of the canal. At the west bank, India began.

Grand Hotel de France, Pondicherry
le 1er Février 1992

Madame/Monsieur,
    Nous avons le plaisir de vous confirmer la réservation suivante . . .

Communicating with the hotel was an unwieldy business, letters winging their way between Europe and south India. Sometimes visitors complained about the difficulty of making bookings, the eccentricity of a hotel without a telephone. *La patronne* was unperturbed. 'We have few rooms. People write to me, I reserve one. Why a telephone?'

'It would help the guests –'

The guests? Since when did the *guests* dictate matters? Oriane was professional enough to remain silent, but any guest in range at that moment, catching the full force of her gaze, the blue gleam dangerous as broken glass, tended to remember a temple that needed to be visited without delay.

The frail, insubstantial figure floated about the hotel like a dried leaf, held to the ground, it seemed, by the stick she used as support and signal. Grown fierce with the years, she bullied her clients and her servants impartially. She was, after all, nearly ninety, which gave her certain rights.

When a guest, hearing her name, exclaimed, 'Oriane! How beautiful!' she said graciously, 'Like Proust's *duchesse*, you know.' Adding, 'But of course you do not. People can't read Proust any more.'

French in name, the hotel was in reality a hybrid: there was a pervasive smell of garlic about the place, but also of drains. There were mosquito nets hanging bundled above the beds, but there was music from an unseen record player blasting out Debussy, and Madame could be sharp with anyone

8

tactless enough to approach her while the music was playing. She was at her worst with visitors from England.

'Why are you here?' she demanded now of one new arrival, her small, shrivelled face grim with disapproval. 'Why are you not in Rajasthan, so picturesque, all those perfectly dreadful forts and kitsch palaces, bits of glass on the ceiling. And elephants. And brass bowls all over the place, that sort of thing. Isn't that what you people like? Nostalgia for the British Raj?'

Servants scurried between kitchen and dining room, moving fast to avoid the lash of her tongue –'Where is the *bouillabaisse*? Is it to be consumed today or next week? What are those devils in the kitchen up to?' She waved her stick, maintaining a precarious balance.

A movement in the drive outside the verandah attracted her attention and she tapped her way to the top of the steps. Two young backpackers, approaching from the gates, had paused at the foot of the steps. Oriane observed them stonily: the dusty sandals, the grubby T-shirts, the Union Jack stitched to the canvas flap of one rucksack . . . The old eyes narrowed.

'*Que désirez-vous?*' She used the French as a weapon, to scare them off, a shot across the bows to discourage would-be boarders.

The girl smiled up at her. 'We're looking for a room –'

Oriane cut in crisply, 'We have no rooms, *mademoiselle*.'

'Oh.' A pause. A silence, hopeful on one side, implacable on the other. 'We've been on the train since yesterday morning.'

'That is not unusual, if one travels in this country.'

The backpackers exchanged a glance and walked away, back to the gate.

A passing guest had witnessed the exchange: 'Poor things, they must be hungry.' Oriane twitched a contemptuous shoulder.

'This is not an establishment for vagabonds! Dirty fingernails and washing underclothing in the bedroom, I know the type. Putting the bread rolls from the breakfast table in their pocket for eating later.'

'When you're on a tight budget –'

'You have compassion for them, I see. This is not a virtue, it is a weakness.' She added serenely, 'No doubt you have heard the expression, *tout comprendre, c'est tout pardonner.* Well that was all very well for Madame de Staël, I dare say. Personally I have other views: to understand all may *not* be to forgive all – absolutely not. I have my conclusions and I do not see why they should be adjusted in the cause of "understanding". *Voilà tout.'*

The hotel stood where it always had, on the corner of the rue Laval, but the stucco had flaked and discoloured with the years. In the garden, palms and tangled creeper grew from the parched soil and a broken fountain cast its shadow on the ground. The garden survived, after a fashion, with desultory watering by the *mali* before sunrise, its morning smell of wet stone replaced by that of burnt earth as the day wore on. What had once been formal and European had evolved gradually into something else, something lusher, wilder, more – in a word – Indian.

Things were different, once. See it on a February day in 1914, for instance, gleaming white in the sunlight, (*tout confort, calme, silencieux*), le Grand Hotel de France welcomes its guests with a shady garden, the music of a small fountain; Monsieur and Madame de l'Esprit have attempted to bring a touch of metropolitan style to the rue Laval.

Over the thirty years since the hotel was established, the owners have worked assiduously: the *parterre* is immaculate, the (regrettably) oriental shrubs tormented into proper geometric neatness, the gravel freshly combed each morning.

The hotel attracts a discerning clientele. People who can discuss politics with Monsieur, literature with Madame, *la cuisine française* with both – for all are agreed there is nothing to be said for Indian cooking other than the freshness of the spices, and then only those, like garlic and fennel, which can be used with advantage. Lost in talk of Europe, they are unaware of events taking place a few streets away; the unremarked activities of an impoverished young Indian in a tall, sparsely furnished house could have no possible bearing on their lives.

But occasionally the two worlds collide. The young Superintendent of Police came to dinner, full of his encounter with 'this so-called political agitator Aurobindo' the British were so bothered about. The Superintendent was irritated: his men were always concerned to give the British any possible help. They intercepted letters, they watched the house day and night. He began to suspect that it was as well they did, for the British were not above planting incriminating documents so that they might be 'found' later – 'They are convinced he is plotting the downfall of the British Empire. Well, I finally went along to the house and we went through the whole place. No documents, no plans of campaign, but in a bureau drawer I found volumes of Homer. In Greek.'

Monsieur de l'Esprit was astonished. 'Greek? In the bureau of an Indian?'

'He is also translating Corneille into English – an impossible task of course, as I told him, but . . . my dear Hubert, the man is an intellectual. We talked at length and I have to say I was impressed. I told the British to leave him alone. They keep harking back to this bomb affair, this attempt on the life of one of their magistrates. Young hot-heads making bombs in their out-houses, you know the sort of thing. I said to them, this is no bomb-garden trouble-maker. I doubt if he knows what a bomb looks like.'

Oriane, well-trained, remained silent at the table, but her wide-eyed interest was noted by her mother. She wondered once again whether they should consider sending the child to school in France, as some of their friends had done. Just last month the Duvilliers put their rather flighty girl, Marie-Hélène on a ship bound for Rouen in the care of a reliable family. These conversations, these . . . influences, could not be helpful. Madame de l'Esprit offered her guest another helping of *gigot*, and talked of her problems with a new cook.

Dear Marie-Hélène,

I shall see you again after all. I am to be sent away from here, quite disgraced. Mama is packing my clothes and ordering new ones to be made in warmer cloth. She is – they are both – upset. No one will talk to me and meals are taken with only the sound of the knives and forks scraping on plates till I long to scream, to drown out the silence. What have I done that is so terrible?

M. Richard, the writer and his wife, had dined with us. He is a philosopher, here on a visit from Paris, and talks much of 'upheavals' to come in Europe. He seems worried about the Germans and the Belgians. Mama is not much concerned. Mme Richard is an artist. She is very small with sharp eyes and she wore a shawl of the most gorgeous colours. Her name is Mira and she has worked with a Monsieur Rodin, we were told. I do not know M. Rodin's work, but Mama said it is extremely heavy, which seemed to cause Mme Richard some amusement. However, the conversation at table is not what caused the trouble – indeed M. Richard congratulated Mama on having a daughter who – not yet twelve – had already heard of Thoreau. Mama, pleased, smiled, you know the way she does.

M. Richard gave me some of his philosophy pamphlets and promised to explain them on another visit. And we spoke of an Indian poet called Rabindranath Tagore who has won something called the Nobel prize which surprised Mama very much indeed for she said she had not known the Indians had a poet and M. Richard said it had also surprised the Indians who apparently had not known either. After this the conversation moved to politics and I stopped listening.

It was the following day that the incident occurred. Mama and I were walking in the cool of the evening on the Promenade. We were passing the statue of Dupleix when I saw M. Richard approaching in the company of an Indian dressed all in white clothes with long hair hanging to his shoulders. When we came closer I recognised him as the prisoner from the Alipore court-house I once told you about, talking earnestly, with slow gesticulations of his hands, which I saw were beautiful. As we drew level I expected we would stop and speak, but it seemed that Mama intended only to bow and walk on. I was so disappointed by this that *I* stopped and bade them good evening. The Indian smiled at me – I remembered the smile well, and M. Richard introduced us –'Madame de l'Esprit and her daughter Oriane. Monsieur Aurobindo Ghose –'

'But we have seen you before!' I broke in, 'in Alipore!' And turning to Mama I said that this was the man in the cage, she must recall it. And then, to M. Richard I explained that I had the strangest memory of Alipore, that Monsieur Ghose had, somehow, made the bars of his cage disappear so that he was free –

(Not even to Marie-Hélène could Oriane bring herself to describe how she had seen the bars waver and vanish like smoke, and how she had floated, like a paper kite over the heads of the people in the courtroom.)

Mama spoke my name rather loudly, and said that we were late, M. Richard must forgive us. But I felt I must learn more and asked the Indian, 'Is it not true,

monsieur, the bars disappeared? And you were free?'
And he said, in excellent French, 'But of course,
mademoiselle. To be free one must simply think oneself
so. Iron bars cannot contain a truly free man.' He
looked at me very directly and his eyes blazed like
Mama's topaz pendant, and he said that for one so
young I had a remarkably developed consciousness!
Then M. Richard said that Sri Aurobindo is a great
teacher, and we could learn much from him.

(And a curious lightness swept over her. It was as it had
been in the court-house and she felt that without difficulty
she might leave the ground and float.)

'Could I too learn? Could I attend your class?' I
asked. At this Mama made an exclamation without
words, took my shoulder and propelled me forward. I
twisted my head to call goodbye, and saw that M.
Ghose was no longer smiling.

We marched on, going straight home without further
conversation, and that was when the silence and the
plans began. Mama has said only that I am to go 'home'
as she calls it, to her cousin in Rouen. For me the word
has no meaning. This is my home and I am not happy to
think of leaving it. But Mama says it is time I was
properly educated, that the 'influences here are
evidently unsuitable'.

It seems that our encounter on the Promenade has
brought about this decision, but when I question her
and ask if I did wrong to mention the court-house, she
becomes angry and says that the court-house is of no
consequence. Then she addresses Papa and says that I
was a baby at the time and she is astonished I should
recall the occasion. I was not a baby, I was nearly seven,
and I recall it very well.

Monsieur Richard too, has become part of the silence and has not returned to visit us. However he has sent me copies of his philosophical journal, the *Arya*. Some parts are in English as well as French and contain writings by Aurobindo Ghose. I told Mama I would like to learn English but she said, what on earth for? 'Who would you want to talk to, in English? You might as well say you want to learn Tamil!' I have found Rouen on the map of France. I see that the Romans were there – as they were here. It is situated on both banks of a river, the Seine – so it is divided by water, as we are by our canal! It is a port of importance, another resemblance, and suffered a long siege by the English. So did we. And its chief industries are connected with textiles – in particular cotton. So you see we are like twins, Rouen and Pondicherry! You have not kept your promise to write to me, and now there will be no time. I shall be leaving here before long, and we will meet in Rouen. Perhaps after all I shall like it there. Though it seems to have been unlucky for Jeanne d'Arc.

Your friend, Oriane.

But, certain actions taken, as usual, history moved on another notch. After all, there would be time for more letters.

A German submarine attacked Madras with shells. Pondi prepared for the worst.

If the Germans should win this war, would they arrive at the pier, the tricolor be replaced by the Prussian eagle? 'Surely not!' cried Mme de l'Esprit. 'Pondi belongs to us. It always has, it always will.'

There was no submarine attack. Instead, a cyclone tore up trees and palms and the storm waters poured through the streets of the town and rose, topping the verandah steps, to the very floors of the house in the rue Laval, which stood like an island as the waves surged past.

No German shells, then, but people and houses were swept away by the cyclone, and far away in Europe, generals gave orders and in trenches and on poppy fields, men in mud-caked boots were heard to groan in agony, in the gaining or the losing of a few square miles of soil.

The Great War was over, the division of Europe engaged the inmates of the hotel. The position of France was of particular interest. While the parents chatted animatedly on the verandah, treating their clients like house-guests, the daughter could be seen in a cool *coin* of the garden with her sketch block, or at her window, reading; a slender, dark-haired figure, head bowed to book, eyes lowered, demure. Oriane had her thoughts and dreams, but prudently she kept these to herself.

Only once did she enter into the general conversation, on a day when the mayor let fall that the British were demanding the extradition of an Indian resident of the town. 'What has he done?' she enquired, the dark eyes following her embroidery needle and thread. The mayor shrugged impatiently. As far as he could tell the man had lived quietly in Pondicherry, more concerned with philosophy and poetry, it seemed, than anything more threatening. But the British were pressing and it would probably be simpler –

'But Monsieur!' Oriane sounded surprised, even shocked, 'the protection of the French flag cannot be denied to a man who is within our territory. Surely?'

The mayor looked uncomfortable. The girl was right. On the other hand, the British ran India, so strictly speaking –

'Oriane,' Madame de l'Esprit said briskly, 'you look quite brown, you must have been out in the sun. Perhaps you should go and rest for a little while.'

The message was coded but clear: Oriane had overstepped the mark again. When would she learn that questions were not socially acceptable?

Later, when the Mayor was undressing for bed, he recounted the amusing incident of the young de l'Esprit girl and the extradition request. His wife did not share his amusement, and wondered aloud that he should be dictated to by foreigners.

In his nightshirt, the mayor squared his shoulders. He nodded to his reflection in the cheval glass: his wife was right. After all, the French flag ... He began to compose a stiff reply to the English.

Chapter 2

The young ladies at the Lycée were well prepared for their first ball. They were familiar with all the appropriate dances, and had been given informal advice on the newer, more doubtful arrivals from Europe. The lessons had been thorough, though the dancing master smelled of garlic and lavender water, and Oriane disliked his fixed smile and pale, spongy hands. She did not enjoy the circuits of the school hall that had to be endured in his perspiring but respectful arms as the pianist went through the sheet music.

She preferred the less predictable experience of pairing off with another girl to practise the steps, taking first the part of the female partner, then of the male. In that way she learned the difference between the passive, doll-like role of the female who did nothing until urged to it by her partner, and the male who controlled the dance. It was comforting to know that nothing more than docility would be required of her.

On the day of the ball Oriane was placed in the hands of a string of women: a maid who prepared her bath, another who laid out her clothes, the *coiffeuse* who smoothed and pinned and prinked the shining black hair into a modish shape. She was eased into her ankle-skimming dress of blue and ivory voile and given a dusting of white powder to cool the flush of her cheeks.

'Everything must be perfect!' declared Madame de l'Esprit. 'These matters cannot be left to chance.'

Flanked by her parents she walked up the steps of the Governor's house. Bats as big as crows flittered and swooped among the trees and the moonlight was so bright that her mother's emerald necklace shone bright green. From within she heard the ominous sound of the orchestra. Her feet felt enormous, her hands were damp. Oriane caught a mental whiff of lavender water and garlic and sensed the encircling arms of the dancing master. It was unlikely she would enjoy this evening.

She glanced about the ballroom with its mixture of military uniforms and *tenues de soirée*, the white arms of women curled sinuous as serpents round the dark sleeves of their partners. Monsieur de l'Esprit watched his daughter compassionately. She looked calm, even a little bored, as she stood without awkwardness by her mother's side, watching the dancers, her pale face composed. But he knew from the occasional sideways flicker of the dark blue eyes that she was nervous.

Madame de l'Esprit had been hoping that one of the officers would present himself, but it was a visitor to the town who was led over to the ladies and introduced to Oriane.

Robert St Denis was not graceful; his evening clothes had a haphazard look to them, as though thrown on while he attended to something more important, and his hair was rumpled, but Oriane found him immediately attractive.

'You have a most unusual flower in your hair, mademoiselle.'

She smiled, pleased. The idea of winding the blue columbines in her chignon had been hers. The plant had been discovered and named (*Aqueligia Espiritia*) by her great-grandfather, she told him, so it was, in a way, a family heirloom. She found his interest was genuine, no mere conversational gambit: Robert St Denis was shortly to embark on a search for unusual flora in the far north.

Over his shoulder she caught sight of her mother's face. 'I think we had better dance, monsieur, or Mama will feel I need to be rescued.'

Monsieur St Denis looked stricken.

'Mademoiselle, I have a confession: I have never danced. This is the first ball I have had the misfortune to attend.' She looked at him aghast, about to confess in turn. Then she straightened her spine with an almost military authority. She had no wish to be passed on to some officer with pink lips and a moustache; Monsieur St Denis suited her very well. Dancing, she said, was not difficult, simply a way of moving in time to the music and not bumping into the other couples. She took his hand, in such a way that it looked as though he had taken hers. She indicated that he should place his other hand in the small of her back. The waltz was quite simple, she would count it for him and indicate, with pressure on his hand or shoulder, which foot to step off on, and which way to turn.

He was surprised, then pleased. 'Lead on, you are the dancing master.'

She halted, struck by an awful thought: 'You must tell me at once! Does my breath smell of garlic?'

From such a poised young woman the question seemed bizarre, shockingly unexpected, but then he saw how anxiously she waited, tremulous, how young she was, barely more than a child. 'No,' he said, 'your breath is cinnamon and cloves and possibly vanilla –'

'Cardamom pod,' she corrected him, 'I chewed one before we came out. Let's begin. And ... ONE two three, ONE two three, ONE,' she murmured below his ear, as they set off, M. St Denis doggedly walking her round the dance floor, apologising when he trod on her toes.

He learned quickly and even followed her into an occasional twirl. They beamed at each other in triumph.

He told her about his travels, about flowers that consumed each other, and ingested visiting insects; about the biggest lily in the world, its diameter as long as a man's arm, that grew on the roots of wild vines in the jungles of Sumatra.

'In the Himalayas there is a moon-flower that blooms once every three years for just one night, between sunset and dawn.'

Madame de l'Esprit saw that they had stopped dancing, stuck like rocks on the dance floor as others eddied past them. This young man seemed somewhat unsatisfactory as a dancing partner. Perhaps, she wondered aloud, Oriane should be tactfully drawn away? Her first ball, after all –

Monsieur de l'Esprit saw the way his daughter was listening to the stocky young man, her eyes intent, her cheeks glowing through the powder. He suggested a glass of champagne to his wife and complimented her on her new gown. 'Oriane,' he added, 'will do what she wants.'

'I trust *not*!' her mother said anxiously. She frowned. 'I see her white satin shoes are quite ruined already.'

Robert St Denis was invited to the house on the corner of the rue Laval and was interested in the brilliant blue flowers that grew round the walls of the terrace. Over apéritifs he told Madame de l'Esprit that, like Louis de Bougainville, the navigator who had become one of Napoleon's senators, he wanted to make discoveries that would increase the glory of France. She was moderately gratified when he pointed out that she herself was proof Monsieur de Bougainville had not travelled in vain; the drifts of scarlet and purple bougainvil-laea that hung over the garden walls were his monument.

Flowers were all very well, Madame de l'Esprit thought, but there were other monuments that concerned her more: 'This house has been the scene of great events, monsieur . . .'

Oriane was embarrassed, impatient. The future, not the past, was the key she reached for, but Madame was not to be denied her vicarious glories. 'Bonaparte might have come to the rue Laval, had certain events gone differently –'

Robert St Denis expressed surprise, curiosity.

'Oh yes, there were plans. Captain de l'Esprit, my husband's grandfather – an artist of some note – was close to the Emperor –'

'Didn't you want me to show Monsieur St Denis the garden, Mama?' Oriane asked, standing up and moving towards the door. Given another minute, her mother would be showing the poor man the family portraits.

He had brought Oriane a book on the flora of the Orient, recently published in Paris, with his name on the cover. They walked in the rose garden and he said he would be leaving soon, on another exploration of the far north.

'Perhaps you will find the moon-flower.'

He saw how she quickened to the description of waterfalls and rainforests, of tiny flowers that bloomed in snow, of creepers that threw out threads fine as spiders' webs which thickened into lianas as strong as hempen rope and brought down trees with their weight.

There was an eagerness to learn, a fire about her that fed on knowledge; she showed him a watercolour she had done of two jungle flowers entwined that he found disconcertingly anthropomorphic. 'Imaginative,' he acknowledged, 'but botanically inaccurate.'

If she had been less delicately built, the hands like silk, skin that must be shielded from the burning sun by parasol or broad-brimmed hat, if she had been a little older, less protected, he might have risked a declaration, but his life was one of hazard and physical punishment, he could take no chances of being held back by questions of comfort or possible danger. And after all, they had met only a few times, it was a congenial acquaintanceship, no more. Or so he convinced himself.

When the expedition was ready he came to say goodbye and she said that perhaps if he found a great many new species he might name a flower after her.

There was a postcard from a town in the foothills of the Himalayas, then nothing more. Oriane put his book among the others on her shelf and went back to her studies of the philosophy pamphlets Monsieur Richard had sent her. When her mother received an invitation to another ball, she was disappointed to learn that Oriane had hurt her ankle and felt unable to attend.

'Well,' Madame de l'Esprit said, making the best of it, 'there will be other balls.' And other men, she added silently.

At the time of the full moon in the festival month of Masi, people congregate on the sea-shore, flowing from the streets and boulevards of the town, and from the villages nearby. Ready by sunrise, they wear their best clothes, saris of crimson and purple and saffron edged with glittering threads. They wear gold or silver nose studs, necklets, red and green glass bangles. Among them walks a young woman in a muslin dress. She shields her face from the sun – and from inquisitive eyes – with a parasol, but there is small risk of her being seen by anyone who matters: among the cheerful crowd surging down to the shore she is the only European. Her parents would be shocked, but her parents think she is at a lecture – 'Oriane attends many lectures,' Madame de l'Esprit tells a guest with some pride, 'she is a truly French young woman, interested in matters of the mind.'

In earlier days, Oriane has heard from the servants, on the rooftop terraces of the nobles in the north, there was dancing on the night of the full moon, and music. In the velvet darkness, the moonlight glinting on their jewels, bleaching their gossamer veils, the women had danced. Supple wrists and outspread fingers caught the light streaming from the sky, the music of their anklet bells tinkled, the sound as silvery as moonlight. Oriane had never seen them dancing, all she knew were the stories, but on the night of the full moon sometimes she thought she heard the anklet bells and in the garden she twirled in her silken dress and saw the way the fountain turned to liquid silver.

At the sea-shore, a white muslin dress is sprayed by the surf, clinging to the slender body. The dark blue eyes watch as the brightly painted Deities are taken from their chariots and given their ritual bath. Bizarre. Alien. The Catholic Brothers would recoil in horror. But she is curious, inter-ested to examine these strange phenomena. Is it not possible that great truths may be scattered more widely than the priests attest? She herself is not drawn to the worship being celebrated on the sea-shore, but neither is she afraid of it. Sometimes, when they are out together, riding through the town in carriage or rickshaw, Mme de l'Esprit catches her daughter gazing openly at some unfortunate manifestation of native vulgarity. 'Oriane!' she exclaims reprovingly, fanning herself, fanning them both, as though the vigorous action will disperse unwelcome influences. Pondicherry is a pleasant place to live; the hotel is a success, but there are still times when she wishes Oriane had been sent home to be educated in the proper manner . . .

The rickshaw turned into the rue Laval and Madame de l'Esprit snapped shut her fan. Yes, a pity. Plans had been made, after that unfortunate business with the political agitator; Oriane's steamer ticket had been purchased, but regrettably, The War had upset everything. Still, no great harm done – the child had been watched more closely. There had been no further unsavoury encounters. Nevertheless, she sometimes feared that at seventeen the girl had been exposed to more Life than could strictly be regarded as necessary. She noticed that her daughter's attention had been caught by a gaudy roadside shrine, its crudely carved figures flaunting themselves in unnatural and to her mind, physically impossible poses. In Rouen there would have been none of that: the practice of religion confined within the walls of church and cathedral where it belonged. One did not wish it thrust in one's face.

'Oriane!' she said sharply.

Chapter 3

Madame de l'Esprit invited suitable young men to the hotel, to make them feel at home in a foreign land, to hear news from France and to introduce them to her daughter. Oriane had no objection to young men, and if their appearance justified it, she would embark on the meeting with an open mind. The young men, encouraged by her welcoming smile, intrigued by the contrast between her confident white bosom and the almost childish lack of coquetry in her social manner, faltered when they encountered her unexpectedly sharp dark-blue gaze. They hesitated. The conversation trailed off. Disconcerted, they fell silent.

At this point her mother generally suggested her daughter should show their visitor the garden, but Oriane would take the opportunity to intersperse horticulture with literature: what were people reading these days, in Paris? What was his view of Monsieur Claudel? Or philosophy: had the visitor met any of the new young thinkers one heard so much about? Or science: was it true that Herr Einstein could bend a beam of light? Earnest questions about their opinions on the life of the mind, the uncertainty of what people called truth, the frontiers of possibility, scared off all but the most tenacious. The visits were not often repeated.

Now and then the young man might persevere, but Oriane's swiftly surfacing boredom, her inability to interest herself in the *salon* conversation of Pondi society, led to the invariable conclusion: Oriane was not a social success. Madame de l'Esprit despaired of the girl: what did she want? What could be more appealing than the comfortable certitude of an appropriate marriage? And the girl was really quite presentable. If only she would refrain from questions . . .

For her twenty-first birthday Oriane had requested a sea trip on a fishing boat 'to look at dolphins'. Her parents could see no charm in an uncomfortable journey that would result, at best, in a glimpse of a number of large fish. This was just another consequence of their daughter's unfortunate addiction to books. However, when alternatives (moonlight picnic, fancy-dress ball, chamber recital . . .) were politely rejected, they gave in and the trip was organised. As her father wryly observed, not for the first or last time, 'Oriane will do what she wants.'

The boat lay alongside the pier, rising and falling gently in the swell, and the fisherman in charge helped the European passengers on board, improvising a sort of gangplank from boards and fishing nets. The town still lay wrapped in pre-dawn gloom, but the first tip of sun appeared on the horizon as the little boat headed out. The Europeans were well wrapped up in shawls, scarves and warm jackets against the chill. It was misty, the sky colourless, the sea pewter, choppy, broken up into little sharp-edged waves. Oriane looked back: in the brightening, but still soft light the Pondi shoreline lay pink and graceful, the houses shimmering like a mirage above the pale sand. She stood in the bow of the boat, her hair blowing in the wind, her eyes scanning the surface. Would there be dolphins?

As they were leaving the bay, the helmsman steered them close to a dirty yellow buoy and slowed the boat. One of the crew leaned out to pluck at a string tied to the buoy. At the end of the string there was a bottle, inside which a tiny fish hung, suspended, in the sea water. The minute creature could probably have got out of the bottle while it lay in the water, but the fish did not know – as yet – that it was imprisoned. It swam tranquilly in its bottle, feeling secure, safe from predators. But as it grew larger it would become increasingly aware of the invisible walls that sealed it off from the larger world. What then? Oriane wondered. Would it fret, languish, hurl itself ineffectually against those glassy constraining walls? What did fish do? Did they think? Suffer? Hope? The crew laughed, amused by the spectacle of the fish in the bottle, knowing the end of the story – this was a familiar game. The fish would outgrow its home, one day it would find itself unable to breathe. The fish would die. Oriane felt suddenly desolate. She seized the bottle and leaning over the side she cracked it against an iron rivet. It broke in two and a fleeting waterfall carried the small fish smoothly into the ocean. She handed the broken bottle to one of the crew. 'Will there be dolphins?' she asked him, but the man spoke no French and merely smiled back at her, showing blackened teeth.

They stayed at sea for five hours, but no dolphins were sighted, and in the end Madame de l'Esprit, feeling hot and seasick, announced that she for one proposed they return home for lunch. It was a muted birthday celebration.

Later that evening Monsieur de l'Esprit saw Oriane by the fountain, trailing her fingers in the water, apparently lost in thought. She looked sad and he went out to her, troubled.

'I'm sorry there were no dolphins for your birthday.'

'Oh, the dolphins weren't important, really, Papa.'

As so often when he was in her company he felt a sense of helplessness, an inability to reach her, as though impeded by an invisible membrane. He found parental pronouncements hampered his normal eloquence.

'Is there anything I can do, Oriane? Rather – what is it that you want?'

28

'I would like to be of *use* in some way – I don't mean good works, that is something we all do to the best of our ability, visit the sick, feed the starving –'

Her face was vivid; she stretched her neck like a bird, restless. 'I want to change the world. Be changed.'

Amused, saddened, touched by her innocence, he said, 'I cannot promise you the first. The second I can guarantee.' And added, silently, 'But not too soon, I hope.'

Her pearl-tipped fingers gleamed in the spray of the fountain and drops of water caught the light, sparkling. Liquid jewels shimmered on her hands.

'Oriane will do what she wants,' her father was fond of saying. But not always. The desire for a life devoted to a search for knowledge clashed repeatedly with the life of a dutiful daughter. Oriane could be ingenious, she had her ways. But to abandon her world for something unknown that lay behind a pale grey wall was to step into the void – and besides, an outsider, a representative of the colonial powers, she might not even be welcome. Risk and fear of failure, too, were part of the equation.

She was tempted, suddenly breathless, to speak to her father; the moment trembled on the verge of deeper things. But her mother hurried out with an unexpected birthday present: a telegram from Paris, informing Mademoiselle de l'Esprit that a new variety of lily had been named after her – *Lilium Oriane*. Her mother was at first suspicious, then puzzled: the name St Denis meant nothing to her – there had, after all, been so many visitors to the hotel. Later a small crate arrived containing bulbs and instructions for planting. The stem-rooting bulbs should be planted fairly deeply and in partial shade, in well-drained soil. The flowers were fragrant.

Madame de l'Esprit gave instructions to the *mali* and the lilies were planted at the far end of the garden. They grew fast, to a height of nearly a metre, and at dusk, from the house, they looked like a far-off group of slender girls clustered together, their pale faces turned towards the light. Their scent was delicate and their colouring unusual for a lily – ivory with a faint blue stripe. Oriane never really liked them.

Occasionally, when she walked by the sea, pausing at the formidable statue of Dupleix, she caught sight of the interesting Indian friend of Monsieur Richard, these days (as she wrote to Marie-Hélène, her only confidante), 'surrounded by disciples, for Mr Ghose now has a sort of school, a circle for study and self-improvement called an Ashram. We do not speak. It is unlikely that he recognises me or recalls our long-ago encounter.'

Once or twice she followed the group, keeping her distance, and stood outside the house where he lived and taught, imagining herself a pupil, a disciple, dedicated to a life of contemplation, a search for the ultimate truth.

But one day, Marie-Hélène, I saw that Mme Richard had returned. Surely she would remember me? So I called out to her by name. She hesitated, seemed about to walk on until I called out again, coming closer. 'We met a few years ago, you dined at our house – the rue Laval,' and she nodded. Then I asked if M. Paul was with her, and Mme Richard looked exceedingly fierce and said that she was alone and I must forgive her, she was extremely busy, and she went into the Ashram and closed the gate.

It seems that I am not to be a disciple. And yet there is nothing else that interests me. Life stretches ahead very long and empty. Perhaps after all, I shall marry one of these young men and return to France (curious, this 'returning' to a place I have never seen). But at least I should see you, dear Marie-Hélène, and admire the new baby – the next one will surely have been born by then, this time a girl as you hope. How lucky you are, to be happy in your fate!

There is a recital this evening at the Hotel de Ville: Rameau and Couperin. It will be quite enjoyable, the music at least, the conversation I have no great hopes of. Meanwhile I have to help my father with the hotel accounts. Mama says the servants cheat one continually, it is in their culture, and they must be watched. As she appears to know nothing of their culture I wonder that she speaks with such confidence. At any rate, father is teaching me the system of accounting he employs.

Write to me and give me news of your life, and also of the wider world that seems so far away from this little corner of mine. Papa says that Major Dreyfus has been awarded the Légion d'Honneur. The Affair was over when I was born, but Papa has told me about it. He, it seems, was always on the side of Dreyfus. I have never met a Jew. Have you? I would like to, for I am told they are all intellectuals. (Mama says they are all money-lenders, but how can this be? Major Dreyfus is not a money-lender. And Marcel Proust is, I believe, at least partly Jewish.) Has André Gide published a new volume? I so enjoyed the last one you sent me.

And in this way seven years passed slowly and painlessly. The recitals changed their style, modern composers – Ravel and Debussy – were introduced, though not always enjoyed. Oriane no longer caught sight of Monsieur Ghose – Sri Aurobindo as he was referred to respectfully by the privileged, who had been admitted to his presence – for he had withdrawn completely from the world and was now as securely locked away in his Ashram as he had been in his Alipore iron cage. But this confinement was of his own choosing. Madame Richard – Mira – sat at his feet and was his conduit to the outside world; she spread the word, gospelist and demi-deity combined. She had shed her old name, as is the way with disciples and converts, and was known now simply as 'Mother'.

Chapter 4

The Hotel de France stood squarely in the French quarter, and Oriane did not often stray beyond it. She walked the Promenade in the cool of the evening, visited the library, attended recitals and an occasional ball at the Governor's house. In due course, she feared, a suitable marriage would take place and she would probably find herself en route to La Belle France, the homeland she had never seen.

Oriane wondered what would become of the hotel. For one day, to be sure, her parents would return to France. She herself, knowing it only second-hand, found it hard to visualise the boulevards, the arcaded squares, the fountains and the public gardens which had been the inspiration of this small, south Indian town.

A hundred and fifty-four years earlier, when Pondi was freshly rebuilt from the last unfortunate encounter with the English, the Hotel de France had been a private mansion. It rose from the ruins of an almost identical house that had stood since 1721. What was once a village, a huddle of fishermen's huts on the Coromandel coast, had grown into a town regularly exchanged between warring nations, sometimes fought for, sometimes formally handed over. Strangers came by sea, the ships rolling in the heavy swell of the Indian Ocean, or travelled by land – armies had arrived by both methods, the men nauseous or footsore, dreaming of France or England, dying in the dusty soil, fighting over territory –

inevitably, in due course, to be restored to the status quo ante bellum by the next peace treaty.

The see-saw was kept in motion by foreigners, British and French. Occasionally they might draw a rajah or a prince into the fray, and from time to time they surged across the Deccan or Carnatic plains to subdue or support a local ruler, but for the most part the game was played by heavily-clad men with red, burnt faces. Men sweating in breeches and jackets. There were officers who urged on the troops, sent them slithering and stumbling through brackish trench water or swamp-land to attack fortifications. The officers kept their feet dry.

When the clash of steel or the musket fire fell silent and the troops dropped to rest, the native sepoys splashed their heads with water; for the European infantrymen there was a moment to ease feet from the deceptive warmth of sodden leather, to confront skin rubbed raw, bleeding. Crying with pain, they washed off bloody, caked mud, hastily wrapped their toes in what was available – rags, leaves, paper – but the feet, released, had swollen and must now be forced into boots hardening rapidly as they dried. The cursing and sobbing of men in boots was a sort of counterpoint to the cries of the dying and wounded left behind, as they hobbled on, to the next glorious engagement.

In 1760 after the siege of Madras, General Lally's French divisions razed the city's Fort David to the ground. A year later the fortunes of war had shifted and it was the turn of the English. Their revenge was savage: the total destruction not only of the Fort but the white town *la Ville Blanche* – of Pondicherry itself. The destruction was so methodically carried out that everything, fort walls, the Governor's house so lovingly built by Dupleix, churches, private dwellings, all were burned and pounded out of existence. Only two Hindu temples were left standing, their intricately carved walls looking from a little way off as though formed from the very rubble surrounding them. The French astronomer, Le Gentil, who was in India at the time to observe the passing of Venus across the surface of the moon, compared the destruction of the place to that of Jerusalem by Vespasian.

A keen eye might have perceived that on what had been the corner of the rue Laval, the stuccoed walls of a fine house lay reduced to the same sad state as its neighbours, wild creeper already spreading across the broken stone. In due course the usual hypocrisies were exchanged and another peace treaty was signed. When the new governor, Law de Lauriston arrived in 1765, he took possession of a shattered landscape. His maps were virtually useless. But these were Frenchmen returning to a place they regarded as theirs. Living in tents and temporary huts, they worked as relentlessly as ants. Clear the rubble. Find the foundation outlines. Rebuild. Within six months nearly two hundred houses were standing. Less than three years later a whole new town had grown from the ruins of the old. Pondicherry was herself again. Until the next foreigner made plans.

'Ah yes,' Madame de l'Esprit says to the hotel's guests, 'this house has been the scene of great events . . . Bonaparte himself might have –'

One day Oriane, changed more than she would have wished, will repeat her mother's words. For now, still young and eager, she rejects the past. But the past has a way of throwing out lures; time itself is an uncertain medium, gaining strength from shifting perspectives. Still, all this she cannot know yet. She dreams of the future, as others have, before her.

Chapter 5

Napoleon, dreaming. On St Helena he dreams of India, of a plan, long ago, to march overland from Egypt, or to go by sea, the Red Sea route, from Suez and snatch that jewel, the subcontinent from the claws of the English.

As a young man he dreamed, like Alexander, of India lying so temptingly before him, and jotted down a businesslike timetable: 'Conquest of Egypt: July – Oct, 1799. March on India November, arriving Feb 1800.'

Thierry de l'Esprit, painting a portrait of his friend the general, requests him to remain still. 'How can I get a good likeness if you keep shifting about?' The general studies a dispatch; stares, head lowered like a bull at the artist. Energy burns in his veins like a fever. His brain boils.

Conquest of India: Arrive February. He begins to shift about.

It seemed workable. Had the money and the will been forthcoming from Paris. 'The power which is mistress of Egypt must become in the long run mistress of India as well,' he wrote the gentlemen of the Directory, but the revolution-makers, like the King before them, were busy with other affairs, suspicious of the risks – and, increasingly, wary of over-ambitious young generals.

There was prevarication. Parsimony.

Talleyrand encouraged him. Nothing practical on offer

but the bait dangled. 'If your eyes turn towards India...'
Ah! The treasures that might follow. And in Egypt, Napoleon's dream grew, took on colour, detail – he pictured himself on the road to Asia. 'Founder of a new religion, mounted on an elephant, wearing a turban and holding a new Koran which contained my own message.' He had a plan, to force history into his service, attack the English power in India, and after that conquest, reopen communications with Europe. It was a grand plan. What he needed now was a trusted emissary. Thierry, perhaps?

Young men hang together: age, daring, ambition unite them. Thierry de l'Esprit was there at the right time. They came from different backgrounds, but they knew where they were going. For a start, Thierry could take a ring from the French general to the Sultan's son and murmur encouraging words in his ear. Bonaparte's letter would be passed discreetly from his emissary's hand to Tipu Sahib. 'You must already have been informed of my arrival on the coast of the Red Sea with a large and invincible army, filled with a desire to liberate you from the iron yoke of England...'

Stirring words. Tipu turned the ring on his finger, a bauble but well meant. In principle, he liked the plan. He beckoned young Esprit to his side.

Years later, Napoleon sequestered on St Helena, pacing hour after hour, dreams of the moment he had it in his reach.

But matters changed: a victory for Nelson in the Nile, politics at home, a coup. The young general, now First Consul, had other priorities. India receded. And all this he remembers later, an old man on a bleak island, sick, tired, disappointed, dreaming dreams of battles and a crown lost. And an oriental jewel.

If matters had worked out differently, if he had landed on the Malabar coast as he planned, approaching from the West, with Pondi forming the pincer, if he had marched on the English then, everything might have been changed. The

French Empire in India! Pondicherry could have been just the beginning.

Napoleon dreamed. And everything seemed possible, at the time.

Instead there was a treaty, a compromise. French territories to be restored, but an end to any ideas of expansion. The revolutionary war was over.

On 15th June 1802 Captain Thierry de l'Esprit sails for India on board the frigate *Belle-Poule*. Once again he is a messenger, carrying a letter to the British Governor-General.

The French force, headed by General Decaen, will follow, as the letter explains, to take peaceful charge of Pondicherry under the terms of the recent treaty.

Also on board the *Belle-Poule* is Decaen's adjutant, Binot (Thierry's comrade and life-long friend), Binot's wife, and a token one hundred and fifty troops. On the voyage Thierry paints portraits of the crew, of Madame Binot, and of astonishing sunsets; he tries to capture the flight of airborne fish, the smile of dolphins. He paints a self-portrait, dispassionate in its depiction of a less than classical profile. He does not minimise his nose.

And Thierry, too, dreams, but his are less majestic visions. He is eager to see Pondicherry; there are family reasons why it should be special. He writes in his journal, the thoughts of a young man who wants fame, fortune and the love of fair women: 'What will this journey bring me? God's will be done. And Bonaparte's.' It is inconceivable that the two should not be identical.

But by the time the *Belle-Poule* reached Pondi, so had fresh rumours of war between England and France. The English authorities diplomatically dragged their heels, waiting for more news. Napoleon's representatives were to be made welcome, but the hand-over would take its time. Just in case.

This was how things stood when the *Belle-Poule* anchored off Pondi and Thierry was sent ashore to arrange suitable accommodation in the town. He was, after all, familiar with India: there had been the matter of the secret messages earlier on, between Bonaparte and Tipu. The young soldier was known to be interested in the culture of the subcontinent, taking the trouble to learn Hindustani, some Persian, and English. He had a passion for the flora of the Orient inspired by a childhood meeting with Louis de Bougainville. 'He may be a politician now,' Thierry was fond of saying, 'but the explorations and the flowers are what he will be remembered for.'

Captain de l'Esprit soon found suitable accommodation: for Binot, a graceful mansion by the charming, tree-lined canal; for Léger, a colonnaded château overlooking the sea. For himself, he requested a billet in a saffron yellow stuccoed house on the corner of the rue Laval where an English family was in residence. The young man was made welcome – the house, they told him, had earlier belonged to some French people, and the English are delicate in such matters. A fountain was being installed in the garden, to replace the existing ornamental fish pond. The daughter of the house, Miss Catherine, smooth black hair draping her head like a silken hood, blue eyes bolder than those of the young ladies Thierry encountered at home, explained to the young captain the reason for the change: 'The *chil*-hawks dive on the pond, snatching the goldfish from the water. The fountain will be more practical.'

'And will it be beautiful also?' Captain de l'Esprit asked. His skin very white, his nose somewhat beaky, he had small bright eyes and a smile that curled up his mouth in a way she found intriguing. She raised her dark eyebrows. 'The importance of aesthetics over practical utility is a rather un-French viewpoint, surely Captain?'

'On the contrary, mademoiselle . . .'

Captain de l'Esprit asks permission to paint the ornamental fish pond before it disappears. He paints the fountain, when installed, the house, and in due course, the daughter of the house.

The English were impeccably hospitable. When the French disembarked, the English Commissioner proposed a toast to the health of the First Consul. He apologised for the unfortunate delay in handing over the territory. Formalities, he explained, mere details. A miasma of hypocrisy floated in the air thick enough to be almost visible. The French fretted, at first impatient, then disquieted.

Thierry, with Catherine, searched for unusual flowers in the surrounding countryside. A few miles away from town, in a quiet hollow of low hills, they came upon a lake shadowed by trees, where buffaloes grazed by the shore. In a fold between two inclines a small temple had been built, square, solid, its carved walls growing out of the earth, an extension of the rock beneath it. It was here, at the base of the temple wall that Thierry found the small blue columbine, its shade and shape new to him, and carefully dug up a root. The French word for columbine, he told Catherine, was *ancolie*, which means melancholie. But he himself felt only happiness. He wrapped the plant in his handkerchief, soaked in the water of the lake, and carried it back to the rue Laval.

Catherine sat for him in the garden, trailing her hand in the stone bowl of the new fountain. Sometimes they spoke English together, sometimes French. He was amused by her accent, charmed by her wit. He drowned in her eyes.

At the centres of power there were shifts of balance. Old suspicions revived. There were orders and counter orders, delays, restoration of possessions postponed. Confusion reigned. Then came a letter from London: there was a possibility – just a possibility – of a rupture with the French. 'You are not only not to carry out restoration, but you are to prepare our forces to take all the French troops prisoner as soon as orders are received.'

Communications crossing oceans can prove untimely in their arrival. The letter reached Pondicherry on the very day the Commissioner had arranged a gala supper and ball. 'Damnably awkward,' he reflected. For the French officers had, of course, been invited to the ball. General Decaen, sailing into harbour that morning with the bulk of the French expeditionary force, was unpleasantly surprised to see the English flag still flying over the town. Surely the hand-over should have been completed? He anchored in the bay and waited for someone to tell him what was going on.

And there they all remained as the sun beat down and the hours passed. In town, women reclined beneath fans, languid. Catherine, tremulous with anticipation, immersed herself in cold water, smoothed French talcum powder on to her cool skin. In the bay, the French fleet lay immobile, sails furled, their fighting men aboard and ashore, helpless, like the English, powerless as chess pieces waiting to be shifted into significant positions. The colourless glare of the afternoon sky softened to the rose of sunset and the first move was made. A ship arrived from France with a message for Decaen: war was imminent, he must leave at once. In the lemon and lavender of the brief Indian dusk, guests prepared for the evening, French and English alike ignorant of the latest news. Catherine padded anxiously at her armpits where treacherous moisture could ruin an elegant *toilette;* Thierry reported for duty. Decaen, anchored off Pondi – so close! – dared not alert his people. Any suspicious action could trigger a violent English response.

Decaen's men, aware of English telescopes trained on

them from the shore, moved casually, making their preparations for departure. Even the next day might be too late – war could be declared at any moment. And Decaen had a personal problem: his wife was ashore, visiting Madame Binot. She had indicated she might stay overnight. To summon her back to the ship could arouse suspicion. He paced the deck, keeping his steps slow, deliberate. If she stayed, he would have to leave without her, abandoning her to the enemy.

A decision that seemed quite unimportant hung for a moment in the balance. But Mme Decaen thought of her husband awaiting her, and requested Captain de l'Esprit to escort her back to the ship.

Catherine pouted, disappointed. 'I shall be besieged by some whiskery old colonel, it will be quite tedious.'

Thierry took her hand, studying the pink nails, the white crescents at their base. He raised them to his lips, kissing each in turn. Catherine, eyes alert for her mother, drew him to the shadowy rear of the verandah, pressed against him yearningly, muslin gown risking damage from all manner of dangers – buckles, brass buttons, insignia . . .

'I shall be back in time to rescue you. I promise.'

He was short with the sailors rowing them out to Decaen's ship, urging them to hurry. Catherine was waiting . . .

The sea was calm enough, but always near this shore there was a heaving turbulence that made navigation tricky. The water rose and fell around the small boat, tossing it almost playfully aloft so that one moment it was poised high, oars flailing helplessly out of reach of water, the next rushing down the black slope, tilted so steeply that it seemed certain they would slide beneath the surface. Madame Decaen was accustomed to the ocean. She gripped the wooden seat and fixed her eyes on the nearest ship. Captain de l'Esprit's agitation surprised her.

Carriages rolled to the door of the Commissioner's house;

the music played, the champagne circulated. When Thierry arrived he was both late and preoccupied. He had secret and difficult orders from Decaen to pass on to Binot. But this was not the time or place. A small locked box was placed in Binot's room to be studied when he retired for the night. Thierry handed him the key as they strolled in the garden, enjoying a cigar: 'Orders from General Decaen.'

Catherine did not regard the evening as a success. First Thierry was absent, then he was abstracted. She sulked, agreed to forgive him, wondered if he truly loved her as he said, asked for a water-ice. As he threaded his way back across the room towards her he glanced casually out at the English ships dimly visible against the darkness of the sea and sky, bobbing as the tide turned.

Next morning, the English awoke to find the whole French fleet had vanished overnight. Only Binot and his men were left, stranded, blandly deflecting questions. No one was at war – yet. They dined, played cards, danced. And waited for the fateful announcement that would end this uneasy peace. They sat it out for eight weeks. Thierry and Catherine, not quite Troilus and Cressida, made plans contingent on survival. She wiped away tears and handed round the teacups to her mother's British military guests in the rue Laval while Thierry, with typical sang-froid, carried elegantly coded messages to the Mahratta princes, trying to drum up allies before it was too late. On September 6th the news came: it was war.

Binot poured a good cognac for himself and the captain. 'Thierry my boy, we have a small problem . . .'

The French had one hundred and fifty men, surrounded by an enemy in full possession of the territory. Resistance was out of the question and the English were already impatient. 'Obey the summons to surrender, or we march in and attack.'

Binot and Thierry had a brief discussion. Thierry had a gift for messages: maybe, he suggested, it was time for a touch of *fierté*, of French panache. He delivered it with his usual grace. 'If an attack is contemplated, General Binot will spare the English half the distance by advancing himself, with his men.'

It might not have been discretion but it was certainly valour. The English respected it and Captain de l'Esprit was sent off to Madras to settle terms with the Governor. As usual, there were less . . . formal orders to be carried out as well, and very soon a new arrival was seen about Madras: an artist of, it seemed, German descent, though conveniently armed with an English passport. The pale young man with his beard, his prominent nose and excellent English became a familiar figure in town. His paintbox and his charm were quite in demand in Madras social circles – for a while – the English have always been slow to recognise the presence of spies. But with time their suspicions can be aroused, and Thierry de l'Esprit's watercolour of a house with a deep verandah and an ornamental fountain was painted in a British jail in Calcutta.

Meanwhile, inspired by Thierry's interest in the local culture, Catherine was taking Sanskrit lessons, to surprise him on his return. She proved an apt pupil and her teacher was impressed – and pleased. Not many Englishwomen bothered to learn more than kitchen Hindi.

She waited anxiously for Thierry to return. At first there had been letters, routed diplomatically through safe channels. Then silence. She fretted, grew thin. Fortunately she had something to occupy her, and the Sanskrit lessons became the focus of her energies. Her teacher consoled her with readings from ancient works where patience was rewarded. But Catherine had never been patient.

Two years later Thierry was back in Pondicherry. The territory remained firmly British but the Napoleonic wars created curious anomalies, and French civilians, cut off from

France, were left to lead their lives in relative peace. The inconspicuous presence of one more civilian aroused no interest.

He made his way to the rue Laval.

Catherine fainted spectacularly: she had thought he must be dead.

'But I promised to return and I always keep my promises,' he said, the corners of his mouth curling in the interesting smile that had first captured her attention.

Thierry requested Catherine's hand in marriage. He was received more cordially than he had expected by the parents. Somewhat to his surprise, they agreed to an early wedding: her mother, he knew, had never considered a Frenchman an ideal match, but she offered no obstacle. She watched her daughter walk down the aisle holding a small bouquet of deep blue columbines, dark eyes demurely lowered, hair smooth beneath the veil. A beautiful girl. Marriage to a Frenchman was not, after all, the worst that could happen. And did, a few months later when Catherine gave birth, prematurely to a boy and failed to survive.

Thierry stared down at the small stranger. The child, skin dark and wrinkled, was not appealing. The captain's gorge rose in momentary revulsion. Then, the delicately veined lids fluttered and the blue of Catherine's eyes gleamed for an instant between the sparse lashes. The man's rough fingers touched the tender starfish of the infant's hand. 'I am blessed with a son,' he said.

Napoleon, dreaming in Cairo, in Paris, on St Helena, sees the great subcontinent rise before him as a mass towering to heaven, bearing down on him, narrowing to a point that dips into the sea like the quill of a pen that will write the words 'My India'. But India eluded him.

In 1840 Catherine's son Maurice, having established himself in Rouen, took a wife. Their youngest son Hubert, in

1880, journeyed to India and made his way to Pondicherry, to the rue Laval, and to the house on the corner. It stood shabby and run-down, the garden a wilderness, the fountain dry. In Rouen he had seen a painting of the house which he had with him now. With dismay he looked at what had become of the immaculate stuccoed walls, the neatly tended garden.

'Put the house in order,' Maurice had directed, 'restoration will not be difficult.' The young man, by no means pleased with the way family affairs had landed him with a dilapidated pile of masonry in an Indian backwater, determined to get back to France as soon as possible. Apart from supervising the natives there was nothing, absolutely nothing, to do here. Reluctantly he attended a reception at the Governor's house and was introduced to a local beauty. Somehow departure became less pressing.

There were balls, boat trips, moonlit expeditions to a nearby lake where servants lit torches that shimmered in the water like underwater flames. There was, finally, a wedding in the church overlooking the sea, with family and guests from France to be fed and entertained. Once more the servants were ingenious, providing music and fireworks for their masters to admire.

Unfortunately, the family fortunes proved unstable. Young Monsieur and Madame de l'Esprit considered their options, weighing the charms of Pondi against the attractions of Rouen. They had energy, and new ideas. They decided to turn their home into a hotel.

They named their youngest, and only surviving child, born in the winter of 1903, Oriane.

In the house on the corner of the rue Laval the past is physically present. In a drawer of a dusty walnut *armoire* in an upstairs room there is a slim mahogany box that holds watercolours, brushes, a sketch book mildewed to a solid, friable block. There is a painting of the house on the drawing room wall showing the fountain new and white in the foreground. Less palpable, in the shadowy corridors drift murmurs of intrigue, a sense of hasty departures under cover of darkness. Secret messages linger in the air.

This had always been the pattern. Fortifications rose and fell, as did flags. The foreigners came and went. The original inhabitants, necessary for labour but otherwise unregarded, kept their heads down, fled when necessary, and got on with living. The years passed. Things, as they have a way of doing, changed.

Chapter 6

On a cool February evening in 1931, Oriane de l'Esprit met a young Indian student newly returned from England. He was not part of her social circle: a Hindu whose Brahmin family had considerable wealth, he would not easily have fitted into the *soirées*, the *diners*, the emphatically French gatherings that were held at the Hotel de France – nor would he have wished to.

Oriane was twenty-eight and though her mother was busy enough with the hotel, she found time to fret, and occasionally resort to action, over the continuing unmarried status of her daughter. 'Oriane is not a difficult girl, not really,' she said to women friends, 'she has interests, moreover her appearance is pleasing.' If only, she thought, as she welcomed new arrivals, summoned servants to carry their luggage, showed them to their table, if only the girl would refrain from her questions. The questions and the books were the problem. The bridegroom was yet to be netted. With this in mind, appropriate outings were encouraged. Some of these Oriane resisted. But she had needed no encouragement to attend the recital given by a visiting European string quartet.

Oriane and Guruvappa were introduced by Thomas Ettridge, an Englishman described by Oriane to her mother as 'a sort of scholar who is researching the history of palm-leaf books'.

'Palm-leaf books? Native work? Is this an occupation for a gentleman? Moreover, is there a living to be made from it?' Madame de l'Esprit enquired incredulously, after Thomas's first visit to the house.

Had she asked him, he could have explained that it was not so much the old palm-leaf books, beautiful though they were with their exquisitely detailed, etched illustrations and frail, brittle brown pages, that interested him, as the letters, wrapped in lace and usually carried by a Brahmin, so often used as messengers: 'Brahmins were a sort of human diplomatic pouch,' he told Oriane, 'they didn't get searched, no one dared. Important letters, negotiations, secret correspondence, could get through.'

So he sought out the surviving manuscripts: he searched the archives and looked in dusty old shops filled with broken pottery and dulled brass, acquiring and restoring where he could, re-tying the slim, rectangular sheets, rubbing the surface gently with citronella oil to preserve it and bring up the Sanskrit writing. And palm-leaf letters too were just a part of his field: a survey of secret communications and coded messages between the colonists and colonised – in its turn an intriguing corner of his main subject: political cryptography: the *scytales* Plutarch described being used by Spartan generals who wrapped their messages round staffs and wrote on the joined edges; Caesar's substitution cipher; the reversal system mentioned by Jeremiah that was used by the Jews; a cipher favoured by Charles I of England, who used numerals instead of letters . . . One day an interesting volume might emerge. Meanwhile he sifted and studied, delving into obscure corners. Oriane might have been intrigued to hear about Louis XIV's Great Cipher or a monumental work by a Frenchman in the sixteenth century, but Thomas was very English and fearful of seeming earnest so he made light of his preoccupation. 'Yes, palm-leaf manuscripts. Charming. Um . . . the delicate calligraphy, you know,' and left it at that.

He had met Guruvappa in London and liked him. He thought that Oriane would find the boy amusing and he had reasons for wanting to please her.

He kept an eye on the door, watching for her arrival at the chamber concert, restraining Guruvappa, who showed signs of impatience, from moving away. He signalled across the room to one of the officials.

'François, have you seen Mademoiselle de l'Esprit?'

'Look, I'll meet her some other time –'

The Frenchman looked puzzled by the boy's impatient tone. Thomas realised an explanation was needed.

'I thought Mademoiselle de l'Esprit might consider giving my young friend here some French lessons.'

'What's wrong with my French?' Guruvappa asked. 'It's better than yours.'

'Oh, for chatting and so forth, I dare say,' Thomas agreed, dismissively, 'but limited, limited. I don't know what those chaps at St Paul's thought they were doing.'

'It would undoubtedly be of benefit to you,' the Frenchman agreed. 'This is, after all, French India, Mr Guruvappa.'

Thomas added, blandly, 'Mademoiselle de l'Esprit is a bit of a blue-stocking, she'll be good for you.' In Guruvappa's experience, things that were pronounced 'good for you' tended to be unpleasant: cold baths, laxatives, team games, over-cooked cabbage and museums furnished with mahogany cabinets. Mademoiselle de l'Esprit would be 'good' for him, ergo Mademoiselle de l'Esprit was unlikely to be much fun.

'Is she a dragon?' he enquired, with visions of a Gallic Lady Bracknell. At nineteen, he considered a woman of twenty-eight very much an Older Woman – his mother, married at fifteen, was in her mid-thirties, after all.

Thomas considered the question for a moment. 'A

dragon? Oriane?' He decided to tease Guruvappa a little. 'Oh no, on the contrary, she's a bit of a shrinking violet. You'll need to be kind to her.'

An elderly shrinking violet! Guruvappa's gloom deepened. Still, as a teacher she would probably be serviceable and it would not be a long encounter. She would presumably provide a reading list, and they would spend a few hours engaged in textual study. A tutorial in which Victor Hugo, alas, would dominate. And that would be more than enough.

Thomas said, breaking into his thoughts, 'Ah! Oriane. Permit me to introduce ... Mademoiselle de l'Esprit, Mr N.V. Guruvappa.'

Oriane paused and turned to acknowledge the introduction. She saw a thin, large-eyed Indian boy dressed in a formal Western suit, shirt with stiff white collar, hair plastered flat to his skull in the style of the day. He looked, she decided, somewhat stupid, his mouth hanging open in a surprised gape, his eyes blinking rapidly. He also appeared to be mute.

'*Enchantée*,' she said and passed on briskly.

It had been a day of tempered sun, later it might even turn chilly, and Oriane wore a frock of flowing silk, cowl-necked, with long, narrow sleeves. It was a dark and subtle indigo, dyed from the plants in the Bengal, woven in Kanchipuram, cut and stitched by a Parisian seamstress languishing in Madras. The line of her throat, her wrists, the turn of her waist had a slenderness that was still girlish, fragile. The smooth oval face was unmarked by experience or age. And the eyes, the blue dark as indigo, had the glitter of a blade-edge that dazzled. Guruvappa felt a sudden ache, as of a wound, the stab of pain delayed that follows a mortal blow. He closed his mouth and watched her move away.

He approached her in the interval, offering a fresh lime sorbet. She accepted it, remembering now that Thomas

Ettridge had mentioned this boy to her. He needed help of some sort. She decided to be kind.

'Did you enjoy the Debussy?'

'I read somewhere that Monsieur Debussy once said he needed to go back to Paris because he longed to see something by Manet and listen to something by Offenbach. I think I admire his taste more than his music.'

The spoon halted mid-way to her lips. Oriane was devoted to Debussy. 'The G-minor quartet is a masterpiece,' she observed, cool, crushing. But she recalled that when she was younger, and heard his music for the first time, she too had found it difficult. 'You will know better one day,' she said, relenting. They were the same height and she looked directly into his eyes. 'So. I understand you are in need of some education.'

'Thomas seems to think I need to do a little work on my French literature.'

A flash of blue, a frown. '*Your* French literature? Such a very Imperialist pronoun, Mr . . . ?'

'Guruvappa.'

'Yes. And what about "your" Indian literature? You must educate me in your masters – name me ten famous Tamils.'

She waited, eyebrows raised, then gave a little shrug, a twitch of her slim shoulders and returned to her lime sorbet.

He was furious. Misled by Thomas, lazily approaching the supposed shrinking violet, he found himself entangled in a thicket of sharp thorns and she had gone straight to the vulnerable spot. She was accusing him of not knowing his own culture, and the worst of it was that she was right. He was absurdly unaccustomed to feeling defensive: in England he had been considered 'too clever by three-quarters' as one of the masters at school once helpfully informed him. At home, his parents deferred to him on matters European, and were indulgent where they recognised inexperience. Caught off-balance, he panicked.

'You must forgive me, Mademoiselle de l'Esprit,' he said stiffly. 'My people have a literary tradition quite as rich as your own and even older, but our culture is a private one and not usually of interest to outsiders. Moreover –' he found he was suddenly short of breath, 'I am not accustomed to . . . ladies taking so active a role –'

'*Ça m'étonnerait*,' said Oriane crisply. 'Were you not educated in England? Englishwomen are not sequestered, to my knowledge. Either you are disingenuous and also rude, or you really are in need of education. And now I think we should go in, the musicians attend us.'

After the recital, the invited audience mingled with the members of the quartet, eager for the latest gossip, the small-change of metropolitan social currency. The wives were quizzed on the new hem-lines, the latest plays; the musicians on politics. The division of the sexes irritated Oriane who thanked her host and left.

Thomas and Guruvappa caught up with her in the drive. Thomas was about to signal for a rickshaw, but Oriane protested that she wished to walk home. Then they must walk with her, Thomas insisted: her parents would not be happy –

'My dear Thomas,' Oriane said, 'you and your young friend do have the most curious idea of women's ability to function. Perhaps one should not blame you; your cultures are to blame.'

Thomas said stiffly, 'Matter of simple courtesy.' Guru-vappa, now wiser, remained silent. She stepped out energetically, her high-heeled sandals clicking on the stone pavement, but she made no complaint when they fell into step beside her. Her confidence in her safety was securely based: here in the French quarter, in *La Ville Blanche*, there were no natives to be seen apart from the rickshaw men and the occasional night-watchman at wrought-iron gates. The sea-front had the look of a small French resort – a miniature

Nice, with its Promenade, its palm trees and white villas. One or two men wandered slowly towards them, smoking cigars, talking quietly. 'How is the writing, Thomas?' she asked, the tone deceptively sweet. 'Are we to see something before too long?' She knew quite well that nothing was completed, that his time in Pondicherry was financed not by publishers but by a slender private income.

'Um . . . still researching . . . early days, you know.'

She led them along the sea-shore, to the statue of Dupleix and paused, looking up at the familiar bewigged stone figure with its heavy features.

'In France, of course,' Oriane said provocatively, 'women have always taken their place at the centre of things, Cartesian women are not happy to be invisible. One of our . . .' she flashed a glance at Guruvappa, 'our *ladies* . . . formed the habit of receiving her favourite poets in her *lit de parade*, and another . . . *lady* . . . Mademoiselle de Scudéry – who was incidentally a successful writer, *mon cher* Thomas, became very angry about people who treated women as if they existed solely for the purpose to be beautiful and to say foolish things. And that was more than two hundred years ago.'

'You're very prickly this evening.'

'Those are my weapons.'

'And must I beware of being hurt?'

'Only if you approach too closely!'

The little exchange, the light-hearted fencing match, was over in a moment – indeed hardly merited the description – but there was something about Thomas's wry comment; about Oriane de l'Esprit's warning note, that made Guruvappa glance up at them suddenly, see her set white profile, distanced, aloof, and Thomas's rumpled, untidily assembled features arranging themselves into a pained smile, and know with absolute certainty: Thomas loves her. Ah, this was more complicated than he had realised.

The moon was small and pale, riding very high in the sky, silvery, a fragile disc so wafer-like it seemed almost as if the light glowed through it from behind. Oriane regretted her lack of scientific knowledge: as a child she had taken for granted a crescent moon that waxed and waned, miraculous and beautiful. When she learned later that all the glittering beauty, the altered states, related to balls of matter hurtling through space, it had removed the magic without providing greater understanding.

This was also the case with people: their faces, pleasing or hideous, their bodies, graceful or clumsy, were merely the visible manifestation of atoms puzzlingly clinging together – rather like flies clustering so close on a lump of horse-dung that they defined its shape. To be told that we are all part of a swarming universe in which nothing is fixed did not reassure her: it somehow took away virtue; the shining face of the moon wavered, insubstantial.

Below the Promenade the inky ocean seethed gently, the surf curling on to the rocks like white fingers waving, beckoning, falling back.

Oriane leaned towards it, expectant, like someone about to sip from a proffered cup. 'Listen how it never stops, it surges continuously. Like Debussy, Mr Guruvappa, no climaxes. Continual change. Secret harmonies of wind and wave.'

'You must explain Debussy to me,' Guruvappa said, 'I can see I have much to learn.'

'But what you must do is to listen,' she said, impatiently. 'If you listen to *La Mer* you will find it is an Impressionist portrait of the sea itself, vast and empty, a landscape without figures . . .'

Below, on the dark, heaving expanse of the sea the moonlight shone like a gauzy ribbon of light floating towards them on the surface.

'I have often wondered about the light of the moon on

water,' Oriane said, 'it puzzles me that it should fall only on one spot.'

'Ah,' said Guruvappa, 'then you and Einstein have something in common. He used to stand on the shore of Lake Zurich when he was young and wonder precisely the same thing.'

Oriane was startled. And flattered. She and Albert Einstein! The same idea! But surely –

'He said as much, once,' Guruvappa added, 'to a young woman he was walking home, but she was not intrigued. He found she was surprisingly uninterested in angles of incidence and reflection.'

Thomas Ettridge broke into sudden laughter. Oriane, nettled, saw that she had missed a joke. She also realised that there was more to moonlight than mere mystery.

'How do you know that?' she asked.

'He told me. I met him once, when I visited Cambridge. He was delightful. He sat on the floor.'

Along the Promenade the lamps glowed like miniature moons, the globes haloed with light and dancing moths. Guruvappa stared up at the sky.

'There's a magic about moonlight and starlight that only physicists can enjoy. The rest of us try to find ways of describing it, poems and similes and metaphors and so on. But the true magic is in the physics.'

She threw him a quick look and said tartly, 'Shall we talk more about this? Then our lessons will not be so one-sided.' He kept his face impassive: there were to be lessons, then. She had decided.

They walked on, past the lighthouse. Above the rooftops to their right loomed the remains of an observatory built a hundred and seventy years before on the foundations of a disused powder magazine by the French astronomer Le Gentil, to observe the passage of Venus across the moon – though Oriane did not know that and Guruvappa did not think to tell her. They turned into the little public park, and on, to the rue Laval. At the gates of the Grand Hotel de France she said goodnight to Thomas Ettridge. Then she held out her hand to Guruvappa. Thin brown fingers took hold of hers, cool, with smooth skin – a hand unacquainted with manual labour. 'We shall begin next week,' she informed him. He looked down at the wrist, bird-boned, the dark sleeve falling away.

'Victor Hugo?' he asked, politely. 'Racine?'

'Mallarmé, Baudelaire, Gérard de Nerval,' she said crisply. 'Do your homework.'

The lessons were not always easy: Guruvappa could unwittingly offend, calling forth irritation, even wrath. She began by bludgeoning him with lists: names, dates, edicts, Rimbaud, Baudelaire, Verlaine, Lautréamont, Laforgue –

'but above all Mallarmé – read the *Tombeau d'Edgar Poe*, listen to that first line, "*Tel qu'en Lui-même enfin l'éternité le change*".'

Guruvappa had no idea what she was talking about but attempted an enigmatic, musing look. 'What is your reading of that line?' he asked, cunningly.

She fell for it. 'Among other things, the frustration of having failed to make certain connections that one is aware of, too late.' She sounded, for a moment, desolate, and Guruvappa felt he should attempt a contribution, something to cheer her up.

'He was a friend of the English playwright, Oscar Wilde,' he said. Adding, as he recalled the fact, 'as was Aurobindo –'

'What? What can you mean? That is impossible!' She seemed suddenly furious. He was bewildered.

'Well –'

'Aurobindo is a saint. A recluse. What can he have to do with a man like Oscar Wilde? This *boulevardier*, this ... *dilettante*!'

Wilting under the blue fire of her eyes Guruvappa back-tracked hastily. 'I remember now, it was Aurobindo's brother who was a friend of Wilde's, they were undergraduates together. I just assumed Aurobindo must have known Wilde too. But of course I have no evidence for that.'

Not altogether mollified, she continued the lesson.

At the beginning they spoke French, but Oriane decided she should improve her English. There were days when she ordered him to correct her, was open to suggestion, when she might agree to listen to Browning or one of the Metaphysicals, and agree that it had a certain something. An occasional line would win her over, make her suddenly vulnerable –

'Annihilating all that's made/To a green thought in a green shade' – ah yes, she said to that, though she never could pronounce the first word of the line.

'Collective nouns,' she said briskly one morning, 'what are these so-called collective nouns?'

'A clamour of rooks,' Guruvappa began, 'an exaltation of larks –'

'You cannot be serious!'

'Perfectly serious. Congregation of plovers, a –'

'This is a frivolous language.' She tried out words on her tongue, tasting them like exotic fruits. 'An exaltation of larks . . . it has a certain charm. Should one create new collective nouns, suitable for Pondi?'

'A chatter of monkeys?' Guruvappa suggested.

'A swoop of *chil*-hawks,' she offered. 'And what could one use for brain-fever birds?'

She peered down at the book before them, absorbed, consumed by the search, flicking her glance up to him enquiringly, unaware how closely he watched her.

When she was feeling generous they spoke English but if she felt irritated or vindictive she would move into French to put him at a disadvantage. Disconcertingly, his French improved so rapidly that quite soon this ploy became less amusing.

'You're behaving like an Aunt,' he said one day, when she was being particularly overbearing.

'Do Indian aunts behave in a special way?'

'Lord no. I meant a Wodehouse Aunt. You know. Aunt Agatha.'

'No. I don't know.'

'Well then, let's say Lady Bracknell. Sometimes you're a bit of a Bracknell.'

This was all very confusing. She demanded clarification, and Guruvappa did his best.

It was hopeless of course – and landed him back in dangerous territory: 'But to attach such importance to a *farceur*, a frivolous playwright!'

She disapproved of Wilde. She read *Salomé* and was troubled by it: 'like being buried in orchids,' she said, '*on étouffe*.' But there was something about the central obsession that, obscurely, she could understand.

Wicked moods overtook her without warning. She could be perverse, wilful, even cruel. It puzzled and frustrated her that her protégé seemed able to deflect her sharpest barbs without losing his calm or his sense of humour.

'She is constantly being exposed to supposedly eligible Frenchmen by her appalling mother,' he told Thomas Ettridge one day. 'I think the old girl hopes that by rubbing shoulders with them her daughter might acquire some of their mediocrity through a sort of osmosis, and live happily ever after.'

Perhaps, Thomas reflected, if she had been allowed to join Aurobindo's Ashram as she had apparently wanted – he was skilled at trawling for information that concerned her – Oriane would have been more tranquil. In her presence he became aware sometimes of a sense of something thwarted. Unfulfilled.

'And how are the lessons going? Are you bored? I feel rather guilty –'

But it seemed the lessons were going well. This should have pleased Thomas, since the idea had been his. Instead he felt put out, and vaguely uneasy. Unsettled.

It was at this point that he discovered she had shortened Guruvappa's name, in an ironical bow to his role as mentor. It was a trivial, conversational thing, but unintentionally it created an exclusivity that formed a kind of intimacy.

'Guru?' Thomas echoed, when he first heard it. 'Am I witnessing the birth of another Ashram?' They all laughed, but Thomas felt, once again, oddly put out.

Oriane felt no need to explain to her parents that she had met a student, a youth lately returned from England where he attended a school for young gentlemen – indeed the same school that Aurobindo had attended. This, as he explained, created its own ironies.

'It's an odd business, being deprived of your own culture, your own language. They sent me off to England to become a copy-cat Englishman. Mimesis. Even our name was tidied up at some point: simplified.'

School had not been a problem. The family had an account at Harrods so a regular supply of first-rate tuck was guaranteed – Rich Dundee cake and Little Scarlet strawberry jam, the best kippers and sardines. From time to time his father changed continents on business trips and carried a group of boys off for extravagant teas at Skindles or the Ritz. Guruvappa's dark skin was offset by his skill at coxing the school's rowing team and adequate cricket. No one locked him in the lavatory or tormented him in the dormitory.

'But – you remember when you asked me to name ten famous Tamils? And what did I know of Sanskrit? That vast literature. I said to my father, do you realise I've been effectively disinherited? There was a bit of a dust-up, I'm afraid. He called me ungrateful. Anyway I'm making up for lost time now.'

He was studying the sacred texts, learning not only Sanskrit but Tamil and Telugu, the Brahmi scripts. 'From nothing, I have to know everything,' he said ruefully, 'it's one of my vices. Ignorance was an affectation that I no longer find appealing.'

Their conversations, which he still referred to as 'lessons' had begun at the Romain Rolland library, formal, seated across a desk from one another. Gradually they evolved, needing no structure, the time allotted ran out too fast, there was always more to be explored, once a week became absurdly inadequate. There was no explicit discussion of the matter; the meetings simply became more frequent. Occasionally they met at a recital or a lecture and then he might walk with her back to the rue Laval, though there was never any suggestion that he should enter the hotel.

Just now and then they paused for coffee or a glass of fresh lime juice at a little bistro on the sea-front not far from the statue of Dupleix, and it was here that Thomas Ettridge caught sight of them one evening, seated on the terrace overhanging the beach. He watched Oriane smooth back a tendril of hair, rest her chin on her hand. The wind drove the surf hard against the rocks and the froth seethed and fretted against the sea-wall. The sound filled his ears, an endlessly repeated sibilance, a murmur of 'She . . . she . . . she . . .'

The two of them were alone on the terrace. She was listening intently while he talked, her eyes on his face. Thomas was about to walk on, reluctant to disturb their privacy, but Oriane saw him and waved and beckoned him over. 'Sit down Thomas, and listen. Guru is telling me about a most wonderful thing called the aberration of starlight.'

Guruvappa broke in, embarrassed, 'Oh Thomas knows all about it –' but Oriane was too filled with enthusiasm to be checked.

'Did you realise, Thomas, that because of the movement of the planets through space it can seem to us as though the stars move their position – have I got this right, Guru? Because we are whirling, and the light from the stars is streaming towards us, the light seems to be dragged or displaced.'

Guru's light, mellifluous voice was barely audible above the hissing of the surf.

'Thomas, you'll remember Bradley described it as like a woman seen running through the rain ... the way the rain seems to slant towards her, so the earth, dragging what he called the aether pulls the light ...'

For a moment Thomas sees Oriane, the black hair streaming loose, running through the rain and the rain slants to meet her face, moulds her flimsy dress to her body –

'Yes, yes,' he says, sounding a little bored, 'apparent displacement of an astral body, caused by the earth's motion and non-instantaneous transmission of light.'

'It's the most beautiful thing I ever heard!' Oriane murmured. 'The abberration of starlight, Thomas. The starlight slanting like rain ... Guru has introduced me to the poetry of the physical world.'

She gazed up at the stars that hovered above them in the breathless darkness.

It was the beauty that Guruvappa found in the calculations and equations – 'the elegance' – that thrilled Oriane. She ached to share it, like a blind woman hearing a description of La Gioconda's smile or the look in the eyes of the old Rembrandt self-portraits; she heard but could not truly share. She watched the stars and knew that those she saw had long since moved their position, she tried to understand Planck's quantum theory and the second law of thermo-dynamics, and at moments like these she was no longer the formidable Mademoiselle de l'Esprit spreading the word of Symbolist truth or Cartesian duality, she was just Oriane, eager to experience revelation.

In the moonlight Thomas saw the radiance in her face.

'It's rather late, don't you think?' he said stiffly. 'Your parents might be concerned. Should we . . .'

'Oh Thomas!' she exclaimed impatiently. 'Have you no poetry in your soul?'

He smiled briefly and bitterly, and said that indeed he suspected he lacked that quality, 'Not much in demand in my part of the world.' But Guruvappa heard other, unspoken words and agreed that it was late and that they should all be on their way.

This was the year the Civil Disobedience movement was launched in British India. There were reports of meetings, boycotts and illegal chanting of 'Jai Hind' and graffiti advocating Swaraj – Self Rule. But in French India matters were less dramatic. True there were visits from Nationalist politicians, and pamphlets distributed. But this was a small, unimportant corner of the subcontinent. It was business as usual for the most part.

Still, one day when Oriane took her sunset walk along the Promenade she met Guruvappa with a visitor – one of the Congress politicians she had been reading about in the newspaper.

She was in her favourite place, by the statue of Dupleix, watching the dying sun gild the waves with a cold, metallic sheen. The sun was hidden by the trees and the sea grew dark while she stood looking down on it. Light thickened, and for a moment, a breathing space, everything was wrapped in pearly grey as the darkness spread from the eastern horizon. Approaching her, Guruvappa thought that in her stillness, with the grey, flowing gown, she looked like a figure on a Victorian gravestone, the bowed head, the contemplative, unseeing gaze. He called out her name while they were some way off, so that she would not be startled, and she turned towards them.

'. . . May I introduce a friend from Delhi.'

The politician bowed over perfunctorily joined fingertips as Guruvappa introduced Mademoiselle de l'Esprit of the Hotel de France. He was plumply elegant, smooth and glossy as an aubergine in his white Congress cap and kurta. He was charming and coolly superior. He and Oriane loathed each other on sight. He glanced up at the statue of Dupleix.

'Ah, Monsieur Dupleix. Poor chap, he didn't quite pull it off, did he?'

Oriane, who knew quite well what the man meant, said, 'What can you mean? He was a great man, a great governor.'

'India finished him though. Didn't he die in disgrace? Sick, in debt – there's an amusing parallel with Clive, he went the same way – went further, killed himself out of disappointment. All those johnny-come-Lately fellows thought they could wear us down. They didn't and they never will.'

'The French are hardly newcomers. And I think we have made some . . . contribution.'

He shrugged. 'The Romans came to Arikamedu and they made some very nice pottery and after a while they went home. And the Mughals had a go at us for a while but it didn't quite work, did it? And the Danes and the Portuguese and the Dutch and the British all moved in for the pickings. And of course you French. You were lucky, having your Revolution while you were here – our fellows felt very good about that: *liberté, égalité, fraternité* – even though your Capucins and Jesuits knocked down our temples and your judges didn't want our lawyers wearing shoes in court because it made them a bit too European for your liking . . . Still, in the end you made us citizens – and best of all, you taught us French! "*Luxe, calme et volupté*" eh? Not that my teacher approved of all that. But even you people are only temporary residents, in due time we will ask you to leave.'

'We *created* this place!' Oriane protested, too angry for

64

irony. 'Mud huts and fishing boats, that was all you had when we arrived!'

'Did we need more?' he asked, his smile polite.

When did *you* last sleep in a mud hut? she wanted to ask him. 'Anyway,' she said forcefully, 'unless you come with hammers, the Hotel de France will remain.'

'Long may it stand,' he said, raising his hand in a gesture of benediction. 'We need these surviving monuments to remind us of the past. To keep us on our toes. Oh yes, the buildings will remain; they change function, they change owners. The visitors go home.'

'*Visitors?*' Oriane exclaimed, disgusted. 'We are your architects, your guides, your teachers –'

'And we have learned.'

Guru found himself torn, different loyalties engaged. The man was right, of course. But . . . he saw something of what Oriane protested. He himself would not want to live without Shakespeare and Donne – and Wodehouse . . . But then again . . . He smoothed back his hair nervously.

'Well, delightful as it is to exchange views,' the visitor said blandly, 'we're late for an appointment.'

In the dusk Oriane's eyes were blue beacons of contempt. 'Yes, no doubt you are planning reforms for your ideal state: the abolition of Untouchability perhaps? Or are you bent on undoing some of the evils of the Colonists – you intend possibly to reinstate the official practice of suttee, make it legal – obligatory? – for widows to burn on their husband's funeral pyre? Bring back Devadasi and encourage temple prostitution? Good evening, monsieur.'

He bowed coolly over his fingertips as she stalked away, then turned to Guruvappa, Oriane already forgotten. 'Now then. This chap Aurobindo. Gandhi-ji speaks highly of him. I suppose I should have a chat. He could be useful.'

'Ah.' Guru tried to keep his face expressionless. 'He's not a politician you know. That's all in the past. He's a recluse, a mystic. He's . . .' He saw the grey gown vanish out of sight as Oriane turned a corner. 'He's regarded as a saint.'

The visitor sighed. 'Heaven protect me from saints,' he said.

Thomas was away for some time, home on a visit, and one day they read something of his in *The Times*, which he sent by Airmail, an account of a walking holiday in Germany and Austria. It began as a description of forests and mountains and foaming, country beers and changed key into something darker and more troubled by its end.

Then he was back, unannounced, and bumped into them at the Library, hunched together over a book of verse. Guruvappa leaped up and hugged him affectionately and Oriane kissed him on both cheeks, pleased to see him. Thomas, less poised than he would have wished, went into an explanation of his presence: he was searching for an early letter from a French governor to one of the Deccan princes. 'I saw a copy of it. Certain ambiguities in the text suggest it might have been in code . . .' He was aware that he sounded drearily pompous. He paused and allowed his words to tail off in mid-sentence. To his chagrin she failed to notice.

That night he sat between them at a recital. In the interval he felt like someone playing piggy-in-the-middle at school, or watching tennis at Wimbledon: Oriane addressed Guruvappa. He replied. She responded, he expanded . . . Thomas looked left, looked right, and listened politely. Finally he cut into a discussion of a Beethoven sonata and said abruptly 'I think there could be war.'

They stopped and looked at him, Oriane taken aback by the non-sequitur, Guruvappa remorseful, aware Thomas had been excluded.

'Beethoven led me to thoughts of Germany,' Thomas explained. 'I'm afraid it's been much on my mind.'

'Who will be involved?' Oriane asked, 'Poland? Czecho-slovakia?'

'Oh, I think you'll find it's rather closer to home than that.'

She looked concerned. 'France?'

Guruvappa said, 'And England, of course. Which means India –'

'Surely not!'

Thomas said, 'No one will be untouched.'

They left the Governor's house, walking back to the Hotel de France along the sea front as they had so often before. Madame and Monsieur de l'Esprit had now accepted that Oriane came and went as she pleased. The old ways were finished. They accepted her friendship with an Englishman. Thomas Ettridge was far from ideal: no money to speak of. The wrong nationality. But this is what happened when a child was not sent home to school.

Of Guruvappa they knew only that he was a young man of a good family and that Oriane was teaching him about French literature. There were precedents for educational links of this sort, and apparently he was a friend of Thomas's. Meanwhile Madame de l'Esprit, ever hopeful, continued to invite 'suitable' Frenchmen to dine. At these occasions Oriane's presence was required and she did not argue.

'Mama has a *diner* tomorrow,' she told Thomas now, 'it is a formal table so I can't ask you to join us.'

'But come and eat with us,' Guruvappa suggested.

Like Aurobindo's father, Guruvappa senior had rejected the taboos of caste and would not regard Thomas's shadow on his plate as a polluting presence.

'Vegetarian, yes. Caste-ism, no,' he would quote, laugh-ing, 'I'm with Gandhi on that one.'

'I have to go back to London fairly soon,' Thomas said. 'A sort of official job I've been offered.'

'Come to tea tomorrow,' Oriane suggested. 'We shall have

those cucumber sandwiches your Mr Wilde is always talking about.'

'That will be splendid.' Though he refrained from adding that they were just not the same made with French bread. Something to do with the crust.

As they went off together into the blue night, Oriane watched them from the gates: the tall Englishman with the curious, half-shambling, half-elegant gait: casual, loose at the hips and shoulders, that came perhaps from his mountain walking. And beside him, the slight, youthful figure looking even more formal in his English suit and stiff white collar contrasted with Thomas's sports jacket and flannels. They were talking, Guru's hands waving graphically to illustrate some point, Thomas listening, head lowered, attentive.

'I've been taking a leaf out of your book,' she heard Guru say, 'a palm-leaf. You're right, some of them are definitely in cipher . . .' And Thomas's deeper voice murmured something of which she caught only, '. . . have a look at Roger Bacon's book . . . code never been cracked . . .'

She expected one or other to turn and look back at her but they walked on, deep in conversation, and she remembered that they had known each other before she met them.

Chapter 7

War seemed a most unlikely condition. There had been war in 1914, but it had affected Oriane only in the sudden absence of M. Richard and the cancellation of her passage 'home' to school in Rouen. This time, it seemed, war was to have a more direct bearing on her life.

She wrote to Marie-Hélène, as she had continued to do.

> 'Everyone is confused. Naturally the Congress Party is against the British: Hitler might well remove their oppressors from the scene for them. Gandhi has even written an open letter to the British people advising them not to oppose Hitler by force, but by "spiritual force" instead. He appears confident that bullets and tanks will be stopped in this way ... Aurobindo, however, says that Hitler is an evil that must be stopped by any means possible. Who will India listen to?'

Marie-Hélène had often suggested that Oriane should see France 'at least on a visit', but it had never happened, and now it was too late. But after the war, they agreed, after the war they must meet again, and Oriane would at last see the children, Etienne and Juliette – now of course quite grown-up. Indeed Etienne was married, his wife already expecting her first child. (It seemed altogether unbelievable to Oriane that Marie-Hélène was about to become a grandmother

69

while she, only two years younger, was still referred to as 'the daughter of the house' in the rue Laval.) Juliette's husband and Marie-Hélène's son Etienne had gone to fight. It all seemed very distant and foreign here, though even in Pondi men were enlisting.

And then, while letters were in mid-ocean, small, domestic plans still being talked of, it was all over. So suddenly. On June 10th the German forces poured across the Seine near Rouen. The French army was swept away like bushes in a hurricane, the dead left by the roadside or in the trenches that provided such brief protection.

Marie-Hélène, her daughter-in-law Isabelle, and the new baby, Raymond, took shelter in the cellar. They heard the gunfire coming closer, and sweeping on. Isabelle tightened her arms round the baby, blank with terror. Marie-Hélène prayed for Etienne. Had she followed the path of a rook skimming eastwards on the wind high above them, and looked down at the field of battle, she might have glimpsed his body in a ditch ten miles away, his blood slowly discolouring the soil.

Four days later the Germans rolled into Paris and the French government sued for an armistice, and on June 21st, in a walnut-panelled coach of the Orient Express, its Lalique glass lampshades unscathed by the brief unpleasantness, the French delegates signed the sad document. The rumble of a distant train drifting through the trees of Compiègne had the sound of a muffled drumroll – the *chamade*, that signifies surrender.

Ten years before, when Gandhi spoke, a subcontinent boycotted Britain; went on strike; men, women and children offered themselves as unresisting targets to *lathi* blows, walked to the sea-shore for a symbolic handful of untaxed salt. Now, he urged Congress to resign, to continue the struggle at a point where the British were at their most stretched. Aurobindo, the ex-fugitive, the man in the long-forgotten iron cage, had come to different conclusions: the mystic who had renounced violence saw Hitler as a force of evil who should be fought in every possible way.

British India wavered, uneasy: the armed forces supported the British – six divisions crossed the ocean – while the politicians worked against them: Stafford Cripps offered Independence once the war had been won. But what if it were lost? 'A post-dated cheque drawn on a failing bank' Gandhi called it, unimpressed.

In Pondicherry matters were arranged differently. There was a moment of shock, of incredulity; a newspaper photograph – Hitler's army at the Arc de Triomphe – was the defining image. French India declared for de Gaulle.

Guruvappa talked of 'signing up' but it seemed that someone had spoken to someone who had spoken to the General, and Guru's languages – and some other skills that Oriane knew less about – had attracted the interest of the French government in exile. He was summoned to London, to de Gaulle's HQ for some mysterious business involving cryptography.

She was furious: this could be dangerous, one heard dreadful things about London, not to mention the perils of the sea voyage: submarines, air attacks. He was not strong, there had been an incident with malarial fever – he could claim his health was not –

Suddenly he began to laugh. 'You're behaving like an Aunt,' he said.

As always with the two of them, she spent her force in ranting and he waited, courteously, and then did what he had already decided. She remained furious while he walked to the gate and stepped out into the road. Then she allowed herself a burst of hot, painful tears. She shouted at the *mali*: the drive was a disgrace, overgrown with weeds! The gates needed washing! By the time she reached the kitchen she was in what

Thomas had once called her Captain Bligh mode. But to her dismay the rage left her and she gave the staff a merely routine telling-off.

Oriane was alone at the hotel now. Her parents had left earlier, choosing a bad time to go 'home', disregarding the warning rumbles. Hubert was over eighty and he wanted to see grey skies again. People talked of war but they busied themselves, settling into a family property overlooking the river. Madame de l'Esprit, to her dismay, felt the gnawing ache of rheumatism in her bones and missed the sun of Pondi. They were visiting cousins in Nice when rumour became fact and they found themselves stranded in the South, exiles in their own country, safe, while war shattered the streets and houses, destroyed the gardens and the countryside they had dreamed of for so long. Oriane did not miss them more than was appropriate: it had never been a close relationship – though she felt sometimes that given an opportunity her father could have played a bigger part in her life; she thought of him with an odd sort of regret, a sense of a lost opportunity, and she found too that the opinions which best stood the test of time had often been his.

There had been a difficult scene when she told them she would not be leaving with them. She intended to stay on, in Pondi.

'But alone –'

'I have friends here.'

'What friends? Thomas Ettridge is in London, and you have never become part of our circle –'

She said briskly, with one of her shrugs, 'It suits me here.'

It was incomprehensible to them. At first they refused to take her seriously. Then Oriane's unwavering insistence wore them down. The girl had always been stubborn. 'Oriane will do what she wants,' her father reminded his wife. And perhaps, after all, to have the Hotel carried on, a family concern . . .

It was her father who told her one day shortly before they left, that there was a small matter of mixed blood in the family.

'Well I knew that. Your grandfather married a British girl –'

'I'm talking about an Indian connection.'

But this was surely impossible – the portraits, the old books, all the documents they had studied together. She was familiar with every branch of the family. Where did this – mixing – take place?

'Before Thierry married his English girl he was away, carrying messages, the usual diplomatic business. And of course there was the war . . . Catherine was lonely. Some kind of – liaison took place, though where and how . . . no one knew. There were rumours about a teacher she saw, language lessons . . . well. The girl died in childbirth less than eight months after the wedding.' He shrugged. 'These things can happen. Thierry took the child back to France. Brought it up as his own. No one outside the family knew. And as years passed –'

She exclaimed, incredulously, 'Your father was half Indian.' He wondered what was coming. She said, 'I wish I had known earlier. I might have learned more of my part-heritage!'

With time, though, Oriane herself almost forgot the small bend sinister in her family tree, but occasionally, a chance remark would drop like a stone into the depths of her consciousness and the ripples would spread.

'Railway people,' someone remarked to her one day, apropos a group of people she had just met at a Government House party. 'Pleasant enough. And the wife and sister, stunning. One weeps for them.'

'Why?'

'Anglo-Indians. Half-castes. Surely you knew? Nobody wants them, not the Indians, not the Europeans. Chi-chi. It's what they call the touch of the tar brush.'

She stared at the man, her heart sinking, reminded of her own background. 'What a revolting expression!'

'Merely a figure of speech –'

But Oriane had lost interest in their conversation. She was tired, and went home early and played Debussy on the gramophone. She stared at herself closely in the mirror. Her mother used to worry about the child spending too long in sun – 'Oriane, you look quite brown!' Her skin shone, luminous in the dim room. 'Nobody wants them,' the man said, 'not the Indians, not the Europeans.' Yet surely she belonged to both?

Some time later Thomas Ettridge called on her, newly arrived from England, bringing her a present of a rosewood bracket clock. 'When it chimes I shall think of you,' she said, pleased.

The uniform suited his loose-limbed body, the cap was flattering. He saluted her ironically, feeling a fraud.

'But Thomas, *cet ensemble farouche*! You're quite the military man. And a major – very impressive.'

'I think they had a spare set of crowns and didn't want to waste them.'

'Were you not a pacifist?'

'I was and am. But –'

'Ah, but. That dangerous word.'

He wanted to explain, to tell her what was happening in the outside world that perhaps she was unaware of, here, so far away. 'There are some situations that make pacifism impossible. In Nazi Germany things are being done –' but she broke in, her thoughts elsewhere.

'Guru is in London.'

'I know.'

Something about the tone alerted her. 'Was it you who did it? Arranged for him to be sent for?'

He nodded. She did not show her anxiety, her fears for how things were. She heard there were bombs, air-raids that were reducing London, it seemed, to rubble as the British had done with Pondi two hundred years before. Londoners were dying, and of course she was horrified in a general way, but the piercing, specific dread was a personal one. To cover it she used irritation; her voice sounded petulant.

'So he's working on codes. I had no idea about this cryptography business.'

'There may be other parts of his life you know nothing of.' A pause. 'He's married.'

'I knew *that*.'

'Really. I wondered.'

It was for the betrothal that he had been brought home from England, before going up to Oxford, before meeting Oriane. That he had never gone back, that he had remained in Pondi was something they had never discussed. Indeed, the bride-to-be seemed immaterial. His father had settled on a suitable girl, it hardly seemed to concern the son. And in any case, it had all seemed a long way off. Until it happened. And then the marriage, too, became somehow immaterial.

Her parents' kitchen boy, Subra, had been promoted to dining room waiter. Beaming a welcome, he brought in a fresh lime juice in iced water and Thomas took it, with a nod of thanks. He held the glass for a moment then put it down, misjudging the distance so that the glass banged on the table.

'They're sending us to Burma. The Japanese are proving quite a problem.'

If he had hoped she would show anxiety on his behalf he was to be disappointed. She seemed distrait, unfocused. He cleared his throat.

'There's something I want to say. I – um – I'm no spring chicken of course –'

'Since we are the same age that is hardly a gallant observation, Thomas dear.'

'You look years younger than me. I don't think Englishmen age well in the tropics. Something to do with our . . .' He stopped, frowned, aware that he had been side-tracked.

'This is not the time, but um, after the war, all being well, you know. I wondered if you'd consider marrying me.'

'What a very extravagant expression of your feelings. Is it your intention to sweep me off my feet?'

'A Sherman tank couldn't sweep you off your feet. Do you want me to go down on one knee? Make a romantic declaration?'

'Not really. You were never very good at that, were you?'

'I didn't have much practice.'

Just once, ten years before, Thomas had found Oriane alone in the garden at dusk, and – misled by her shining eyes and the smile she gave him, had attempted to kiss the blurred softness of her mouth.

She had recoiled violently, taken by surprise (frightened by the intensity of the botched embrace, though he had no way of knowing that) and he released her immediately, stepping back, almost losing his balance on the loose gravel. He felt ridiculous and began to burble an apology.

She said crisply, 'Please stop that, Thomas.'

He flicked an agonised, embarrassed glance at her white face, luminous in the dusk. 'I just wanted to explain –'

She was shaking with nerves, uncertain how to deal with the situation: a woman approaching thirty who was behaving like a green girl. But how should she have behaved? She had denied herself the easy, fleeting excitements of youthful passion. There had been no tentative fumblings and snatched kisses in secret corners from eligible young Frenchmen to whom she was showing the garden. None had ventured past the cutting edges of her protective armour: the sarcasm, the earnest intellectual façade.

Thomas had been different. She had thought of the Englishman as a friend and found herself in a false position.

She turned away and left him stammering his unsatisfactory words, calling over her shoulder 'I think Mama is expecting some people. I must go in.'

He had hoped in the following weeks to find an opportunity to put his case more elegantly – perhaps even in French, though the lines that ran through his head came from an English poet, one who knew about women and disappointment, who captured the moment a loose gown fell from smooth shoulders, 'and she caught me in her arms long and small' . . . long and small, odd words, but yes, the flow and slenderness of Oriane's arms, their weightlessness caused a contraction in his chest when he saw her.

But the poet never had Oriane to deal with, the sceptical glance, the blue flash that left men floundering. Thomas had memorised suitable phrases, worked out strategies for bringing about an ideal encounter. She seemed to have forgotten the garden incident altogether, her smile once more encouraging. He had begun to hope. And then at the Governor's house one evening he had introduced her to a young student.

'Oriane, may I present . . . ?' And walking home after the recital the three of them had paused on the Promenade and Oriane had been, playfully, sharp with him.

'You're very prickly this evening,' he said.

'Those are my weapons.'

'And must I beware of being hurt?'

'Only if you approach too closely.'

He wondered if this was a warning or merely banter, part of an elaborate ritual. He too, after all, was not experienced.

Then young Guruvappa had said something quite banal – about the night sky, was it? – and he had been aware of a sharpening focus, of a certain intentness in the way she glanced at the boy. It was a turning point, but he saw that only afterwards.

He never did get the opportunity for the polished proposal, the right time and place to advance his cause. And ten years later he slammed down his glass of lime juice on the dark, polished table and botched things again. But this time he would not give up so easily.

'At risk of sounding ridiculous, Oriane, I just want to say I've loved you for the last ten years.' *The thought of you beats in my veins like blood, your voice runs in my head like music, your perfume is a memory I carry with me wherever –* He cleared his throat. 'I think I can – um – make you happy.'

'And I know I would make you miserable.'

'Couldn't I risk that?'

She shook her head.

'Do you intend to grow old like this? Alone?'

She did not reply but he saw her face, the expression of pity for a man who simply did not comprehend her situation. And understanding everything, his body burning with a longing he would never have expressed to her in words, lamenting the separate sadness that he foresaw for them all, he burst out angrily, 'I wish I'd never bloody well introduced you!'

She smiled. 'Oh Thomas, you always have to place yourself in the position of power. If it had not been then it would have been another day. Fate has its ways.'

'Karma?' he said contemptuously.

'Did you organise London to get him away?'

'Yes. But not for the reasons you imagine. Not for me. For his sake.'

Then, his throat cracking, he had gulped down the lime juice and left.

Chapter 8

Oriane had never minded being alone. As a child she spent hours gazing into the fountain in the hotel garden, or out over the rooftops towards the sea, feeling the warmth of the stone beneath her fingertips; an occasional breeze lifting the wing of dark hair at her temple. She liked the feeling of aloneness.

Now, for the first time, she found the condition irksome. She was learning the difference between being alone and being lonely. She had grown accustomed to the presence of another; she had become dependent – unpleasant word – on that presence. They might not speak or even meet for hours on end, but the cord was there between them, humming with life, and when they next spoke, the conversation would continue as though uninterrupted.

Guru, his sardonic, sceptical eye, the slanting cheekbones, his fingers moving across a page, his laugh, all these things had become as necessary as breathing. She had never shared a gesture more intimate than a clasping of hands, yet her body ached as though a part of it had been amputated; she was incomplete. This was intolerable. The servants felt the lash of her irritation.

One day, when a hot wind blew the dust into angry swirls in even the sheltered streets, when the trees drooped as though the sap had dried up within them and the sea heaved itself on to the rocks beneath the Promenade, grey and ominous, the movement lethargic, but signalling the possibility of danger, like the unhurried sinuosity of a snake, Oriane strode down the drive and out on to the rue Laval at an inappropriately hasty pace. Her bias-cut frock became trapped between her hot, moist legs; her wide-brimmed hat flapped and struggled to escape the steel pins that skewered it to her head. It was not the season or the time of day for hurrying. But Oriane's wishes had always directed her actions and now she wished to be in a different part of town without delay.

The idea had come to her quite suddenly, and now she wished it already accomplished: she would visit Guru's wife.

Bending her head to shield her eyes from wind-blown grit, uncomfortably aware of sweat trickling beneath her armpits, she built a mental picture of what she would find: perhaps the wife would be strolling in a scented garden, or reclining on a shaded charpoy, the woven hemp covered by some richly coloured cotton, softened with cushions. The woman would be a plump, smooth-skinned matron, round-cheeked and bright-eyed or else a thin, haughty matriarch, secure in her position – perhaps chilly. She might be unaware of Oriane's existence; the encounter could prove embarrassing: how under those conditions would Oriane explain her presence at the house?

He had never discussed his marriage in detail. The bleak day, six years before, when he had announced the event, had been painful for them both.

He began without preamble. 'I'm to be married. It can't be put off any longer.'

'So have you come to say goodbye? Is that it?'

'Why on earth would I do that?'

The marriage was not something that entered into their world. It was necessary for family continuity – for a child in other words. But now the wedding was to take place, on the correct, auspicious date. She sat listening, occasionally smoothing her hair at her neck, touching her sleeve as though to straighten it. She asked no questions until he came to a stop. Then she said two things. First she asked, 'Was there no other way?' And when he shook his head, she asked, 'Are you content?'

He looked at her, frowning uncomprehendingly. 'Content? *Content?* What has that to do with the matter? My discontent, my despair, my . . . revulsion, are irrelevant.'

She was angry, but more than that, she was astonished: he had seemed so independent, so detached from the absurdities of caste and tradition. Now she saw that he had merely *seemed* to be free, like a monkey on a very long lead. They had twitched the string and brought him to heel.

Disappointment pulled the muscles in her face downwards so that her mouth curved in what looked like disgust.

'What happened to all those grand theories you talked about? Bergson and all that. The assertion of free will?'

The small, ironical smile showed fleetingly. 'I *chose* to submit,' he said drily.

She gave one of her small shrugs, less a movement than a tiny adjustment of her posture. It said a great deal and no further words were necessary.

There had been one other conversation, a year after the wedding. He missed an appointment, sent apologies. Next day he appeared at the hotel, his face grey with fatigue.

'Kamala has lost the child. There were complications, I'm afraid. It seems she will not be able to have children.'

Kamala, Oriane registered mechanically. She had told him once she did not wish to know his wife's name, and he had maintained the interdiction, referring when absolutely necessary to 'my wife'. Now 'Kamala' had lost the child. And no more to come. What, then, was the use of Kamala? Why should she sit there in the big house, occupying space, causing her husband inconvenience and pain – ('my revulsion' he had said, that first day) – with no offspring to justify her presence? Divorce her, Oriane said briskly, but silently, divorce her, she implored, silently, divorce her she screamed, silently.

'Divorce,' Guruvappa said, as though she had spoken aloud, 'would not be appropriate. All this has been very hard on her. She is a sick woman.'

But if there could be no child, the point of the marriage was lost. Surely the family would expect . . . He had accepted the bonds of duty then, but now seemed able to disregard them. The anger mounted in her like fire, roaring in her ears. 'So –' Her vision blurred and even her speech thickened as she attempted to reach him. 'So what will happen?'

Nothing would happen, he said. 'She will remain.' Misfortune would be accepted; it was the right thing to do. His own desires did not enter into the matter.

Oriane watched his face, looking for signs. Did she believe him? The proof that would have convinced her – for him to behave badly for her sake – would have itself rendered the gesture useless and ultimately destructive. Because by behaving badly he would no longer have been himself.

She wondered about the faceless, unfortunate wife ('Kamala has lost the child'), who was perhaps more important than she had realised. How much time did they spend together? She had assumed too much, a marriage could build ties even between unlikely partners. There had been no further discussion of the matter, but for a while Oriane had required Guruvappa's presence for increasingly long periods of time: she had become interested in Tamil literature and his teaching skills were needed. She worked ferociously, and brought up the subject of a project they had often discussed: the translating from Tamil into French of some ancient poems. They would begin without further delay, she decided. The compactness, the liquidity of Tamil made the task almost impossible, one phrase in the original requiring two lines to say the same thing. But she tried, searching for the *mot juste*, the most accurate choice of expression. Guru-vappa did not wear a wristwatch, and she never caught him glancing at a clock. But she sensed a weariness, a goaded quality to his responses that distressed her. And then, shuffling the pages, she came upon a draft of a rough translation, one of the ancient Tamil poems, in his hand-writing.

> You tell me I am wrong, my friend,
> That I should stop seeing her.
> Yes, of course it would be right
> If I could do as you say.
> But the pain is like butter melting
> On a sun-scorched board
> While a man without hands or tongue
> Tries to save it.
> It spreads through me
> No matter what I do.

She stared down at the page, feeling the pain spread through her, feeling his pain.

'I've decided I need a holiday,' she announced the next day, and left for the Nilgiri hills. She went for long walks, searched for wild flowers to be transplanted to the hotel garden. On her return she was out of touch for a while, busy, postponed the idea of the translation. Then things returned to normal. She did not ask about the wife.

The house was some way off, in a quiet turning off the rue Ananda Rangapoullé. She crossed the canal, feeling she was venturing into foreign territory, aware that the houses, though substantial, were different. Even the smell was different – no hint of sea-breeze here; the trapped air smelled faintly of spices, incense and drains, sharp in her nostrils.

It was a big house, three stories high, decorated on the front and around the windows with ornate plaster scroll-work. She walked to the door and knocked, conscious of the curious dimensions of the door, wide but not tall enough to be in proportion. The paint had long ago discoloured and worn away so that the wood seemed stained a pale, washed-out blue. The door was opened by a Tamil who listened impassively as she gave her name and asked to see Mrs Kamala Guruvappa. He stood unmoving, staring at her, and she wondered whether he had even understood her words. Then he closed the door and she heard him padding away. She waited, conscious of the sun on her shoulders and the backs of her legs. A bead of perspiration formed in the hollow of her throat and trickled down between her breasts. Perhaps there would be no response. She wondered how long she should wait. Then, without warning, the door opened and a silent female beckoned her in, waved her hand towards the stairs. It was all a disconcerting blend of the expected and the unfamiliar: the cool, dark rooms furnished with heavy oak pieces, tiles underfoot, wall hangings. But there were jarring touches, a charpoy, a woven hemp bed, pushed against one wall, a young servant glimpsed through an open door, squatting on the floor to chop up vegetables.

Guruvappa's wife sat cross-legged by the window of a bare upstairs room. She seemed neither surprised nor put out by Oriane's appearance at the door. She waited while the Frenchwoman haltingly explained that she had come to see her, to visit her, because ... 'because with your husband away, it must be lonely for you.'

The woman spoke neither French nor English, and Oriane was suddenly reluctant to use the Tamil she had acquired with Guru's encouragement. In the slow, musical phrases of the wife and then the uninflected voice of the interpreter, Oriane heard, twice-over, of the agony and despair of the woman by the window, a woman who had outlived her reason for existence. She was not more lonely now than when her husband was at home. She would like to share his life but did not know how. Perhaps if she had learned English? But surely at home, their own language should be spoken . . . She was at pains to assure the visitor that her husband was kindness itself. Few men would have been so gentle.

'One of our poets wrote of the power of a child to hold a man to his home. Perhaps if I had produced a child . . .'

Perhaps this friend of his, who had been kind enough to think of her, might advise on how she could win back her husband?

Kamala was thin, not slender. Her fine bones were covered too tightly by her dark skin and her eyes were strained. There was no lustre to her hair. She looked away, to the window, while her words were retold, then back, with no change of expression, to Oriane.

Oriane said hurriedly, 'I'm sorry, please tell your mistress it was simply a call of friendship. I have no knowledge of these matters . . .' and fled, stumbling down the stairs, out of the gate, back along the street, eyes blurred with tears. The unfairness of it! How dare the ineffectual wife presume, reveal her predicament, make Oriane feel *sorry* for her? Distraught, she found her way home and lay on her bed in the darkened room, listening to the squeak of the overhead fan, dully watching the slight movements of the mosquito net. She was more alone now, in her awareness that she was not unique. Across the canal, another woman languished, diminishing her own suffering.

Kamala's cousin was shocked: 'To speak of such personal matters to a stranger – a foreigner! How *could* you!'

Guru's wife closed her eyes. She saw again the French-woman blundering out of the room like a blind person, saw the way something died in her face. Sometimes shame must be endured in self-defence.

Chapter 9

The war in Europe had ended. Guru was on his way home. In India, the end seemed imminent – 'It's all over, really, isn't it?' an Englishwoman called to Oriane as they passed on the sea-front. '*Ah oui, ils sont foutus, les japonais,*' concurred the man at Government House. Yet the Japanese were still there, in Burma, on the Andamans, and news of peace celebrations across the ocean seemed premature. Of Thomas, Oriane knew only that he was in a prisoner-of-war camp near Rangoon. She had written, sent food parcels care of the Red Cross, though she doubted if any got through.

She was vague about the details of Guru's home-coming. She waited at the hotel, aware that his family would be meeting him at the station – or would he come by car? Was he still, officially, under the wing of the army? Would he be in uniform? How odd that she did not know the answers to these questions.

She threw herself into household tasks: the place needed redecorating. People would be travelling again; guests could be expected before long.

The garden had been turned to growing vegetables, shortages had made them all more practical. Now, she acquired seedlings from a friend at the botanical gardens, sent the sweeper for manure, encouraged the small blue columbines that had managed to survive round the walls of the house. She found herself straying frequently into the drive, discovering reasons for checking the gates, the state of the gravel, finding fault with the cleaning of the fountain.

Oriane had resisted the fashion for short, skimpy skirts that Englishwomen had adopted in the big cities. She found the square-shouldered little outfits in stiff cotton or tussore ugly and lacking in grace. She preferred the droopy, longer frocks that hung in her wardrobe.

Wearing one of these, dark blue with lace collar, worn almost threadbare but good enough for gardening, she was supervising the pruning of a thornbush at the side of the house, arguing strenuously with the *mali*, so that she failed to hear the light footsteps on the gravel drive and glanced up to catch the *mali*'s surprised smile and call of welcome, directed over her shoulder. She turned, startled, and her crêpe skirt caught on a particularly vicious thorn which snagged and tore the flimsy cloth.

She cried '*Merde*!', tugging at her skirt and pricking her finger so that a bright drop of blood flew on to the bush and hung on a dark leaf like a single holly berry. Sharp as the thorn, tears pricked her eyes.

He stood, dressed in a white kurta and cotton trousers, smiling, carrying a small package wrapped in brown paper.

'I'm sorry!' Guru exclaimed, 'I startled you, oh heavens, you're bleeding –'

'Don't be foolish!' She tore the dress free and stood facing him, tears trickling down her cheeks while she sucked her pricked finger. For a moment neither spoke or moved. Then, laughing and crying she reached out her hands and gripped his. There was a hesitation, a moment when, in the French manner she might have kissed him socially, acceptably, one cheek then the other, but the gardener stood by, grinning, and the heartbeat of the moment passed. She was still holding both his hands, gripping them hard, and she exclaimed, irrelevantly, 'Your skin has grown rough!'

'We were packed off to a stately home in the countryside.

A sort of neo-Tudor château. Hard water. And the most awful soap.'

The tension evaporated, and she released his hands, leading the way indoors. 'We read about the rationing in England, two ounces of butter a week –'

'But we heard you were starving here –'

'Oh, eating cats and dogs, just like the siege of 1760 – rats were quite a delicacy –' He was looking horrified and she relented, laughing. 'No, not that bad. There were shortages, kerosene dried up completely, but not for long.' And she said to herself, what is this? Are we to be polite with one another now?

They went up the verandah steps and he handed her the brown paper package. 'I brought you a present – some stuff by a chap called Camus. Essays. I think you'll like them. He's rather rude about God.'

'Whose God, yours or mine? I see you've gone native. Is this a new affectation?' she enquired, raising her eyebrows at the kurta and cotton trousers.

She began to tear off the paper wrapping and with the stepping through the door of the drawing room the frontier was crossed; already she was asking questions, her eyes on his face and everything was as it had always been.

'Welcome home,' she said almost absent-mindedly, when they paused for breath.

Chapter 10

Thomas wrote to say he would be passing through Pondi in due course. The prisoner-of-war camp in Burma had left him with certain lasting souvenirs: he was deaf in one ear and he would no longer be able to challenge Guru on the cricket pitch, but he considered himself fortunate nevertheless. The letter carried the authentic Thomas tone: rueful, self-deprecating, deliberately unemotional.

'He doesn't say when he'll be here,' Oriane complained. 'As bad as you. No consideration.' She intended asking Thomas to explain about the atomic bomb. Had this really been necessary to end the war? Guru said not, that it was more a gesture, a statement of power. But others thought differently. There was much to discuss.

She prepared a room and then forgot about the matter. She and Guru were already busy with a new project, another translation. They were working, surrounded by books, at a table on the verandah when a taxi drew up at the gate and Thomas got out, moving awkwardly.

Oriane had leapt up and was about to hurry down the drive. She paused, narrowing her eyes against the glare. Ah, Thomas had lost that careless, graceful manner of walking, that way he had of seeming to be shouldering his way through the impeding air. He limped. 'Someone is helping him,' she said. 'Is it the taxi driver? No: he has a child with him.'

Guru looked more carefully at the person whose hand was on Thomas's elbow – a small, fragile figure in a green lunghi and cropped blouse, hair drawn back from a face pale and pointed as a blanched almond. 'It's not a child. It's a woman.'

And then Thomas, limping up the drive, waved happily, and the two of them went to meet him, hugging him, all three of them talking at once, the small, pale woman at his side waiting silently until he introduced her: 'This is Kyung. My wife.'

There was a moment's embarrassment, and on Oriane's part, an odd dismay: Thomas had always been – well, *there*, not that she wanted him, not that she would ever have considered – still, the last time she had seen him, he had asked her to marry him, professed enduring love, and now here he was, standing in the drive with a foolish smile on his face introducing this Burmese child as 'My wife'.

There were handshakes, welcoming phrases. ('Does she speak any civilised language?' Oriane wanted to ask him, since the creature had not yet uttered a word.) Then the girl said, in a soft, undeniably musical voice, 'Thomas taught me English and I taught him Burmese. He learned more quickly than I did. But we are equals now.'

Oriane drew them out of the heat and into the house, making Thomas comfortable, talking rapidly, recalling the past, explaining to the stranger some reference or allusion that might have puzzled her. She was talking too much, she was aware of that, leaping from subject to subject, her manner almost feverish. Thomas should have warned her; prepared, she would not have found the woman's presence so unsettling. Kyung sat gracefully on a low stool; her legs, wrapped in the long, narrow lunghi, were drawn to one side like a mermaid's tail. Her cropped, long-sleeved top occasionally revealed a glimpse of smooth, honey-coloured skin at her midriff. Her face remained impassive as she listened.

She had an enigmatic tranquillity, a repose that even

Oriane could see must have been valuable to Thomas. ('Men often marry the women who nurse them,' she commented to Guru later, 'they develop a psychological dependency. Most unhealthy.')

Thomas regarded Guruvappa's cotton outfit with an ironic smile.

'We have abandoned Savile Row, I see.'

'Do you disapprove?'

'It's that man Gandhi's fault,' Oriane broke in. 'He's got top politicians walking around trying to look as though they weave their own cloth. Thank God I'm not British, I hear the Indians are rioting all over the place, demanding independence.'

Thomas caught Guru's eye and they burst out laughing. Once again Oriane sensed a bond that excluded her. She remembered the night she had first met Guru. He had said something about Einstein and moonlight and Thomas had laughed. She had blamed her lack of English – how should she understand their jokes? The famous irony? But it was not a question of language. With a feeling of desolation she sensed that at a certain level there was a link between the two men that she would never be able to share.

'I shall have to give you another room,' she said briskly. 'Do you prefer two beds or the *lit matrimonial*?'

If she had been hoping to discomfit Thomas she failed: 'Oh, a double bed if possible!' he exclaimed. 'I like to feel Kyung's presence even in my sleep.' There was a tiny silence. Oriane noticed that a framed portrait of General de Gaulle on the facing wall was hanging crooked and strode over to straighten it carefully. How callous men could be: it obviously did not cross Thomas's mind that she had no one whose presence she could feel, sleeping or waking. No one whose smooth skin might touch hers, as limbs moved carelessly in the dead hours. Years ago she had read something by a writer whose name she no longer remembered, who said that there were books which ranked in one's life with lovers and passionate experiences. She had agreed, but she had not known, then, that for her they would end by taking the place of the possible alternatives. With a grim smile she wondered now whether this might be considered an 'English joke'.

Thomas watched her slender back, the long arms upraised to straighten the picture and regretted his words. Had they been intended to wound? He was not a vindictive man, but she had hurt him. Did she even know that?

Guruvappa and the girl sat quietly, each thinking their thoughts. They did not exchange glances. Over dinner Thomas told the story of how the village girl, half-starved herself, had cared for him, dragging him to safety when he was left for dead by the retreating Japanese; crippled, sapped by dysentery, feet festering, body destroyed.

'I wouldn't be here,' Thomas said, 'if it hadn't been for Kyung and her ancient remedies. She used plants, herbs, oils –'

'You make it sound like a marinade for a gigot of lamb,' Oriane cut in lightly.

They all laughed then, but the next day Oriane said disgustedly to Guru, 'He's lost all his *edge*, didn't you think? He kept giving those terrible sickly smiles! I thought he looked ridiculous, didn't you?'

'I thought he looked happy,' Guru said.

PART TWO

Chapter 11

The diary began on a Thursday. *Thursday 6 September 1736 or 25th Avani of Nala ...* At the beginning he hardly knew what he intended: *I proceed to chronicle what I hear with my ears, what I see with my eyes, the arrival and departure of ships and whatsoever wonderful or novel takes place.* What he described along the way was something more: the rise, the zenith and the first failure of nerve; the decline of French power in India.

Thursday 6 September 1736 ...

He wrote in bound volumes the size of large account books – this at a time when paper was not always in use, when letters were scratched on palmyra palm leaves with sharp steel and rubbed over with sesame oil for protection. But Ananda Ranga Pillai, son of a wealthy merchant, twenty-seven years old, robed in his gown and turban, his sword and dagger worn for show rather than defence, passing through town in his palanquin, wrote his Tamil diary in many large bound volumes and it survived while its author and those he observed decayed and turned to dust.

Sunday 14 January 1742 ... He chronicled the comings and goings of men and ships, the flogging and branding of felons, the flight of meteors across the skies, defeats and triumphs, the deaths of children, the rise and fall of Governors. There had been earlier Governors – Lenoir who bought a hundred slaves, boys and girls aged between eight and twenty-five and shipped them off to the Ile de France – slaves were cheap in Pondicherry because of the famine that followed the Mughal wars … There was Dumas and François Martin, and there were others, afterwards, Godeheu, de Leyrit, but the one he remembered best was Dupleix.

This morning at 6, under the constellation of Asvini, when the rising sign of the zodiac was Capricorn, M. Dupleix the new Governor, and his wife, with their retinue, descended from the ship from Chandernagore under a salute of 21 guns from the fort.

A big man, the Governor, heavy thighs, jowls that would sag in time, rough Northern skin looking pallid next to the olive smoothness of Mme Dupleix – Jeanne – with her cascading black curls. *The road from the beach to Government House was decorated with plantain trees and coconut leaves. All the Europeans, members of council and the rest, were waiting on the beach, and they walked to the church to hear the service, then walked to Government House. Thus, on an auspicious day, with all state, and amidst music and dancing, he assumed the reins of government …*

Ananda noted the way she hung on her husband's arm, her sparkling eyes turning constantly to his face. Tightly corseted, jewelled at throat and wrist, she glowed in the heat. The mother, of course, had been half-Indian, so she would feel at home here. Dupleix, forty-five and overweight, suffered with the climate: boils, fevers, bowel problems, but by the end, for him too, it was home. This was his place. Hopes, drive, ambition, he had them all, and knew he would succeed magnificently.

Madame Dupleix's mother was half-Indian, Oriane noted grimly. It did not seem to have caused her social embarrassment. Had society been so different, then? Or had Dupleix overridden prejudice?

'Are you looking for a word, Oriane?' Guru asked.

She returned to the page.

... today the Governor entertained the Nawab Unwar-Ud-Din-Khan ... with great pomp and with a roll of drums, a clanging of cymbals and the sound of wind instruments, the procession moved off ... later, at the Governor's house a table was spread, groaning under the weight of silver plates, cups and dishes (some of which, it was discovered later, the Nawab's mace-bearers hid about their persons with the intention of pilfering). Musicians with flags were mounted on elephants, camels and horses, playing kettle and one-headed drums. There was a salute of fifty guns and later, fireworks ...

What do old men remember, feeble, sick at heart, disappointed with life? Do they remember the first battle they won, the bright day when everything went well, the women in silk, the touch of the Royal hand that elevated them from the crowd? Joseph François Dupleix, Marquis, not so old – only sixty-six – dragging out his last days in poverty and debt, waiting for the letter, the word that will justify his life, acknowledge his services to his country, his mind a turmoil, what does he remember?

Dupleix, dreaming: When was it, that day, with the dancing girls, the flags and pipes ... I'd just been installed as Governor, a cool February morning, and we went ... somewhere ... outside the city. Ananda the Tamil was there and Jeanne wearing her jewels as always, diamonds that lay heavy on her breasts ... We rode in palanquins decorated with peacock feathers, mine up ahead, the noise of the music making the horses rear and buck ...

The palanquin of the Governor went first, followed by others, and fifty soldiers, horses, dancing women, tom-toms, horns, drums, pipes, clarionets and flags ... The party set out early, by moonlight for my choultry. When we arrived the soldiers fired a 21-gun salute. The choultry was ornamented with leaf pavilions, cords hung with garlands and mango leaves, and when the Governor sat down to refreshments again a 21-gun salute, and again when he drank wine, and when he rose from table ... the whole day was like a festival, exhilarating. That evening the Governor went home, to Pondicherry, I remaining at my choultry –

'What is this *"choultry"*?' Oriane asked. 'You can't use words that no one will understand.'

Guruvappa was studying the bound volumes, the faded, cramped Tamil writing, the foxed pages, and replied absently, 'a *choultry* is a sort of hut, resting place, temporary dwelling – you could call it an arbour ... a gazebo.' He wondered where Ranga Pillai's had been built; where would a prosperous merchant choose for a secluded retreat?

The *choultry* had been built by Ananda's father, a place for quiet and peace, overlooking a small lake. There was a temple nearby, modest, shaded by neem trees and a banyan. When the Govenor's party had gone back, Ananda stayed on. The Governor had been gracious, the day had been a success, but Indians and Europeans together, it was an unnatural grouping involving effort on both sides and he felt a need to rest. At sunset the lake was a dark, rosy red, the light reflected on to the pearly-skinned cows that came down to drink so that they glowed like statues chiselled from rose-quartz. Ananda Ranga Pillai stayed the night. The following day he presented himself at the Governor's house.

For the next twelve years they would be partners, sometimes too close for comfort, when Ananda told Dupleix he was wrong, too harsh in a judgment –

... three lascars employed in the fort made away with some bags of pepper ... apprehended, they were sentenced, tied to a tree, received fifty lashes; were subsequently branded with the figure of a dog and their ears cut off ... they would

have forfeited their lives but for divine mercy and my intervention. I pleaded with the Governor and begged that capital punishment might not be inflicted on them . . .

There were days when Dupleix's brilliance, his courage, caught the imagination of his courtier – *Luck was with the Governor in those days – he might tear his coat but he would be sure to find a use for the pieces. He possessed the nectar of help, otherwise called the favour of God . . .* But there were days when even the loyal servant thought Dupleix was too greedy for profit, or foolish to trust a Mahratta prince whose motives were ambiguous; or when Dupleix in turn accused him of laziness or divided loyalties – apologising later, knowing he was unfair – the criticism prompted by Jeanne, who disliked the Hindu, mistrusted him and above all was jealous of his closeness with Joseph. Years later, when all three were limping towards their end, Jeanne – fat, flatulent, with painfully swollen feet and legs, shivering with cold in the alien grey climate of northern France – remembered the presents he brought her, the cloth of gold and fine muslin printed with flowers, the turban studded with jewels, crimson and green velvet, rose-water. She recalled his excellent taste in china and silver. The way he wept when her child died half an hour after he was born –

Wed 10 Oct. 1742. Half past 12 this afternoon the Governor M. Dupleix blessed with a son. 21-gun salute and church bells rang for half an Indian hour. But the life of the infant was limited to this period and his soul then returned to God. The child remarkably well developed: he was as large as one of a year old. The surgeon who measured the body said it was full two and a half feet long. He had never seen an infant of such a size at birth.

– she recalled that the Indian wept more bitterly than she herself: there had after all been other children, other deaths. Later he watched her take more and more control of the

Governor's affairs, using her knowledge of languages to displace him at Dupleix's right hand. Her father the doctor had taught her Persian and French. She spoke Portuguese to her mother and Tamil to the servants. English, French and Dutch were for merchants: fluent in their own tongues she felt no diffidence in explaining the necessities for certain . . .practical arrangements to be arrived at.

There were still days when Jeanne smiled at him, complimented him on his robe or a jewel he wore – Ananda had perfect taste, more refined than her own – and sent some new thing from Paris to his house, a book or a picture as a mark of appreciation. She knew how much her husband owed him. On other days she tore through the great rooms of the Governor's house, seething in fury. The Indian. The Tamil. A *native*, criticising her silently, with his eyes, or – less prudently – in that diary of his.

They had an edgy relationship, these three: two men linked by admiration and affection, and the woman close to both, ambitious, clever. Jealousy came into it and a desire to protect, and suspicion of one sort and another. Ananda was appalled by Jeanne's greed, her incorrigible attitude to bribes and so-called gifts. In the diary he described her as *a Hindu goddess with a multitude of hands ready to accept offerings.* It was too good a phrase to keep to himself, and someone made sure it reached her ears.

She had ways of getting her own back, coming between him and the Governor, making sure that any shortcoming was brought to Joseph's attention. Finally she won the day, edging him out, depriving him of power. It was not difficult: it was the language that did it, Jeanne's fluency. Moreover she could translate for Joseph in ways the Tamil would have found it difficult to match: mixing politics and pillow-talk; giving Joseph her views of a foreign diplomat while he admired her naked back in the tub.

The Governor and his lady were not in church on the day of the 'scented harlot' affair, but she used her closeness to the Capucins to make the most of it.

A wall had long been erected in the church between Caste Christians and Pariahs . . . The priest of Kârikâl, visiting, was offended by this and ordered the wall to be demolished. The following Sunday all mingled . . . and native Christian females came also. The wife of Asarappa Mudali . . . went to church decked with all the ornaments that are worn by the women of her caste, and arrayed in muslin gauze which was perfumed. She approached the altar where the senior priest was ministering, knelt down and was absorbed in listening to his exhortations. As soon as he smelt the sweet odour diffused by the lady's clothes he stopped preaching, held his nose, thrust the cane which he had in his hand into her hair-knot, and angrily addressed her thus: 'Art thou not a married woman? Art thou a dancing woman? Has thy husband no sense of shame? Can chaste ladies appear at church dressed in muslin gauze and exhibit their limbs, bosoms and the very hair on their bodies? Thou art a blessed woman indeed! Rise and begone to thy house!'

The matter might have ended there, had Jeanne not had a few quiet words with the Capucin brothers, who in turn advised the priest . . . *He summoned all Caste Christians, told them they should not deck themselves in thin cloths, ornaments of the kind worn by Tamilians, should tie their hair after the manner of the Eurasians. Should not wear perfumed muslin –*

'What does he mean, "perfumed muslin"?' Oriane demanded. 'Is this some native custom?'

She was intrigued, and Guruvappa had to explain to her the custom of perfuming clothes and linen with appropriate scents. 'Vetiver, cool in the hot season, or patchouli in the winter.'

She found the idea appealing; to waft through a room

swirling a subtle perfume in your wake. The Capucins had perhaps been too harsh. She returned to the diary. *The town in uproar, disorder and riot threatened, the Governor forced to forbid gatherings of more than four natives . . .* In due course another wall was built – of chairs piled one on the other – and services were resumed. But the Tamils had been shown their place.

Ananda, who had refused to accept Christianity, was unsurprised by the less than Christian attitude of the priest. But Jeanne could surprise him in other ways: her rapacity pained him, and he found her lack of moral scruples astonishing:

She wanted to hang me for keeping a letter addressed to her for one day, forgotten in my drawer – but she opens and reads and re-seals letters addressed to me!

Jeanne, an old woman in a strange country, huddled against insidious drafts, rubs a throbbing varicose vein and groans aloud, despairingly, at the thought of all the glory that slipped away. What a partnership it had been, hers and the Governor's! Even on the worst days, with the English taunting the French –

When all looked gloomy for Pondi, the Governor brought his energies to bear, and turned the tide of misfortune. Possessed of riches, courage, an indomitable will and a spirit which refused – even in this time of trouble – to look upon the English other than with contempt, M. Dupleix rose superior to the occasion, lavished his wealth, repaired the fort and ramparts, enlisted Mahé sepoys and others, secretly collected provisions for the army and to prevent the desertion of Pondi by its inhabitants, gave employment to every one of them –

Jeanne had always been the practical one. The vein stabs, her flatulence is getting worse. And the Court delays with a decision about reimbursing Joseph for his money, his own money, their personal money, spent to save the town. Thank God she had held on to a few of her jewels.

And Jeanne, too, dreams. But bitterly: I saw the way things were going. Someone had to look out for the revenue, Joseph was too busy worrying about wars and the English, betrayals by the princes – and see where his loyalty got us . . . I sold my last ring yesterday.

'Dupleix was the man who should have been honoured, *après tout*,' Oriane said. 'He had the vision, they should have recognised that. Imagine how it must have been for him, at the end. Bones aching with cold. Dreaming of Pondicherry. And Jeanne, with her tainted blood, the touch of the tar brush, dreaming of her lost splendour –'

'And the Tamil Pepys,' Guruvappa said drily, 'he died sick and disheartened too. They outlived their dream, I'm afraid. They knew the dying fall.'

'I don't want that,' she said. 'When the time comes, Guru, I want you to finish me off - *le coup de grâce* – like they do with old horses.'

'It doesn't have to be like that, you know. The British don't do that, they find a nice field, a quiet corner where the poor old thing can be at rest and they put him out to graze.'

'You'll find me a quiet corner then.' Oriane returned to the page, then paused. 'You said you have one of these gazebos, this *choultry* thing . . .'

'Well, it's my father's really. Family celebrations, that sort of thing. We hardly ever go there. I haven't been for donkey's years. Not since –' He paused and frowned.

Silently she completed the sentence for him. 'Not since the wedding.' They might have gone again for the celebration of a child – if a boy – but Kamala had lost the child.

'I'd like to see it,' Oriane said. 'Can we go? Is it allowed?'

A few miles outside the town, along the old sea road, the taxi turned inland and bumped along a track, through open countryside at first, then a winding route through palm groves and peanut fields, following the coastline so that now and then, when they crested a rise, they glimpsed the sea. Guru directed the driver until the path petered out and they came to a stop. They left the taxi and walked on, up a gentle slope, and stood looking down at a small round lake, lying in the hollow, surrounded by red earth. It was fringed on one side by neem trees and a banyan. A small, roofless temple stood between them, a neem tree growing through the middle, its branches forming a roof. Around its ruined walls small wild flowers grew in profusion, blending in the dim light so that they formed a haze of luminous blue.

'My *ancolies*,' Oriane exclaimed. 'How extraordinary that they grow wild here.'

The *choultry* was set back, among trees, a curious hybrid, a cross between a pavilion and an orangerie, a once elegant little structure now shabby, almost derelict, its palm-thatch roof sagging, the slender poles of its verandah splayed at crazy angles.

Oriane stared across at it, picturing that last visit, the wedding festivities, the bride in her jewels, the families laughing, servants bringing food in gleaming steel dishes, offering cool drinks, lighting flambeaux as the dusk deepened. There would have been musicians, but no dancing-girls, no twenty-one-gun salute . . .

They skirted the lake, the earth softened by layers of dried leaves, their feet crunching on fallen seed pods and empty husks, and stopped in front of the little wooden house. Oriane, suddenly tired, sat down on the steps. She had long ago given up high-heels and wore floppy Indian *chappals*, bazaar sandals which she would once have despised. She kicked off the sandals and sank her bare feet in the dried leaves and sat there while the silence grew in the space between the trees and filled the cup of the lake and wrapped them in its stillness.

The sun was very low, glowing red through the trees and the lake was already in shadow. A man came over the hill opposite, taking his cows home, waiting patiently as they paused to drink at the edge of the lake. He called a greeting, nodding up at them, his voice hanging for a moment like an echo in the still air.

Oriane tentatively steadied one of the sagging poles. 'You should restore this place.'

'Maybe I will,' he said, pushing cautiously at the creaking door. 'Would you like the guided tour?'

'Are you about to carry me across your threshold?' she asked.

Guru gave his ironical smile. 'I wouldn't have the temerity.'

The sun had gone by the time they drove home. In the gloom of the taxi they sat far apart, saying nothing. Her hand rested on the cracked leather seat like a pale bird. He covered it with his own and the fingers curled into each other. As the light faded, the rosy dust of the track turned greyish white while the sky at the horizon brightened almost to crimson, as though drinking the colour from the earth.

The diary took up more and more of their time, the papers spreading on to table after table. Hotel routine was quickly dealt with. She appeared at mealtimes to greet the guests and checked the accounts. The rest of the time was her own. The project itself was swathed in ambiguity; there was excitement, the thrill of unravelling a rare document, the frustrations and triumphs of bringing it to life again. But for Oriane there had been something more, at the beginning. She had set herself on what in her mind she called *une entreprise intime* , unwilling – or perhaps unable – to call it what it was: a literary seduction. No one knows what songs the sirens sang, nor in what tongue they sang them. Oriane, however, knew her power: language was the thread that would bind and hold him. But what began as a calculated exercise in temptation moved into something quite different – a shared obsession.

'What page?' she would enquire when he appeared each day, she, too, impatient to be started. Stratagem had led her into the trap of sincerity.

There was an interruption in August 1947. 'Independence, madame!' Subra from the kitchen exclaimed when he brought her breakfast. 'Midnight tonight! British going home!' He giggled.

'What is that to us?' she asked sharply, and saw his smile fade. She felt guilty. *Après tout*, the British had crushed the French, as well as the local opposition. There was no reason why she should be upset at their end of empire.

For once, she agreed with Ananda Ranga Pillai when he exulted at their defeat. *They are like the jackal who burnt his skin in stripes in order to imitate the tiger – and perished in anguish.* Alas, in the end it was the jackal who had gained the day. But now they were going home.

'Well,' she said, when Subra brought her coffee, 'we can all celebrate the British flag coming down. You can have the evening free. After dinner is served.'

Sunday 16th December – a celebration, the town decorated throughout with garlands, streets lined on both sides with lights . . . the cloth market in the fort where the Governor and his wife were to sup, was painted anew, embellished and supplied with wax-candles, silver plates and dishes . . .

Jeanne loved rich materials, precious stones, excess; the diaries listed her possessions, presents given to her, in columns, with their number, their value, their colours glowing on the page, the cloth shimmering, the jewels gleaming. Guru studied the list. The words, so imbued with a sense of themselves, so satisfying in Tamil, so musical, must be brought alive in another language.

The French word *chatoyant* means iridescent, glistening, changeable in colour or lustre, like shot silk and certain jewels. Could it be applied to eyes, he wondered. Oriane's eyes, could they be called *chatoyants*? Changing from a glitter amost sapphire-like they could dull to granite when a dark mood overtook her. Guru glanced up now and saw her bent over the page, lips pursed in concentration, frowning as she sought for the exact equivalent of a Ranga Pillai description – adjectives were particularly tricky, nuances could be lost, cultural differences could shift a word into unintended territory. She had lost the flawless surface texture of youth, her face had hollows and shadows now, but the flesh clung firm to the bone. In English he could describe her perfectly, in English the curve of a cheek, for example, could be tender or sweet and you knew where you were. Or it could be fine-drawn, taut, something you could trace with your finger, follow the contour as though holding a fine goblet. In French, did the word –

'Guru,' Oriane said, 'is something wrong? You're staring at my face. Have I a smudge?'

'Just searching for an adjective,' he said, and turned back to the text. *Their retinue consisted of an elephant bearing kettle-drums, horses with large drums on their bags, another elephant carrying the standard –*

'Do you find this interesting?' Oriane asked impatiently. 'All these lists and details –'

'The life is in the detail,' said Guruvappa. 'He was a good diarist.'

'The Goncourts went in for a lot of detail too,' Oriane retorted. Her eyes flicked down the page.

The mounted force of Mir Asad ravages the towns and villages on its line of march, setting fire to the houses and

plundering the inhabitants of everything they possessed . . .
they, having lost their all, and suffering from want and
nakedness, dispersed and fled in all directions . . . How lucky
for the local people,' she said mockingly, 'that Dupleix was
there to protect them at times like that . . . from savagery and
fraud and double-dealing by their fellow-Indians –'
  'And by the French.'
  'What?'
  'Double-dealing. Your precious Dupleix . . .' He had
coined the word dupleixity for the Governor's not unblemished career – a pun she did not appreciate. They returned
to the text:
  These, certainly, are troublous times. A star being visible by
day, one having been seen to fall from the heavens in
daylight, and a comet appearing with a sweeping tail of the
length of two picotta-poles –
  'What? What poles?'
  'You've seen farmers using picottas, Oriane, for raising
water. Those long levers of bamboo. Don't interrupt all the
time' – *all these prodigies bear out, it would seem, what the*
wise men have said in the past, namely, that they are signs and
portents of coming evil . . .

She heard the news by chance: a visitor calling, exchanging a
few words over a glass of wine. 'Aurobindo's died, did you
know? I just heard.' Later there were the official announce-
ments from the Ashram – 'On December 5th 1950 Sri
Aurobindo left his body' – but for her it came as gossip from
a passing acquaintance.
  She looked into the kitchen and threw some mechanical
orders their way. Subra and the others politely ignored her
and went on with what they were doing. She could see that
they were clearly in control of things. She, for once, was filled
with uncertainties. She went to bed early and next day she
remained in her room. It was as though the weight of the

years, held back by sheer will-power and an obstinate refusal to acknowledge their passing, had suddenly overcome her and she crumbled, feeling tired and useless. She lay under the mosquito net and lamented a lost life. She could have served, she too could have dedicated herself to his ideas, one of the faithful. There was so much she could have done. Instead she had wasted her days, entertaining strangers for money, watching others build lives while she fretted in the rue Laval like a cuckoo, restless in a nest she had had no part in building. Emptiness mocked her.

She had never seen Aurobindo again after that childhood meeting on the sea-front, but she had followed his life with bitter interest. If only . . .

Now, when it was too late, she made a brief pilgrimage to the grey-walled house and stood in the courtyard with the other mourners. She felt she was observed and looked up to see the hooded eyes of Mira Richard, the Mother, peering down at her from a terrace. Later she was summoned to the Mother's room and the two women spent a short time alone together. Oriane never spoke of the meeting and did not return to the Ashram, but when, some years later, the idea of Auroville was born and volunteers asked for, she went at once and put herself and all she had at their disposal.

But on December 5th she did nothing, listless beneath the slowly turning fan, her eyes closed, ignoring the anxious knocking on the door and Subra's repeated 'Madame? Madame all right?' Madame was not all right, but there was nothing to be done. She was forty-seven and she felt a thousand years old.

It was inevitable that with the British dispatched, the French would find their days numbered. It was just that Oriane found it impossible to visualise a Pondicherry without the tricolor. Their long occupation could not be coming to an end – could it? Would they prove to have been merely visitors after all?

By June 1954 everything was in short supply: no kerosene available in the town, no buses running to Madras, electricity cut off for hours on end. Oriane complained officially to the authorities: how was she supposed to run a hotel under these conditions? What was she to tell people who had travelled across the world to be here? At least the arsonists were taking a rest, no fires were started in the night, unlike the spell four years earlier when over a hundred houses were burned down. But predictions were gloomy: when the cyclone hit and the old Pier crashed into the sea, there were those who made unaccustomed libations to the gods and prayed for a peaceful outcome. The rioters had rioted. The politicians had talked, and now the time had come. Merger.

They were at the desk early on the morning of November 1st; Oriane nervy, questioning his adjectives more than ever. She concentrated on the page, unwilling to acknowledge that this was a special day. A short walk away from the rue Laval, Kewal Singh, the representative of the Government of India, was received with full honours at the Governor's palace by Pierre Landy embodying the Republic of France. They signed the instrument of power and with the drying of the ink, the *de facto* merger of Pondicherry with the Indian Union took place.

As one tricolor replaced another, as the Indian flag was hoisted on the Governor's palace to general applause, soldiers fired a 21-gun salute, the sound floating over the tree-tops to the surrounding streets . . .

Oriane stopped translating in mid-sentence. In silence she listened to the firing of the guns. Then, as though it had been merely a noise that interrupted her train of thought, she continued the translation.

At the Governor's palace R.K. Nehru, who was attending

the function on behalf of the Government of India, assured 'the people of Pondi' (who of course were not actually present) that 'any change in the state will be effected only after ascertaining the views of the people'. There was cheering from those who heard the words, their relief echoed by those who read them in the newspaper later, or who heard the news in the market place. No fears, then, that Merger might bring problems of its own, or awareness that a power-shift is seldom accomplished without pain.

'No trumpets, no tom-toms, no elephants,' Oriane said suddenly apropos nothing in particular. 'A 21-gun salute! Dupleix got that for taking a glass of wine. Government celebrations are not what they were.'

The diary was to be in both English and French. Sometimes there were difficulties: they fought over descriptions, inter-pretations, when a particular word might – in Oriane's view – cast a pejorative light on a neutral action by Dupleix, or – Guruvappa might feel – did not give full due to Ranga Pillai's observations. To his stature. Oriane's original comment that no one would know who the man was, still rankled.

'Of course not,' he had snapped, for once irritated, 'it's another case of the invisible Tamil. We don't exist.'

'We?' She twitched a shoulder. 'Don't try and ally yourself with the Tamil in the street, my dear. You're a fraud,' she said, but affectionately, and he side-tilted his head in rueful imitation of the familiar Indian gesture.

'Maybe with Merger, things will be better.'

'No they won't,' Oriane said violently, 'everything gets worse. You taught me that: entropy. Just wait and see.'

To punish her, he chose a diary entry about injustice. Injustice was always a problem.

When we plundered Madras, the merchants abandoned their wealth and fled, terrified. 'The French,' they tell each other, 'will make us all Christian by force. They are not

tolerant, like the English. Their punishments are too severe.
They will hang us and cut our ears off –

'And what about education? What about the Untouchables?' Oriane retorted. 'What about citizenship, and all we did to try and create equality here?'

'Cultures are not comfortably grafted, like apples or roses. Ultimately rejection takes place.' She thought back to '47. They got rid of the British. If we are kicked out . . . thinking the unthinkable, she confronted her secret fear. Where would she go? Would she end her life like Jeanne Dupleix, shivering in the grey northern winds, remembering the warmth, the coconut trees, the palms and scents, the green and gold of Pondicherry? What would become of her?

'Shall we all be kicked out, Guru?' she asked.

'Not you,' he said, evading the real question. 'You're a fixture. You belong here.'

'Don't patronise me!' She was taken by surprise. His unexpected gentleness must mean things were worse than she had realised. 'I can face the truth.'

'Face it when you have to,' he advised. 'Shall we do some work?'

He opened the big, shabby volume. She tried to concentrate on the page. Everyone was tricking everyone else; the merchants, the councillors, the Governor, the army . . . Madame Dupleix, scheming with the Catholic priests, grasping, indulging her passion for jewels, finery, luxury. But she had loved him, Oriane reflected. Long before they were married, she was imprudent, jeopardising her reputation as a respectable married woman. They had been passionate lovers. The Dupleix marriage, when it took place, was described as the public confession of a long-standing clandestine admiration. Oriane, who was not narrow-minded, could see that poor M. Vincens, the first husband, had been complaisant indeed until his quiet, convenient death. This was David and Bathsheba, Anthony and Cleopatra. Jeanne was immoderate in all things: she plated the walls of the great salon of Government House with silver that reflected the faces of visitors, hung green-laced velvet curtains at the long windows, installed carvings and filigree and gold-embroidered velvet couches, coveted diamonds, flaunted pearls – but above everything, what she loved most was Dupleix.

Oriane, sifting through the pages, tried to visualise the reality: the public show, the pomp, the jewelled elephants and ceremonial swords, the glorious days. But with all that went the secret letters and negotiations with perfidious princes who promised but did not deliver assistance. The endless, exhausting correspondence with Paris, begging for the funds needed to finance the trade that benefited the King. And gradually the great idea of French India slipping away. The ignominy. But between the council meetings and the sieges, the quarrels with the Government and the appeasing of covert enemies, there had been a fierce, enduring love, they were bound by flesh and spirit; at the end of the worst day there was physical union, the sweaty exploration of each other's private domains, the soaring, the glory of oblivion –

'Ah, she was a lucky woman,' Oriane said aloud.

'Yes,' Guru agreed, his eyes on a line detailing Madame D's shameless demand for yet more bribes disguised as 'interest-free loans'. 'Lucky to get away with it. She was a monster.'

'But how she loved him!' Oriane exclaimed. 'How she loved him!'

He frowned, perplexed. 'Which page are you on?'

August 2 1754. M. Godeheu has landed with orders recalling the Governor and authorising his arrest if he hesitates to obey. At the Council meeting the reading of Godeheu's Commission was greeted by the fallen Governor with a cry of 'Vive le

Roi' . . .

'Ah!' Oriane exclaimed, close to tears, 'the unfairness of it. Betrayed by his own government, his own country!'

They have recalled the great and valorous man, the Duc d'Orléans *has sailed for France, taking him home –*

'But this was home to him!' Oriane exclaimed.

. . . sailing without the square flag at the masthead which the Governor of Pondicherry was entitled to . . . He used to say he would like to lay his bones in this city which he raised to so proud an eminence . . .

The ship headed for the grey north. If Dupleix looked back, he would see the town already growing smaller. He would have had to look ahead to see the magnificence of his creation dwindling, its greatness crumbling like the unsound belfry which he built, and which almost crushed his successor in its fall. The coin outlasts Tiberius, and time creates its own ironies. The belfry was rebuilt, stronger. And in due course a statue was raised, to Dupleix.

'And if the King had given him the money he needed,' Guru said, 'he could have held the Carnatic, all south India would have been theirs – yours,' he added mockingly.

On November 10th 1764, Joseph François Dupleix received the last rites.

Did he die remembering the disappointment? Or Jeanne as she was in the early days, the black curls, the lustrous amber skin scented with sandalwood, the jewels competing with her eyes, her breath sweet as cashew blossom?

He had outlived the faithful diarist. Weakened by dysentery, sick and weary, disheartened by the corruption and intrigue which followed the recall of Dupleix, Ananda Ranga Pillai was observing and writing to the end, as the English laid siege, yet again, to the city.

Within the walls provisions are now so low that soldiers' rations are cut to a half-measure of rice, a loaf made of palmyra fruit, and 8 ounces of pounded, maggoty biscuit every other day, with an issue of meat – camel, horse-flesh or whatever can be found – once a week.

Outside the town, the *choultry* built by his father, the shady pavilion where Dupleix and his retinue had once drunk wine to the sound of a 21-gun salute, had been destroyed by maurauding tribes. Only the small temple remained, high on the bank above the little lake, the blue flowers throwing their reflection on to the crumbling stone walls.

That final day the Diary ceased to be a journal and became an account, in another hand: *He got up, put on his glasses and signed a note – 'This must be considered my last letter.' Four days after his body was carried to the burning ghat, the English flag was hoisted over Fort Louis.*

'And now,' Oriane said sombrely, 'we have another flag where the French tricolor flew.'

'This is India, Oriane. It's only logical –'

'Boff,' she said.

Chapter 12

It was some time before 'the people' realised that Merger had been a beginning, not an end. That change meant not just shedding the French tricolor, casting off the French yoke, but being linked to something very large and close at hand. Moreover the bonds were being pulled tighter than was altogether comfortable. Panic rumbled.

'I probably won't see you tomorrow,' Guru warned Oriane, 'Nehru's arriving and I'm bidden to a meeting.'

'I know. I read it in the newspaper.' She flapped it at him and read aloud, 'Jawarhalal Nehru promises Pondi its individuality will be preserved –'

'Now I'm really worried.' He waved the newspaper away. 'When politicians promise . . .'

At the meeting everyone was charming – and charmed. Except for those who exchanged ironic glances over their chilled lime juice and murmured 'Wait and see.' And soon it could be seen that the status of the southern territories was being . . . regularised.

A few weeks later Guru reluctantly joined a deputation to Congress. In a cool, well-furnished office he met his old school friend, Oriane's 'pompous aubergine'.

This was a private audience: Guru had a realist's scepticism for official meetings.

The politician sighed and pushed irritably at his paper-work. 'Oh God, what's all the fuss about? I mean to say old chap, Pondi's not even a big city. You're just another piece of India, why should you be any different from Mysore or Bangalore?'

'Because it *is* different. Don't you retain *any* understanding of the claims of individuality? What did they teach you at St Paul's?' They shared hollow laughter at an old boys' joke.

Tamil Nadu lapped round Pondi like an ocean preparing to engulf a very small island.

Then, unexpectedly, on December 28th 1962, the fourteenth amendment to the constitution offered the reprieve: Pondi, Karikal, Mahé and Yanam were now officially the Union Territory of Pondicherry.

Oriane was exultant. 'Thank God! At least we're not just a corner of a south Indian state. We've kept our independence.' Guru said nothing. He had his links with Delhi, and he had a feeling bad news was on its way.

Meanwhile the monumental translation proceeded; the checking, revising and polishing. They catalogued the plays, the concerts that Ananda had financed, the poets for whom he was patron.

They searched out the songs composed and sung in Tamil and Telugu, the flowering of the local tongues that had already produced a rich literature, an ancient, vigorous culture. Oriane was not always quick to appreciate them. When Guru read her some verses by an eighteenth-century Tamil poet, she sighed impatiently. 'All right, he's pretty good. But he's not Baudelaire.'

'He doesn't celebrate evil, no. I expect it's naive of me but I rather like that.'

To Oriane's intense irritation she found herself for once without an appropriate rejoinder.

January 26th 1965. Congress in session . . .

Guruvappa was at home when the call from Delhi came through. The telephone sat in his hand, snug as a bone, a smooth black bone carrying the germ of bad news. He held it away from his ear, superstitiously reluctant to get too close.

'NV? Are you there?'

He sighed. 'Yes.' He listened, nodding as though his friend could see him. 'Thanks for letting me know.'

'Well there it is. Progress old boy. Had to come.'

Delhi had decided and the word was law: Hindi was to be the national language of India.

Oriane, when he told her, was taken aback. 'No debate? *Fait accompli*?' She shrugged. 'Is this how your democracy works?' Personally, she did not feel strongly about the matter one way or the other, but still it seemed wrong. This was Tamil country. Were the people to be deprived of their own voice? The language that linked them with their beginnings, that dated back to 500 BC? Were they now to be outsiders in their own land, forced to stumble in Hindi where they flew in their own tongue? French had been imposed on them, but only as a second language. Now it was Tamil that took second place. Aurobindo, she recalled, wrote that language was the index of the cultural life of a people; diversity of language was valuable because in its absence there was a danger, almost an inevitability of decline and stagnation.

'I'm sorry my dear.'

'This is a north-south thing,' Guru said, 'they've tried before; this has been building for a long time.'

Realpolitik creates unexpected bedfellows. All at once Pondicherry felt unthreatened by Tamil Nadu, as they fought common cause. Tamil Nadu, Madras, Karnataka, the whole of south India vibrated with the anti-Hindi agitation.

Partition had been a shuddering upheaval, an earthquake that changed the whole landscape of British India, sundering families, shattering established structures. The maps had been redrawn, the wounds had begun to heal. Now the planners and the law-makers were at it again, and this time it was not territory but language that was under threat.

At the Hotel de France it was business as usual: the foreigners kept coming, unconcerned with local strife. This was not a problem for outsiders.

Meals were served, linen changed, the fans turned lazily. But Oriane was seen less often: she and Guru withdrew into study, they lost themselves in translation. The diary was finished and they had moved back in time, sifting through the ancient anthologies of Tamil poetry.

The old poems looked unblinkingly at lonely wives, separation, loss, the sheen on a concubine's breast, the drum-beat of battle in the blood, the bleakness of death on the field of conflict. They examined the taste of fruit on the tongue, the way moonlight lies on a leaf, they knew about love –

> My father and yours,
> Were they kin?
> You and I
> How do we know each other?
> Yet like rain and red earth
> Our hearts have mixed together.

He looked over at her, and back at the page: 'That's as close as I can get it at the moment.'

'What's all this about her father and his being related –'

'That's because, traditionally, cousins marry each other.'

She nodded without comment. So Kamala, was she the traditional cousin? The poem dealt with an exception, with two whose fathers were not kin. Two not previously connected who had blended as inextricably as rain and red earth, two separate substances mingling, through some force of alchemy becoming one. She studied the words: so few, and saying so much.

'Yes,' she said, handing back the page, '*pas mal.*'

At the beginning of February Pondicherry college students went on hunger strike against 'the imposition of Hindi and the police excesses in Madras state'. From the roof terrace Oriane watched them marching, shouting slogans, hundreds of them, heading for the railway station, erasing Hindi letters from signposts. Some of them tugged at the purple bougain-villaea frothing over the walls of the houses they passed, wrenching them from their roots. It was probably a mistake for the police to use force, perhaps the youthful mob would have run out of energy. But someone threw a stone, there was a *lathi* charge, and then a policeman opened fire.

By the end of the day the students had set fire to the railway station, scrawled in Tamil on Hindi signposts all over town. When police reinforcements arrived and the shooting began, everyone lost control. Fires blazed at the post office, the telephone exchange and the Sri Aurobindo Ashram. Guru stayed away from the hotel: the mob was raging down the streets round the canal and Kamala, sick and frightened, could not be left alone. Oriane relied on Subra to keep her informed. The giddy kitchen boy was a family man now, with problems of his own.

'Twelve policemen hurt in the stone-throwing, madame, and army has been called in. Demonstrators injured. My son included. My cousin at the hospital told me four people are dead.'

Pilgrims and tourists were outraged. Where was the tranquillity, the sleepy charm they had been promised?

And Oriane, for the first time, did not feel at home.

Chapter 13

Marie-Hélène dreamed occasionally of India. In her memory Pondi was a green and white place – the green of trees and palm leaves, lawns and creepers. The sea, too, could be green; a pale, angry green on windy days when it dashed angrily against the rocks and sent its frilly surf hissing across the sand, the waves mounting so that the fishermen's catamarans canted over almost perpendicular, held to the heaving surface, it seemed, only by their bulging nets weighted with a ballast of living fish. On calmer days it lay like shot-silk, its pale turquoise turning to bronze as the wave curled against the light.

The white blazed all around, its source the sun, so bright it burned through closed eyelids, reflecting a sky of glaring pallor. The white light hit the white walls of the houses, the verandahs casting sharp black shadows, the windows black as eye-sockets in a skull. Everything glittered hard-edged in *La Ville Blanche*; there were courtyards with the sound of fountains where crystal drops flashed like diamonds, the roofs jutted against a glaring sky that acquired colour only at the sunset hour when the tide of night washed it lavender and indigo before the stars swam into view.

All this Marie-Hélène had described to her son. He had planned to visit her birthplace – 'after the war', studies finished, life ahead of him. But that dream ended in a ditch outside Rouen on a June morning in 1940 when the German army drove into France across the fields and flesh of the defending troops; of young men like Etienne.

Raymond did not remember his father – sheltering in the cellar, clutched in his mother's arms he heard noise, but felt no fear. Later, his grandmother told him stories, of a green and white place where the curving arms of the Promenade held the sea in check and where it was always warm. She remembered it imperfectly, hazily, but there were Oriane's letters, each another link in a chain that held the years together. Oriane's tirades, her enthusiasms, her descriptions brought the Orient to the grey northerliness of the Seine Inférieure; the contents of those flimsy envelopes released a spicy, heady scent that Raymond grew addicted to.

It was a childhood lacking in hostility: a young mother who had subsided, resigned, into widowhood, a doting grandmother, indomitable in her own losses – he found it easy to make them happy – all they wanted was for him to be so.

When he announced that he wished to become an architect they encouraged him: why not? Frenchmen had always excelled at creating beautiful buildings. But Raymond's drawings sometimes puzzled them: his early designs – stark, modernist blocks as was the mode – gradually gave way to strange, fluid shapes, structures that grew organically from the soil, echoing plants and rock formations.

It was never discussed, but India was always part of the plan.

Oriane's latest letter spoke of her involvement in a project to create a new kind of place for people to live, a city called Auroville. Raymond's grandmother read the letter aloud. His mother sighed heavily, her reaction to news of any sort. He asked to see the letter. It described plans for a new city . . . They would need houses. Raymond announced he would be spending some time in Pondicherry that winter.

'We will build a place where people can live in harmony,'

Oriane had written, 'not driven by commercial forces, belonging to no one and to everyone. This will be a place for love and peace. Utopia, perhaps.'

Chapter 14

They arrived in twos and threes, in groups or alone, some bowed under backpacks, some empty-handed, not knowing what to expect. They trailed in, volunteers from the Ashram, and outsiders, visitors who had heard about this new place that was to be built, the city of dawn. There were, of course, many foreigners. The Indians present studied the newcomers with their pony-tails and beads and wondered if the enterprise could survive such an unpromising beginning.

'This will never work. I can see it developing into one of those Kathmandu-type communes for pot-smoking hippies,' one Bengali commented apprehensively.

Most of the volunteers had thought there would be something there already – a camp, or a few shacks at least – a centre of sorts established. But when they turned inland off the sea road, leaving the village behind them, they faced a scene of unmitigated bleakness. Before them the land lay like a rusting desert, broken only by a few palm trees and scrub. Someone did get a hut started – just a roof with open sides, but at least it provided shade from a sun that beat down from above and bounced back off the hard surface of a plateau worn away by centuries of wind and monsoon rains. The new arrivals felt trapped between two fires, one that blazed from above, the other formed of the soil they stood on, burning the soles of their feet. Some lost heart. But others stayed, and still more arrived each day. Raymond was one of them.

Oriane brought him in the minibus she had learned to drive. In her bleached-out cotton skirt and old kurta, hair tied back in an untidy bunch, skin brown and shiny with sweat, she dashed about, full of energy and resolve. She told the new arrivals that this was the shape of the future and they were the people who would build it.

In his mind's eye, remembering his grandmother's descriptions over the years, he had pictured a landscape riotous with crimson flowers, a tropical place where bananas and mangoes grew and where the surging breakers of the Indian Ocean left gleaming shells on the pale sand, sea snails whorled from mother-of-pearl, striped with fantastic colours, spun into subtle coils by their frail occupants. He visualised a land pulsating with life, vegetation bursting from every crevice; his houses would grow in a green Eden.

The old town matched his mental image: the palms, the sea, the bougainvillaea. But when he got to Auroville he found a scorched emptiness, a bare place baked as hard as rock. Beneath the surface, when they hammered and chipped away a few feet, they came upon fragments of petrified wood: there had been trees here, once, whole groves of them shading this dead land. Now there was nothing except for thorn-bushes, here and there a palm tree, the villagers' cashews and an occasional banyan. The red earth was scarred with gullies gouged out by the liquid fingers of the monsoon.

'We will plant new trees,' Oriane said. 'Life will breed life!'

Raymond, surprisingly, did not lose heart. The beard, newly grown, itched in the heat, and the thin brown hands, used to nothing more abrasive than a pencil, blistered and grew calloused as he hacked and dug his way into the bitter ground. He helped to sink pumps for drinking water, cleared undergrowth, binding palm struts and woven leaves into the fiirst of the huts, the rough hemp cord rasping through his hands like a rope woven of splinters leaving tiny needle-sharp fragments in his skin. The reddish-grey dust lay on them all like fur. Their eyes blinking through the clogged lashes were the only visible sign of moisture.

There were no formal gangs, people dug aimlessly, offering help where it seemed needed. Raymond found himself one day working alongside a young Indian who looked too frail to survive the regime, but kept on doggedly, pausing occasionally to gulp at the hot, dusty air, tongue flicking out like a lizard.

'I must introduce myself,' he said formally, at one of these breathing points, 'A.D. Chetty. We are fellow pioneers.'

Arjuna Chetty had looked, when he arrived, the sort to wilt at the first heat of the day, his feet in cheap city shoes, his clothes incongruous in these surroundings: he wore badly made trousers that looked like part of a suit, and a shirt styled for office wear. He kept his sleeves rolled down and buttoned, and occasionally wiped his face with an increasingly grubby handkerchief.

Curiously at odds with the rest of his possessions was a briefcase of the finest leather, polished to a deep mahogany glow, its straps fastened by heavy silver buckles. Far too grand, and inconveniently heavy, it had been a parting present from a tearful mother and he kept it with him at all times. It held two volumes of Aurobindo's works and a fat book by Herman Hesse. That apart, the briefcase was empty. On the first day he looked about anxiously, placed it carefully in the shade of the hut, and started to dig.

As the hours passed, his mouth and nostrils became caked with dried mud; the dust mingling with sweat, formed a mortar-like substance that threatened to seal him off from the air – Raymond wondered how he breathed at all. At midday they collapsed, shovels and pickaxes by their sides, waiting for the bullock-cart to arrive with a meal of sorts and drinking water, rationed out daily to the workers. Raymond watched Arjuna's crumpled body, wondering if the boy had died on them. Then there was a momentary gleam from between the furry lashes. 'Onward and upward!' he muttered, flexing his hands cautiously, reaching for the shovel with a stifled groan. They ate little, drained of appetite by the heat, sustained by the precious liquid from the bullock-cart.

Arjuna looked into his beaker, at the gleam and flash of water and steel. 'How fortunate we are,' he said. It was the sort of remark that could have seemed gratingly Panglossian, delivered differently it might have irritated Raymond. But Arjuna Chetty looked at him and broke into a smile of such sweetness and wonder that the Frenchman felt a sudden lightening of the spirit and marvelled yet again at the miracle of the boy's faith.

'A joyous occupation, architecture,' Arjuna remarked thoughtfully one day as he watched Raymond measuring out the dimensions for a dwelling. 'Our parents have grand dreams, of professions that could bring success. They would like us to be doctors, lawyers, accountants. But all these are depending on people's problems and tragedies. Architecture is about love and life.'

Raymond, who had yet to discover that architecture was also about frustration and strife and the intransigence of inert materials, felt his own faith confirmed. They dug on happily.

The first huts were built near the sea and the road to Pondi, made of bamboo and casuarina poles, woven palm and keet – plaited coconut fronds. An earlier arrival had worked out a plan for a tetraoctahedron structure with a raised platform floor and a pointed thatched roof. He called it a capsule, a modular cell that could be added to, built up like a crystal from the basic one-person model to family-sized complexes. For Raymond, whose expectations had included concrete and steel, it was at first sight disconcerting. But he saw that the hut was big enough to sleep in, sit cross-legged and meditate in, even read inspiring works in while there was daylight. It kept out the rain, the breeze blew through its open sides and when someone felt like moving to another settlement, a few friends could pick up the whole thing and put it on an ox-cart.

'Tell me about your plans, show me your ideas!' Oriane had exclaimed when Raymond arrived, carrying a portable drawing board, portfolio and instruments – none of which had proved of much use on the empty plateau.

She sparkled, avid for explanations, for names, styles, possibilities. When Raymond talked of Corbusier and Frank Lloyd Wright she built up a picture of an architectural Auroville that would rival Corbusier's Chandigarh. 'We shall have a wonder, it will be unique, our place,' she declared, throwing herself into the idea, elated by the new doorway opening in her life.

The hotel virtually ran itself these days – Subra no longer relied on her instructions. His son Selva, too, was on the staff. She spent more and more time out on the burning plateau, ferrying new arrivals and delivering food.

The translations had tailed off and she was at something of a loose end. Worse, she no longer felt at ease in her white town. The resentment she sensed among the locals was not directed at her or her compatriots, the time for that was long past – she was an irrelevance – but the town had been drawn into a wider conflict, it had taken its place in the web of its own politics. It was part of India now; its problems were Indian problems: the tension between the secular and the sacred; the delicate balance between tradition and new technology. The choices: socialism or market force? Oriane felt – and was – an outsider.

And there was something more. Guru was occupied with family affairs and there was much that needed doing. The family business had provided comfort for two extended generations, but Guru had never taken much interest in it.

When the Institut Français was formed, he became part of the Indology department. Not, his father suggested, an activity likely to bring lustre to the family name. 'I was a disappointment to him,' Guru said regretfully, on one of the few occasions the matter was discussed. 'I rather think he would have liked a businessman – or at least a diplomat – to follow him. My sort of dilettantism was not appreciated.'

When he tried to explain once, that his aim was to spread awareness of Tamil literature, his father had looked at him in incredulity. 'Who cares? Who actually gives a damn about Tamil *literature*? We can't even use the language in business. The civil servants behave as though it doesn't exist.' The old man had lost heart and Guru let the argument lapse.

There were other ways in which Guru had perhaps disappointed his father more. Oriane never told him about the day Mr Guruvappa senior appeared at the hotel, asking to see Madame. He stood on the verandah, brushing away flies, a small, erect old man in a formal western suit, touchingly like his son in looks, but with a slight air of self-importance, a touch of pomposity that Guru was incapable of.

Oriane offered refreshment; he refused, and remained standing when she indicated a wicker chair. He embarked suddenly on what seemed to be a lecture on the vulnerability of traditional life and *mores*, moved on to the matter of family honour, responsibility. He did not look at her while he spoke, his eyes wandering about the verandah, dwelling briefly on the etchings of Paris and Rouen, the copies of *Paris Match* and *Le Figaro* on the round table. There was a pause.

'I most earnestly implore you to cease your . . . relationship with my son.' It reminded her of the scene in *Traviata* where Armand's father makes a similar plea, and she found herself falling obediently into the role of Marguerite, wondering if the old man thought she was a whore.

'Why are you asking me to do this?' she wanted to demand. 'What harm have I done you? Or your family?' But she knew that honour (he must mean caste, she supposed) and family responsibility were areas she had no right to intrude in. So she had not asked the difficult questions and he had made no attempt to extort promises, merely left it to her conscience – that was how he put it. She was at first amused, then enraged, finally quelled by a sort of exhaustion, a sense of loss – of something she had never had.

Then one morning Guru told her the old man was dead. And Oriane saw that she had misread her operatic encounter: Mr Guruvappa had been putting his affairs in order, and he wanted to set his son on the straight road to patriarchal continuity. It was not long afterwards that she decided to burn the unreliable past in her own auto-da-fé: nothing too dramatic, just a bonfire in the garden, but it served.

Auroville had been the Mother's idea. She was the one who said that somewhere there should be a place where people could live and work without the materialist pressure that destroyed so many. And she, from the beginning, had been determined there should be a meditation chamber. Already frail, she gave the nod to the architectural model of the city that was put before her – a Galaxy model, where a central house of meditation was ringed by four districts: residential, industrial, cultural and international. It was to be a place for all nations, owned by none. 'Auroville,' she repeated, 'belongs to no one and to everyone.'

Even in Utopia, alas, bills needed paying and building materials had to be bought. The Ashram was generous, UNESCO chipped in, others followed. The experiment was under way.

Oriane, like the others, desperately needed it to succeed. It was irresistible: a way of making sense of a mad world, of bringing Aurobindo's yoga to everyday life. To a visitor those first Aurovillians had the zeal of the early Christians;

they were the few, messianic, bringing a new doctrine to the world and – if necessary – sacrificing themselves to do so.

Behind the pale grey walls in Pondicherry, the Ashramites concentrated on self-transformation, thinking their way towards the next evolutionary stage promised by Aurobindo: 'Man is a transitional being,' he said. If they concentrated hard enough, might they themselves embody the next stage that was to come, when they would be able to rise above the limitations of the flesh? Already in their seclusion they were preparing themselves: purity, celibacy, restricted diet, the attainment of the quiet mind. There was the corporeal problem, as the Mother herself said: the race against time, the body's disconcerting habit of decaying. It was a question whether they could attain the supramental before the cells betrayed them. In the Ashram school, the children's bodies were drilled as strenuously as their minds: they spent time not only on academic subjects but on athletics, gymnastics, swimming. They learned to meditate, but also cultivated a powerful forehand drive. On the private tennis courts beside the sea-shore immaculate young Ashramites sent the ball stinging across the net, calling out the score in French or English. The ball-boys, skinny as rats, recruited from the town population, scurried to keep up, eyes big in their pinched faces, muttering to each other in Tamil. At sunset, young female Ashramites strolled the Promenade in pairs, wearing a uniform of shorts, aertex shirts and neat white turbans. Slim, glowing with energy, confident, they moved past the locals as though breathing air from another planet. A visitor might have been forgiven for thinking that Aurobindo's yogic evolution was already under way.

Things were done differently in Auroville. They had their dream, but the dream must be made reality through the sweat of their brow. They were the builders. One day there would be a place for meditation, to be called the Matrimandir, the house of the Mother, a chamber with a great crystal, set in bright gardens; there would be an auditorium for dance and music, an art gallery, but meanwhile they sweated out their karma in manual labour, greening the desert, making the dead land breathe again.

Chapter 15

Judith first saw Raymond one evening across the Ashram courtyard as they sat cross-legged with the others in meditation, the homespun cotton shirts, beads, embroidered headbands, leather wrist thongs and flowered garlands of the westerners sprinkled among the more conservatively clad Indians.

He had touched her before they met. Judith was struggling with her necklace, the beads caught up in her pony-tail, when she felt cool fingers on the nape of her neck, a sure touch untangling the beads, releasing her. She turned her head and everything changed: as her hair was freed, she herself fell under what she later, laughing nervily, called the spell. At the time she thought, astonished, 'Is this what falling in love is like?' Or was it a touch of heat-stroke? Whatever the cause, there remained that sense of falling, of a loss of equilibrium, giddiness, a movement of the heart.

They did not speak – in the courtyard, talking was out of the question. She smiled her thanks, and tried to concentrate. *Om,* she murmured to herself, *Om* ... peace, peace, peace ...

Aurobindo's courtyard tomb was decorated with fresh flowers every day. The Mother, very much alive, was now the driving force. The privileged were admitted briefly to her presence, one by one. Sometimes she spoke. Sometimes she remained silent. Sometimes she asked questions, sometimes she prescribed action. Judith always felt she was lucky to have been granted an audience at all – the Mother had already seen Raymond, and Judith claimed to have got in on his shirt-tails. Afterwards she wryly described the experience: 'The old girl gave me a long look, patted my head and swivelled her eyes to signal "Next!" It was a winnowing process and I'd been instantly identified as chaff. Ah well.'

Raymond was one of the chosen. The Mother, glittering eyes embedded in her small face like beads stitched into a wrinkled ivory silk cushion, had said little. Just pressed her hand down on his head, stared hard into his eyes and murmured some words. Raymond could never quite recall what she said. He stumbled out of her room, dazed, shaken, unable to speak. Next day he could say only that she had instructed him to build the city – he would help to build the city.

People often asked – visitors, that is, outsiders, asked – 'Where is the city?', not grasping that there was no city, but that in a sense the city lay all around them amid the cashew trees and the baked red earth. Judith grew used to the question, became as fluent as any other guide at explaining how Auroville, the City of Dawn named after Aurobindo, planned for 50,000 people would stand here one day, existed already as a sort of promise; that the present population was the handful working to build it.

The visitors – smooth-skinned, well-groomed north Indians; Europeans with peeling, sunburnt noses – would listen, giving sympathetic glances at her battered bicycle, her worn sandals and sweaty, dust-streaked face. Admiringly, they would wish her well and make a contribution to the Ashram funds.

Originally she had intended to be a bird of passage. It was meant to be part of her education: the India trip, the toe dipped in Eastern mysticism, then back to London and art school, sketchbook filled with vibrant watercolours, joss sticks in her rucksack. She was there on a visit.

In Pondi Judith had joined the pilgrims streaming to the Ashram – 'You've come at a really good time,' they said, 'it's Aurobindo's birthday.' She was so ignorant that she thought he would be there celebrating it with them, but 'only Mother will be physically present,' someone explained, making it clear that Aurobindo's spiritual presence was taken for granted. She sat cross-legged in the Ashram courtyard, taking part in the mass meditation, floating on a sea of shared ecstasy. She lined up for the tour of Aurobindo's rooms.

She had expected a monkish cell, but there were armchairs with white satin dust sheets thrown over them, a bed with a tiger skin. On the walls portraits of Aurobindo as a young man: thin-faced, dark-eyed, fierce. And older, when he had grown more solid, the dark hair streaked with grey. In the last years he worked in his room, never leaving it, pacing to and fro for hours on end, in time wearing a groove in the stone floor.

'What did you think?' a glowing-eyed fellow visitor murmured as they came out on to the street.

'Quite an experience.' Judith was reluctant to damp the joy. Quite an experience, but alas, not a mystical one. Her most vivid memory would remain the two notices on the staircase: the first one read 'Cling to the truth'. Mother. The second, below it, said, 'Do not lean against the wall.'

She felt a fraud: she was looking for significant experiences to enrich her work. She would take from this gathering, not contribute. But at least she would be learning something. At the Ashram guest house she had a clean, bare room and a bucket of hot water to wash in every morning. And she listened to others talking about a place called Auroville. One day she joined a group, squeezing into a minibus, to spend a day there. At the wheel was a Frenchwoman, energetic, burning with enthusiasm, her wind-blown black hair streaked dramatically with badger stripes of white. 'It will be unique. *Un miracle*. We will create a place for a different sort of life, an alternative, *un autre moyen de vivre*.'

Judith wondered how this vision of a brave new city was to be made real in the red desert she found herself standing in, given that no one seemed to have any money, but she refrained from asking. Madame de l'Esprit was gracious, vivacious, but her dark blue eyes could harden, go cold like frozen splinters of the Indian Ocean, if she was upset.

It was on the trip to Auroville that Judith met Raymond again, measuring out the ground for some future structure. Like his idol, Corbusier, he rejected metric measurements and used what he described as the *Modulor*, invented by the master, a rule of elbow and thumb, pacing out the plan by foot.

Judith had lost her sunglasses. Against the glare of the sky he was a silhouette, gaunt, not quite human. Lightning flickered round his head like snakes of fire, thunder murmured a warning. A god walked. Others, remarking the thunder, said the monsoon was on its way. Judith knew better. He strode about waving his arms in a very French manner, explaining how this parched strip would grow and blossom, how in this wilderness the settlements would develop, buildings of tomorrow would house the pioneers, how newcomers would in turn build more houses, there would be schools, a hospital –

'It will be *une vraie utopie* –'

'*Oui, oui!*'

They fell into French together, Raymond and Madame de l'Esprit, in what sounded to Judith like jewelled phrases, the words flashing to and fro, low across the net, fast and accurate. They picked up each other's references, one would extend the other's thought, embellish it.

When the pre-monsoon storm broke, they all huddled

under the great spreading banyan tree that towered at the centre of the plateau – that had, some said, stood here for centuries – and talked. And dreamed. Thin, dark and fiercely young, Raymond was full of certainties and vision. He sketched small palaces in the air, planned a microcosmic arcadia, his kurta and baggy cotton trousers hanging from his bony frame with an unexpected elegance, eyes flashing, thin jaw masked by the beginnings of a beard. Judith looked at him and her heart leaped in her floral cotton breast. She touched the nape of her neck where his fingers had fleetingly lingered, and cancelled her planned departure for Kerala: the Marxist experience would have to wait.

There were many variations on the legend of Auroville, the story of how it all began. That day, with rain dripping through the banyan branches on to her head, Judith listened to a version Raymond had seen in a book, contradicted now and then by one of the pioneers who had got it from someone else, and prompted occasionally by Arjuna Chetty when an ancient detail needed clarifying. But she heard only Raymond.

Once, long ago, a green plateau overlooked the sea, the land rich with trees and fruit. Beneath a banyan tree a *sadhu* sat, meditating, as wise men do. The local people ignored him, except one young girl, who had been to the well. The old man was thirsty and the girl gave him water to drink. On other days, passing, she again gave him water and she talked to him.

It was the custom for the girls of that neighbourhood to dance in public when they came of age, and the day arrived when she was to dance. In the village, people gathered. The *sadhu*, whom she had invited, was among those watching, seated round the performing space. As she was about to begin, the old man noticed that one of her anklets of silver bells had come loose. Leaning forward as he sat, cross-legged

137

on the earth floor, he re-tied the leather thong, secured the anklet, and the girl smiled in gratitude. They had sat in the tree's shade and talked; they were at ease together. When his hands reached out to her slender ankle, there was familiarity in the gesture. The watchers exchanged glances, eyes lowered. Later she came to him in tears. There had been talk, gossip: the villagers had accused her, had accused him, accused them . . .

Old men in old stories have a way of over-reacting: daughters are cast off, wives condemned, wars embarked on. This time the violence took a slow form. He cursed the land. The fertile plateau would wither and shrivel; the plants die, the rich earth turn to dust. The villagers would pay for their unfounded suspicion with slow starvation.

They could have shrugged it off but they grew uneasy: with old men you never knew, some had powers . . . So they played safe: they sent messages of apology. Begged, pleaded for forgiveness, for the curse to be lifted. She too, the unwitting cause of it, cast herself at his feet. The *sadhu* replied, what is said cannot be unsaid. The curse cannot be undone. But perhaps it can be modified. He concentrated for a long time and then he said: one day, many years from now, strangers will come, men from across the sea, and make the land green again.

Was it drought, or dry wind or something more? The land died. The centuries rolled. The people, generation after generation, waited, forgot the reason for their suffering, scratched at the red dust . . .

(She looked at Raymond's feet, thinking how beautiful they were, the skin brown and unblemished. The thongs of his sandals accentuated their nakedness so that she had an almost irresistible urge to reach out and stroke the flesh.)

. . . and – Raymond ended – here is still a banyan tree at the centre of Auroville. And the land lives again and is green.

Oriane retold the story to Guru the next time she saw him. She found it somewhat harsh – '*Un peu dur*, I thought.'

'That's in the nature of legends, my dear. They're implacable. The dragon must be hunted down, the giant killed, the dwarf cheated of his negotiated fee.'

But there were other explanations to draw on.

'Some might see it as neo-colonialism masquerading as folk-tale. Men from beyond the sea bringing their language, their skills, making things grow. Perpetuating the idea of inferiority. You'll find some of the locals classify Auroville itself as neo-colonialist, ask young Chetty, he'll tell you. As to the plateau, it was covered with trees once, plants, medicinal shrubs. There were forests –'

Then, certain actions taken, others inevitably followed: 'The scrub jungles were cut down to build the town, people moved in. Deforestation, bad land-management and over-grazing – what can you expect? With the trees gone, the monsoon and the sand storms did the rest.'

But Judith heard only Raymond recounting a legend that fired her imagination. When he told her he meant to be one of the builders of the new city, devote his life to it, she thought no more of St Martin's, wiped curriculum and portfolio from her mind. She had come to Auroville by chance, so she had thought, but surely it was fate?

'You are cold, Yoodeet,' Raymond said, aware of her shivering in the thin cotton shirt as they sat waiting for the sun to rise, to begin work. He had acquired a shawl of unbleached wool and now he wrapped it round her shoulders. She gazed up at him gratefully, into the brown eyes and the amused, angular face. 'Shall we be lovers?' he asked, knowing she wished it. 'Oh, yes *please*!' she replied without hesitating.

One day, in the Ashram courtyard, the Mother had put one

of her ritual questions; she asked, as she often did, for a definition of yoga. Someone said, 'For me, yoga means to come home,' and was rewarded with a gleam of approval. At the time it might have seemed predictably gnomic. But later, as the huts and tents proliferated, as the settlements began to form, the sense of that description became increasingly clear to Raymond: to come to Auroville was to come home.

He said as much to Oriane one day, and she repeated slowly, 'to come home', as though testing the words. Was this what it had all been leading to, all these years? Had it really been a journey and was she now seeing a place where she could finally be at peace? Her magpie striped hair dramatic above the bright eyes, her bony grace, seemed particularly appealing that day and Raymond responded to a yearning he sensed within her. 'Why don't you come to Auroville? Why don't you come home?'

It seemed so right, so natural that she did not even question the wisdom of it. The emptiness, the sense of a useless life, of rushing downhill towards an ominous conclusion, were washed away in a surge of new energy.

'Why not?' She could live there, in a hut until Raymond could build her a dwelling. 'Show me some more of your drawings.' She felt at home already. They were, of course, speaking French.

She drove out next day, before dawn, impatient, already filled with the new idea, wanting as always to put it into action.

The first plantings had been done, the beginnings of an irrigation system laid out. The land drank greedily and on the bald red soil, here and there, patches of green had appeared like bristles on a hairbrush. In the coolness Oriane, alone, wandered along a winding path, one signposted *Aspiration*. The sky was pearly and against it the trees rose like smudged, restful shadows. She walked through a grove of date palms, saw strange fruit ripening on bough and branch. The air was fresh against her skin, the soil dark with moisture, and as she walked, the scent of bruised grass from beneath her feet mingled with the smell of growing things all around, coriander and mint and wild fennel. She stood, feeling the movement of life about her, new shoots bursting from hidden roots, worming through the soil to reach her, circle her ankles, climb her body, tendrils winding round her like the clinging fingers of a Morning Glory, binding her fast so that she was rooted to this place for ever. And on a breeze that was no more than a movement of the air there came to her a hint of a tantalising fragrance, one that had something of fruit in it, but also of sweetmeat and spice. The scent of cashew blossom.

She was brisk with Guru and kept her explanation minimal: she was moving to Auroville. She would bring in a manager, retain ownership of the hotel, but the profits would go to Auroville. He watched her carefully, as though some clue to this aberrant behaviour might be found in the movements of head and hands. As always when she was ill at ease she became very Gallic, extravagant gestures and little grimaces underlining her words. But there was something new today, a zeal, an air of purpose that he mistrusted. He had seen this before, in westerners, this evangelical energy, and it had a way of proving short-lived. He voiced his doubts only once, and lightly.

'A straw hut, Oriane? Is that quite your style? Where will you keep your books?' But he saw her eyes blaze and realised things had gone too far for irony. Tentatively, he added, 'Utopias have a bad record you know: it's a built-in problem – the second law of thermodynamics has a way of coming into force.'

'What can you mean?' Oriane exclaimed. Guru's rarely expressed reservations had a way of undermining her soaring enthusiasm, and she was determined not to be side-tracked now.

'I've told you: Et in Arcadia Entropy. There's a winding down. When Yeats said things fall apart, it was another way of saying the same thing. The loss of energy ... the inevitability of disappointment.'

But he refrained from any further word of discouragement: what could he say? He could have said don't go. Don't leave me. I shall dwindle away without you, grow parched, an old sea snail drying out in the sun, all that will remain of me a husk, a shell; deprived of sweetness, delight, provocation, the wayward pleasure of your quick laugh, your illogical anger, your greed for knowledge, your utter trust. How shall I go on living?

But he said nothing. After all, what could he offer instead? What right had he?

As they talked she was clearing drawers and cupboards, filling sacks with letters, papers, photographs. 'Subra!' she called, 'ask *le petit* to carry these outside for me.' Her parents' kitchen-boy had grown silver-haired and diplomatic with the years. Guru had insisted on teaching him to read and write, and knowledge had brought gravitas to the young boy whose high-pitched giggle had irritated Oriane long ago. His son carried out the sacks, as she directed, and she followed, arms filled with more papers, envelopes, magazines from France. The contents of the first sack burned quickly, the paper flaring up and crumpling to grey ash, and she fed the fire with letters, old newspaper cuttings, creased and folded copies of a philosophical journal from fifty years ago. Leafing through a cardboard box of photographs Guru protested, 'Oriane this is excessive: your life is here, why are you doing this?'

'For that very reason, *mon cher*. I'm starting a new life. None of this is part of me now. I mean to begin without any baggage from the past.'

He paused at a snapshot showing the two of them, taken outside the hotel gates, Oriane laughing, caught at a moment of total unself-consciousness. He smiled and she asked, 'What have you found?'

He held up the photograph. 'Just a bit of baggage.'

For a moment she relented, allowing the past a nod. 'That ghastly politician friend of yours!' Her old enemy, the Congressman, now rather powerful, had been visiting Pondi, making speeches, mouthing the usual promises. He had decided to pause on his princely progress through the town to call on Oriane. Perhaps to give himself the small triumph of seeing the disinherited interloper. 'This is our place!' she had cried, at their first meeting, nearly twenty years before his trip; 'Pondicherry is French and will remain so!' Well she had been wrong, and he could afford to be gracious. As a grass-roots gesture, he came by horse-drawn carriage. If Gandhi-ji could travel Third Class . . .

At the gate, as he stepped down from his carriage, the horse decided to relieve himself. There was a sudden flurry in the crowd, the horse shied, and a huge dollop of fragrant yellow shit landed on the polished political shoes.

He glared down, stupefied, as the crowd cheered and whooped. And Subra, with the cheap camera he had acquired from a friendly American guest of the hotel, snapped Madame, head flung back in a paroxysm of laughter, with Guruvappa by her side, relishing her delight.

She held out her hand for the photograph but at just that moment a shower of sparks from the bonfire distracted her and she hastily threw on more letters, so perhaps she was too busy to notice that Guru had held on to the snapshot.

The paper burned quickly, the flames almost invisible in the sunlight, and she fed the fire with everything she could find, the informal documentation of a life. She sensed his dismay. 'A new beginning!' she said, defiantly.

It was also, of course, an ending; a parting of the ways, but neither of them felt able to mention that.

She watched as the flames censored an old letter, line by line, as a snapshot for a moment became a negative before crumbling to ash. A gust of wind blew smoke into her face, causing her to blink, eyes watering. He offered her a handkerchief but Oriane waved it away: 'I'm covered in bits of ash, filthy, I'll get a tissue,' and she hurried inside, rubbing at her face.

Chapter 16

The first time Raymond and Judith shared a bed in Auroville, the palm-strut floor of their Aurocapsule collapsed under them. Raymond had been mending a hole in the roof – 'To see the stars is beautiful, but the monsoon will be with us before long, so . . .' He rearranged the palm thatch of the little hut, stepped back, tripped and fell heavily on to the woven palm floor, which proved unequal to the strain.

From a nearby capsule a solemn Dutch couple watched the frail structure shaking on its stilts, the sounds of merriment clearly audible. 'The French must always go too far,' Jan commented. 'Even their love-making has no discretion.'

Later, when the floor had been patched up, the love-making began, but there were no shrieks or cries of delight. The floor did not shake though possibly for the two involved, the earth moved.

It was a matter of small moans and muted groans and one limb adjusting to fit another, of stroking and exploration, a sense of levitation and a star-burst, an expanding personal universe with everything rushing away from everything else at the speed of light.

'Ah Yoodeet, Yoodeet,' sighed Raymond, happy himself and happy to have made her happy. Judith smiled in the darkness, ignoring the mosquitoes. From the palm roof, rain began to drip on to her nose. Another monsoon had begun.

There were days when Oriane's legs ached from wading through the wet soil, the dry terracotta transformed – a miraculous inversion – into a spongy field of potter's clay that sucked at the workers' feet like a morass as they slogged across it. It had been a bitter summer, the fierce rays blackening the tender growth. Raymond did not become despondent; one day there would be gardens here, he assured her. They would mantle the bare red body of the earth with green.

'*Rappelle-toi*, Oriane, the original Arcadie in the Peloponnese was not a garden, it was a harsh, rocky place . . . *sauvage*. It was the artists, Poussin *et les autres*, who created the landscape we believe in, on canvas. But we will create a real landscape.'

And Oriane felt again the tug of the tendrils circling her ankles, holding her fast to Auroville, to a landscape of the mind.

After the wells were sunk, dikes were built to create irrigation channels. The Aurovillians began to plant trees and crops, collecting compost from the puzzled villagers who could understand using cow-dung for fuel but not for fertilising – they had chemicals for that. As trees grew, the birds began to come back. The dead, silent plateau rang with the songs of migrating birds using Auroville as a visiting place – even, in some cases, settling in.

Occasionally she made the trip to Pondicherry – only six kilometres, but a journey to be reckoned with on the old sit-up-and-beg bicycle she now used. In the Ashram courtyard, with its flowers and the scent of incense, the pilgrims cross-legged round Aurobindo's bloom-decked tomb, she emptied herself of jangling thought; she sought for the quiet mind. She would call in to check that the hotel was running smoothly, reassured by the manager's enthusiasm, his well-kept books, though there seemed to be fewer guests these days. Afterwards she walked for a while on the sea-front, watching the young Ashramites on their way to gymnastics, so trim and clean in their regulation shorts and aertex shirts, the girls with their slender necks, their hair confined by the neat, turban-like bandeaux. And she would straighten her shoulders, aware of her crumpled dress of village cotton, her hair untidy in the breeze.

She avoided the Institut Français. The fervour of the move to Auroville had blotted out the pain of rupture for a while, but the sight of Guru was more than she could risk. In any case, he had his own life. And wife.

Occasionally she would see Arjuna Chetty, coming out of the library, his small, anxious face breaking into a smile of greeting. Once, Judith was with him and the three of them sat together at a run-down café on the Promenade and sipped a milky south Indian coffee, listening to the seethe and fret of the waves.

'Don't you ever get impatient?' Judith asked. 'Frustrated? We achieve so little and time is passing. We'll grow old before the city is built.'

Oriane thrust the thought away with a twinge of panic: the child had no right to such fears, that was for others, those who could hear the ticking of the clock. She twitched a shoulder, dismissing the question, but Arjuna reached for a phrase from Aurobindo or the Mother, something about experience justifying faith, and gave his tentative smile and encouraging side-tilt of the head. 'Love and work,' he said, 'that is the way. Divine pattern.' And the three of them cycled back together, along the sea road.

Between the settlements and the coconut groves lay the villagers' cashew plantations, the trees shimmering in the sunlight, bushy as hawthorn and starred with pink and yellow blossom. Their scent drifted across the fields, warm, spicy, exotic. '*Anarcadium Occidentale*,' Arjuna informed Judith when he came upon her admiring the cashew blossom for the first time. 'Pretty, but do not attempt to pick the nuts off the tree, or you will regret the action.'

She thought it must be some local custom, some taboo he was warning her off, but there was a simpler, more practical explanation: the shell of the fruit was hard; breaking it to reach the little kidney-shaped nut at the base, the village women got the juice on their hands, bitter black juice that burned like acid and went on burning. The cashew harvesters' hands blistered and peeled, the skin shiny and horribly pink, like plastic gloves – or bright new scar tissue, which is what it was. Their hands were skinned, flayed by the cashew acid.

'Can nothing be done to avoid this?' Judith asked, horrified.

'Rubbing wood-ash over their hands would protect them, to an extent, but no one has the time, the fruit is waiting.'

And later, when she thought back to Auroville, that was what Judith remembered most sharply: the scent of cashew blossom was the smell of Auroville. It combined the sweetness of first sight with the burning bitterness of experience.

The place was difficult for couples, someone warned her, too primitive, too demanding. Emotions were easily aroused, the labour physically draining. The combination of idealism and exhaustion, the isolation and consequent enforced closeness of the group, all created an unstable environment in which relationships foundered. 'It can be hard to be a woman in Auroville,' they said.

Judith was puzzled: their settlement was to be Arcadia, they were building something important together. Surely life was perfect? And Raymond was wonderful, so kind. Two years later, spilling tears of anger and unhappiness, she told him she was leaving: she was sick of being last in line for his attention. 'I can't spend my life waiting for you to find time for me, while everyone else seems to have a prior claim on you and your kindness!' And, unspoken but printed on her tear-streaked face there was the other resentment – the question that had sparked off the bitter rebellion: how far did it go, the kindness? The women he comforted, how much did he comfort them? Raymond was always available.

'And then he is so very beautiful, isn't he?' an American woman said one day in Judith's hearing, watching Raymond at work. 'And it's so hard to be well-behaved *all* the time . . .'

He was regretful, surprised by Judith's vehemence. 'I thought you would understand, these people are our friends –'

'*Your* friends. They ask nothing of me!' Then she told him she was going back to England.

They stood, helpless, divided. 'You are tired,' Raymond said, 'the work has been too hard. *Repose-toi un peu*, you will feel better when you have rested. Return in the autumn, in the coolness.'

But she had not returned. The coolness had spread through her, insulating her against the feverish influences of Auroville, the heat she felt when Raymond's body touched hers, the magic of the moment when the newly risen sun lay warm on her skin like a benediction, before it bounded into the colourless sky and began the day's punishment.

Moreover she was carrying a child. She had been cavalier with her pill-taking.

Her mother added to the chorus of advice: 'No hospital . . . and the germs . . . no running water . . . no proper roof over your head . . . You'd be mad to go back. You owe it to the child.'

She owed it to the child, she told herself. But the truth was, she wanted a rest from all the demands and the altruism. She couldn't take it any more: the price of ecstasy was too high.

Chapter 17

Raymond came upon the woman in a rocky canyon, out beyond the coconut plantation. She was standing, head bowed, staring dully at the infant on the ground at her feet. She turned, then stopped, turned back, sinking to the ground and rocking, silently, in despair. Raymond waited for the Aurovillian engineer to catch up with him. 'What's going on, Dilip? What is the problem?'

The engineer shrugged. 'Oh this is nothing unusual. She has given birth to a daughter and so she is bringing the infant here to abandon it – well actually she should be disposing of it to be on safe side.'

'But why?'

'Well, sons are for prosperity, a son will work, will be supporting you in your old age and so forth. Daughter will be only added burden. You know the old saying: raising a daughter is like watering a neighbour's land. Husband must be found, dowry provided. This can bring ruination. Simpler to dispose of the child before these problems arise.'

Raymond was appalled. 'This woman is being forced to murder her child! Look at her!' Dilip, who came from Bengal, regarded the woman, the tiny bundle on the ground, without curiosity. She did not weep. She squatted, one hand to her head, as though shielding her eyes, still as a statue. Her rough cotton sari had been washed so often by the monsoon rains, dried by the punishing sun, that the pattern had been bleached out of it, leaving only vestigial touches of colour here and there – faint traces of blue, a shadow of vermilion – like old carvings that offer hints of what was once poly-chrome. She was thin, her bones gaunt in her face, knees sharp as sticks when she squatted.

Dilip murmured, 'This has always gone on, to an extent, in the south. Quietly. But not in my personal experience. Now in Bihar, those chaps up there are forever slaughtering each other, exposing infants, kidnapping bridegrooms, burning brides and so forth. But times are hard all over.'

'It's barbaric!'

'It is a sadness of course, but practical. Better for everyone. The child will not live to experience the pangs of hunger, and worse, the shame she brings to the family –'

'What shame?'

'Of being a girl. Causing additional hardship. And before long the woman will conceive again and possibly bear a son – you see the general effect of such an action. Judged on Utilitarian standards, this abandoning of the infant would be judged a Good Thing.'

Raymond could not and did not wish to see it as a Good Thing. He saw the woman's face. He saw the way her fingers moved slowly over the child's body, touching the frail skin, delicate as the sheath of a plum. She sat, watching the child, her hand supporting her brow, hopeless; her despair envel-oping her, wrapping her more closely than her mud-stained sari. She seemed to be somehow sinking into the ground, as though burying herself.

'She intends to die with the child.'

'It is possible but unlikely. They will find her. Matters will be arranged. She will return to her husband.'

'Will you ask her,' Raymond paused, uncertain how to phrase the thought, 'will you ask her whether she will accept my help? I can build her a hut. And I will provide food for her and for the child in due course.'

Dilip looked astonished. 'Why should you do this?'

It was Raymond's turn to look surprised. 'How can you need to ask? What is our life in Auroville? If we want a better world, do we not have to create it?'

Dilip began to speak to the woman, haltingly. As a northerner he spoke Hindi, and had acquired some Tamil only since he came to Auroville, to communicate with the surrounding villagers. She listened intently to the offer. Then without a word she gathered up the child and stood, expressionless, waiting. Raymond led the way to the clearing. Auroville lay around them, a parched wilderness they had set out to tame. Areas of dense undergrowth here and there, with tall palms rising out of the harsh red dust. The villages, scattered around the perimeter and between settlements, were enclaves of shade and beaten earth. A pump, a scattering of huts, cattle – compared with the pitiless nakedness of the new settlements, the villages looked civilised, restful. Even Raymond could see that an Auroville capsule on stilts with no running water fell short of luxury. But it was a beginning. The settlement of *Arcadie* had been staked out; soon they would begin to build. Meanwhile, his hut, a frail, thatched structure of woven palm leaves, stood some way from several others of similar design. He waved the woman towards the hut and she climbed silently into it. When he glanced in a little later as he passed, the child was at her breast, feeding contentedly.

Raymond intended to build a second hut. He meant to give her no more than shelter and sustenance. But everyone said he was crazy to sleep on the ground meanwhile: snakes, scorpions . . . why after all, had they decided on stilts for their shelters? He could see that what they said was true, but by now they were all busy on the first of the proper houses, so – 'well, we shall share the hut,' he said, 'she must be used to sharing sleeping quarters.' He gave her a name: Félicité.

Propinquity and gratitude are potent bed fellows. One

dawn, she touched Raymond's feet with her hands, then put her fingers to her eyelids – the traditional Tamil greeting of a wife for a husband. The relationship had altered.

It was a pity that after so much kindness, such loving care, the child died soon afterwards from a gastric infestation. But the woman stayed on. The village would not have taken her back, and in any case by then Raymond was committed to the consequences of his act of kindness. Judith had written from England to say she was not coming back. In due course, Félicité bore another child, another girl: Raymond called her Dorothée, shortened to Dolly.

Chapter 18

Oriane was not, at first, aware of things changing. Work dominated her consciousness and at the end of the day, a scrappy meal and high-minded discussion led swiftly to sleep. She had never been more tired or so happy, her own desires subsumed in the creation of the City of Dawn.

Visitors sometimes asked 'Where is the city?' and Oriane, like Judith before her, grew used to the question, and, like Judith, explained how the City of Dawn planned for 50,000 people would stand here one day, existed already as a sort of promise. For Oriane, as for the others, the city already lay all around them amid the cashew trees and the baked red earth. But of course outsiders found that hard to grasp.

And the new visitors, the usual well-groomed north Indians and Europeans with peeling, sunburnt noses, would listen, and wish her well and head back with relief to the paved streets and tea-shops, the plumbing and comforts of Pondi.

Meanwhile the pioneers worked on, no more than two or three hundred still, but more would come of course, and the ground must be prepared, the houses built. The house of meditation was under construction but the crystal to sit at its heart proved harder to acquire.

It began like a fairy-tale: *and the king sent out his messengers to the four corners of the earth, seeking –* They sent out the message to the four corners of the earth – well, letters to a dozen countries, asking who could manufacture a crystal 70cms in diameter – the dimensions specified by the Mother. They discovered that they were asking a different question: they were asking who could make them the biggest crystal in the world. A crystal that would be transparent, translucent, perfect. At the beginning they did not go into detailed explanations – mysticism, spirituality, a meditation chamber, all smacked of fortune-tellers' tents and hocus-pocus. They stuck to the practicalities: they required a flawless glass globe of the dimensions specified. Could such a crystal be made?

Responses trickled in slowly. Murano in Venice wrote to say *non, magare.* The Firozabad glassworks in Uttar Pradesh did not reply. An American firm said maybe, then went silent. Baccarat in France at first said *'c'est possible'* – but changed their mind. Waterford in Ireland, Glassexport in Prague, regretted, but saw no way it could be done.

The flagging Aurovillians began to think the idea might have to be abandoned. Then someone remembered a firm in West Germany – Schott, in Mainz. Off went the question. And back came the answer: 'Why not?'

All that remained to be found was the money.

Years before, to keep the clamorous demands of administration from penetrating the grey walls of the rue de la Marine, the Mother had put the Ashram's real-estate purchasing into the hands of a group of businessmen. And not long after the day when Arjuna Chetty came hobbling in – his feet had never recovered from those early, burning days, digging the stubborn ground in unsuitable shoes – to inform them that 'Mother has decided to leave her body', things gradually began to change.

The men meeting in committee rooms, discussing the affairs of what had once been a simple Ashram and was now a prosperous enterprise, took charge. The Ashramites themselves could still concentrate on the attainment of perfection.

The businessmen had practical tasks to attend to: there were, the committee pointed out, branches overseas, mailing lists to be serviced, accounts to be kept, books to be balanced. Auroville, they said, must be properly run.

'But *we* run Auroville!' Oriane exclaimed, 'Auroville runs itself.'

She had her own concrete cube now, hotter than the capsule, but with a proper door and window. Those who could afford to, built houses, and the architects gave advice when asked. It was not always wanted, and some of the more eccentric dwellings that sprouted from the soil leaned and settled into curious shapes, but others proved more durable, with domes and courtyards and airy rooms. Most of the original palm-leaf capsules had gone, there was water and electricity. Children had lessons at their own school, the sick were cared for. And everywhere the trees grew, shading the earth, the tall Acacia Longifolia that the Mother had called Work Trees and instructed them to plant. Oriane's bougain-villaea flourished, and flowering shrubs grew beneath banana and mango trees. The villagers who came in to help were often baffled (why refuse to spray crops with DDT? What was the point of this so-called organic farming?) but their children had a good time in the makeshift schoolroom and no one in Auroville stood around giving orders. They worked together in – Oriane's favourite word – harmony. It was indeed arcadia, and she had named their settlement in that certainty. True, they were not self-sufficient: once a month they drew up their modest lists for toothpaste, soap and other basics, and someone drove off in jeep or minibus to collect supplies from the Aurobindo Society's beach office. Still, water was now criss-crossing the plateau, they had their own bakery and carpentry workshop, things were slowly improving.

But inescapably, the new order made itself felt. The administrators thought it only logical that they should take over Auroville: as one of the Society's possessions it must take its proper place on the books.

'This is absurd! Auroville belongs to no one and to everyone, it is free. Mother always said so. Auroville is not part of anything. It is Auroville.' The pioneers, gaunt, sunburnt, shaggy-haired were mutinous, obstinate. They went back to their digging and their building and planting and ignored the Society.

The Society responded by cutting off their funds.

Gradually, building work came to a halt. As cement and bricks and steel ran out, the builders and the dreamers realised they were back where they started: worse – not just raw materials but food was in short supply. One day Oriane heard that plans were afoot to send a deputation into Pondi to demand justice. 'Justice?' she echoed, mouth turned down in a cynical curl. 'Rather ask for mercy. Justice has a way of proving unsatisfactory.'

Probably no one meant things to get so out of hand, but bitterness and resentment are sharp seasonings and there were other, more fundamental differences: the Ashramites in their clean white robes lived a calm, ordered, ascetic existence. In Auroville they saw a messy, undisciplined way of life: meat was consumed, and alcohol, there were rumours of free sex, drugs in circulation. It should be controlled. She looked at the opposing parties and her heart sank. This would not be harmoniously resolved.

There were ugly scenes, shouting matches, 'fisticuffs engaged in', lamented Arjuna, shocked. There was the ultimate indignity of Ashramites and Aurovillians finding themselves, briefly, in jail.

Oriane would have been among them, but Subra had established a connection with the policeman who injured his son in the riots – guilt and remorse and a sum of money had cemented the relationship. The policeman failed to include

Oriane in the round-up. Furious, she attempted to join those in jail.

'Go home, madame,' said a young uniformed constable, adjusting his red képi, 'we're not arresting old ladies today.'

What began as a confrontation grew into a battle and then a war of attrition. The villagers had been in favour of Auroville, because they remembered the legend, the prophecy. Now they became reluctant – hostile even – hearing the denunciations coming from the Ashram. 'They are turning the villagers against us,' Oriane heard people saying, 'they are telling them we're Europeans and it will be colonialism all over again.' Sometimes the Aurovillians woke to find their water pipes had been cut in the night. There was a sourness in the air; a dispirited pall that hung like a shadow over the plateau, so that even the brilliance of the sun seemed grey, the light tarnished. People dragged themselves about, lethargic, starving.

Raymond was worried about Oriane: she hardly ate, her hair had become quite grey – possibly with dust, for she seemed not to be washing too strenuously. Her face was gaunt, the flesh falling away, revealing the structure beneath it. The wide, clean sweep of brow was more prominent and the eyebrows had faded, no longer providing a dark frame for the deep sockets of her eyes. The nose was sharper, its arch more pronounced. The lips were puckered, the cheeks drained of moisture, scarred with fine lines that caught the light like blade strokes on an etching. She was like a full, soft fruit that had lost its vital colour, its firmness, shrinking, wrinkling as a shining plum retreats into prunehood, as grape dries to raisin. Raymond saw all this with the pitiless eyes of youth, and after all, he had never seen her as she used to be. But he was worried about her.

She told him to press on with building – she would provide the materials, and she went into Pondi, to consult her lawyer.

'I have the hotel,' she said, 'I can borrow money against that security. We must build the beautiful city.'

Raymond had started work on a house he was to build for her, a place of inner courtyards open to the sky, linking one room with another to create a spatial flow, but he was finding that in practice the work of an architect lay not in dreams but in making sure the walls did not fall down and the roof kept the rain out. He no longer talked about the golden mean but of the durability of ferrocement and mud bricks, the red bricks which he and his village helpers were making by hand, using the rusty laterite soil from around them. It all took time. The beautiful city was there, safe inside his head, but slow in execution.

The house lay out beyond the fertile belt, on a slight crest overlooking the sea. Driving with Oriane to check progress, he had taken the wrong path once, and was quickly lost. He drove on, winding through the fields and cashew plantations, until they found they were among trees, sloping down to the hollow of a small lake. The sun was high, the trees that ringed the lake casting shade no further than their roots. Reflecting the blinding sky, the water had the sheen of a moonstone. It lay, as though weighed down by the sunlight, heavy, almost viscous in the mid-day heat. There was a tiny temple, little more than a ruin, and on the opposite bank, among a grove of neem trees, he saw what looked like a derelict orangerie. Intrigued, he got out to explore further, but Oriane, sitting silently in the jeep, staring down at the glassy water, flew into a rage that puzzled him, crying 'We're *late*, we can't waste time here!' and some passing villagers waved him away, calling out that the land was private.

When they got to the house her mood changed and she walked through the raw shell, touching the walls, the archways as though to reassure herself they existed. She was impatient to see the house finished; it would house a family, a colony even. She intended to occupy only one small wing, and there would be a communal kitchen, rooms for them all to work and make music – 'and live in harmony,' she said, laughing. In those days she could still laugh – just.

The system allowed for private property; a house could be handed down from parents to children. But it could not be sold. If the owner decided to leave Auroville, the house became communal property. Oriane, of course, had no intention of leaving. Her money was swallowed up by the arid soil as fast as water poured on to its surface. She borrowed more, though her lawyer advised against it. One day she collapsed, and lay all day, threshing feebly on the thin mattress, unable to call for help, her body burning, her gut infested with amoebic dysentery. Medical supplies had long ago run out except for emergencies and for the children. Women looked in on Oriane and made her as comfortable as possible. Raymond, arriving one evening, saw that the fever had taken a different turn. She lay still, sunk in a sort of coma, so frail that her head barely dented the pillow.

He knew only one person who might be able to help, and was unsure even how to make the approach. Without any definite plan, he begged a ride into Pondi, and stationed himself on the Promenade. The statue of Gandhi stood, back turned to the sea, surrounded by slender, ornately carved pillars of sandstone. By the statue Raymond waited, knowing he could stay only till sundown, refusing to acknowledge his helplessness.

As the sun was dipping towards the trees in the little park, the sea beginning to darken into a chill gunmetal, he saw Guruvappa walking towards him in conversation with another man, head bowed as he listened, nodding from time to time. Raymond stepped forward into his path.

'Mr Guruvappa.'

Chapter 19

Oriane slowly surfaced into consciousness, a drowning swimmer rising towards the light, too exhausted to help herself, spiralling out of the silence and the darkness that had enfolded her. She became aware of an unaccustomed sensation: the feel of smooth sheets against her skin, a cool breeze. Where was she?

'Where am I?'

A small laugh from somewhere nearby. 'Waking into a cliché, my dear.'

She kept her eyes firmly closed. If she held her breath, refused to breathe, perhaps she could end it now, drift back into the darkness, avoid the ignominy, the facing of facts, the . . . *ennui* of real life. She, who had directed her life – and those about her – with flair and confidence, now to be –

She was aware of a cooling perfume . . . not lavender, not bergamot . . . Despite her desire to escape, she sniffed enquiringly.

'Vetiver,' Guru murmured, 'the aromatic root of *Andropogon Muricatus*, we Tamils call it Vettiveru –'

Her eyes flew open. She stared up at him angrily, fearful. 'Why are you here? Why am I here? What is going on?'

'You're a very lucky woman. If your sensible young friend had not informed me of your condition you might very well be dead.'

'Sensible friend?'

'Raymond.'

'Oh . . .'

She was drifting again. She was back at Auroville, the next day's work must be planned, and they needed food – rice and okra, but there was no money, and the villagers –

Guru wiped her face with a cool, damp cloth. She slept for a while and when she woke it was cooler, the light dim. Guru sat reading nearby. He saw that she was awake and put down his book.

'I'll prepare some soup. I'm not talented, limited kitchen experience I'm afraid, but –'

'Where's Subra?'

'Ah. Well, I'm afraid he and the rest of the staff had been given the push by the time I got here.' He sighed. 'You were extremely naughty, Oriane, to go to a money-lender without talking to me. Really! Were you aware that he was your manager's brother-in-law?' She shook her head, lips pressed tight. The shame! Why hadn't she died? It would have been better for everyone.

'The debt was called in and the building taken over. There was apparently no need to inform you, under the terms of the loan.'

'Then why have I been allowed in?'

'Because I know how to deal with these people. I'm one of them after all.'

He looked at her with the old, ironic half-smile but her face did not soften. She knew she looked terrible. He too had aged, grown thinner, the glossy black hair sprinkled with grey. His face looked smaller –

'You're wearing glasses!' she exclaimed.

'There it is. Time's wingéd chariot I'm afraid.' He paused. 'I'll get your staff back, but I wanted to make sure you were well before I –'

'Have you been caring for me?'

He coughed, cleared his throat. 'Must you always interrupt my sentences?'

'Who's been looking after me? Doing everything? You?'

'Yes.'

'But – you can't do that. You'll be polluted.'

He laughed incredulously. 'Isn't it rather late to be worrying about that?'

She frowned. 'You've been here all the time?'

'I made up a bed in a little room down the corridor. It's really quite comfortable.'

She felt she had been a fool, which was not a consoling realisation.

'At least they left the furnishings intact,' he said, 'I feared there might have been a house-clearing.'

He was hesitant to advise her – something she had discouraged in the past. For a while they said nothing. At last he ventured, 'You're very weak. You'll have to take things carefully for a while.'

She said, the words a lament: 'Am I fated never to be of *use*, Guru? I so much wanted to help.'

'You did help. You made Arcadia a reality.'

She looked down at her hands, resting on the smooth white sheet. They stood out shockingly, scarred and roughened from work, burnt reddish-brown. Her arms were scrawny, she noted, the veins standing out like cords. It was years since she had looked in a mirror, smoothed her skin with creams or coiled her hair with thought of style rather than convenience. She realised with a sense of deadening despair that she was an old woman.

He misinterpreted her expression and said gently, 'Perhaps you can go back –'

She broke in, violently, 'No!' Auroville was for the young and vigorous. For the strong. She had no desire to provide them with their first funeral.

Remorse was not something that came easily to Oriane,

and her condition was in any case complicated here by all sorts of unspoken and unacknowledged emotions. She said abruptly, 'You can't stay here.'

He raised his eyebrows, the obstinately dark wings contrasting comically with his grey hair. 'You want me to leave? Dear me, that will complicate the – er – domestic arrangements somewhat.'

'I mean you've done too much. I'm not going to start thanking you, it's gone beyond that. But. You have a home. A –' she paused, 'wife.'

'Kamala died last year.'

She cast about for something to say but the right words eluded her. Three sentences spanning a lifetime. 'I am to be married.' And later, 'Kamala has lost the child.' And now Kamala had died. An unregarded life, then. Fruitless, pointless, lacking satisfaction and issue. How like her own! Two women linked by this unsatisfactory man, a man who could give neither of them what they wanted from him: his complete loyalty. But would even that have been enough? Passion might have sufficed; taken the place of the service she had been balked of. So might an aspirant saint have felt, ready for martyrdom, only to be told the fire had been prepared for someone else.

Cheated of her destiny, she felt she had turned bad, rotted from within, the amoebic dysentery no more than a metaphor of a greater malaise. She was tempted to slip away, slide down, away from the light. But the fight, it seemed, was not to be abandoned: she felt thirsty. And, disconcertingly, hungry.

She said cautiously, 'Perhaps I should eat something.'

He got up at once, and she added, 'But none of that awful brown Windsor soup you got us to make once.'

He gave the smile that, so long ago, had made her heart turn over, that brought her to the edge of tears now. Even to see him leaving the room left her for a moment bereft.

She held out her hand – it took effort, like lifting a weight – and he took it, gripping the thin fingers. She blinked fiercely, but it was no good: the tears could no longer be held back and she wept, for lost years and foolish anger and the chasms that could not be crossed, and for them both. Her tears were the thanks she found it impossible to speak aloud. He passed her a handkerchief – paper tissues had never been his style.

PART THREE

Chapter 20

Madras 1992

'Is it holiday, madam?' asked the driver. 'Visit to Ashram, temples, beach?'

Charlotte disliked the Indian way of asking questions. In the street, on the bus, in a restaurant, they embarked on conversations that skipped the preliminaries, that jumped into areas not normally shared with strangers. 'Do English ladies believe in free love? Can you find work for me in London? How much salary are you making? What is your name? Your age? Have you one husband?' As befitted people whose lives were lived so much on the street, they regarded intimacy as natural.

She and her mother played it differently, keeping things light, the waltz spinning, the jokes coming, not dealing with the difficult areas. This was their way of coping. This trip, for instance.

They had talked before she left, the basement kitchen dark, with a grey, almost liquid quality to the light. The street above their heads, the area between railings and barred windows, swam in the miserable, flocculent February gloom.

'You're all set then?'

'I have a reservation,' Charlotte said, 'at a hotel in Pondicherry. At least I hope so. They don't seem to have a phone.'

Through the barred windows the legs of passing Kentish Town residents intermittently shadowed the basement room, like telegraph poles flashing past the windows of a train. It gave the room a restless feeling: the changing light, the unidentified, hurrying limbs. Outside, people were on the move. As Charlotte too would be, soon.

'Is there a pool?'

'I shouldn't think so. It's incredibly cheap.'

Judith said, 'Of course the whole scene – it's not going to be what you expect.'

'But I expect nothing,' Charlotte said, 'or rather, I'm keeping an open mind. The soup's boiling over,' she added. 'Does that mean we can eat? I have to push off early.'

No mention of doubt creeping up on her, of nerves, a growing desire to cancel the whole thing. No word from Judith to indicate emotional turmoil, fear of sleeping dogs, anxiety. 'At least you're going British Airways,' she said, 'they won't force curry down your throat.'

Visitors travelled by train or coach, or took a taxi from Madras, bouncing over pot-holes and swerving to avoid lorries that confidently occupied the crown of the road, giving way only to the languidly trundling bullock-carts whose drivers led a charmed life: no truck or car would endanger a bullock. Pale as sand, unhurried, they tossed their painted horns, safe, sacred. Their skin, wrinkling like the surface of clotted cream, glowed in the sunlight that shimmered through the leaves of the roadside trees. Moped drivers slalomed fearlessly through oncoming trucks and rickshaws. Everything else on the road effortlessly overtook Charlotte's clapped-out vehicle. The car, suspension long ago expired, lurched its way along the dusty road in spasms that resembled the motion of an exhausted kangaroo.

Already Charlotte hated India; she disliked the way no one could be trusted to keep to what they said yesterday, the way they told you what they thought you wanted to hear, reluctant to descend to a reality which would almost certainly prove disappointing. 'No problem,' was a phrase she learned to dread: they used it like a mantra, hoping that the words would make it so. She resented the way they refused to be kept at arm's length. ('They expect me to share my newspaper,' she wrote to Judith. 'In the coffee shop a man clucked impatiently when I was a bit slow turning the pages . . .') She was appalled by the dirt, discomfited by the contrast between her modest affluence and the life beyond the windows of the car. And the contrasts in the street itself, where a huge hoarding for an electric rice steamer loomed above families living in drainpipes and cardboard shanties by the side of the road. Gleaming stainless steel, requiring a plug, socket and power carried effortlessly along wire and flex, the electric steamer hovered alien as a space-ship over the heads of squatting women who stirred earthenware cooking pots feebly heated by a few twigs thrust between two broken bricks. Men washed at street-corner pumps. Little black pigs snuffled among the roots of a gnarled tree pushing through the concrete outside a Xerox 'center'. Children, emerging from hovels, immaculate, carrying satchels, made their way along the busy road, bound for school. The girls wore jasmine in their tightly combed and bound hair; boys had neat shirts and shorts. Naked toddlers – the have-nots – bare-footed and dusty looking, stood watching the school-bound privileged. A poster outside a military barracks read 'Join the Army. It offers handsome pay. Adventure. Prestige.' Some passer-by had scrawled encouragingly, 'And killing also'.

As the driver swerved wildly to avoid a particularly large

hole in the road, Charlotte suddenly recalled the headlines that had caught her eye in that morning's newspaper: 'FORTY DIE IN BUS CRASH', 'SIX DROWNED WHEN TAXI FALLS INTO CANAL'.

To her horror she saw two men on bicycles, heading straight for her. She closed her eyes – ('TWO CYCLISTS CRUSHED'). When she dared to look she saw that the driver had simply cleaved a path through them – normal Indian roadmanship. Earlier he had been cheerful, offering conversation.

'My name is Joseph,' he told her, 'Paul Vincent Joseph. Peewee for short.'

'Please keep your eyes on the road,' she said, and saw his disappointment. When she requested a 'rest stop' he halted by what he called a suitable bush. She returned, legs lacerated by invisible thorns, and sat hunched in the back of the car, applying antiseptic cream and longing for London. For zebra crossings and buses with room to sit down and pubs with Ladies and Gents and toilet paper. Clean towel dispensers. She was filled with self-pity and frustration. And she had not even reached Pondicherry.

In a pharmacy she saw a lurid poster advertising the Kama Sutra. Was this a daring attempt to spread literacy? Erotic literature as reading aid. Then she realised that Kama Sutra was a brand of condoms. This was a place where past and present, myth and actuality merged into one chaotic, kaleidoscopic whole. And she did not care for it.

'Soon now, madam!'

He did his best to sound confident, watching her in the rear mirror – the only time he used it – smiling ingratiatingly.

'Watch the road!' she said sharply, and closed her eyes.

She had fallen into an uneasy doze when his voice woke her, calling cheerfully, 'We are arriving!'

She sat up and gazed around. The wide road had become a dual carriageway. Something looked different though: the policeman directing traffic wore a red képi; a signpost read 'Pondicherry welcomes you – *soyez le bienvenu.*' Despite herself she felt the beginning of excitement in her stomach, something between apprehension and exhilaration. She was almost there. The road was lined with fine houses shaded by tall trees. But looking closer she saw that it was all falling apart: the dual carriageway into town, part of the original, majestic plan, was pitted with pot-holes, and cyclists pedalled blithely up the wrong lane towards them. The avenues that intersected it, the arcaded shops, had sunk into decrepitude. The mansions of the bourgeoisie, once white and resplendent, were lichen-encrusted, the walls cracked and peeling. Some had thatched huts perched on the roof terraces, visible behind stone balustrading. The once-grand streets were piled with filth and rubble; in some places the surface had reverted to sand. Men squatted by the roadside to urinate. Shanties had grown on to the sides of the palatial buildings like barnacles on to the hulls of ships; secondary life-forms, supported by the carcasses of now-defunct hosts. Another grubby hoarding welcomed her to 'Pondicherry, City of Peace.' The smell of drains was overwhelming.

Gazing about, trying to take in the jumble of impressions, she saw the sign, a square board, mud-spattered but still legible: an arrow indicating a turn-off, and then the words 'Auroville, city of universal harmony'. Before she could call to the driver, 'Stop! Turn here!' it was gone. She became aware of a dull ache at the base of her skull.

The streets became narrower, packed with people and colour, bicycles and noise. The pavements were lined with small shops selling cloth by the yard, wooden carvings, necklaces, kitchen equipment, radios, T-shirts, saris, jeans, incense, nuts, cheap furniture, garlands of marigolds and frangipani, purses, bangles, sandals, sacred statuettes, every inch filled with goods for sale. Cycles and mopeds were parked eight deep by the curb in a crazy, metallic jumble, reducing the navigable road space to a cramped lane. Tinsel and plastic glittered in the sun, spilling from doorways, hanging from ceiling hooks, piled in heaps. The air was filled with the sound of cycle-rickshaw bells, car hooters, music from transistors, loud-speakers, street-cries and the squeal of brakes.

At an intersection the driver pulled up, uncertain, calling out for directions, waved, nodded and turned right. Charlotte stared about, eyes sore from the dust. They appeared to be driving along some kind of quayside, along a bank edging a dried-up drain or canal. Men were at work, labourers in loincloths, with bare feet, moving slowly along the cracked and ruined canal sides. The car crossed the canal and turned into a quieter street. Rubbing her sore neck Charlotte became aware that the town had changed its character: the shops and cacophony were left behind; the streets were cleaner, quieter. It was as though the canal had formed some kind of boundary, and they had crossed it.

A long grey wall was pierced by a high gate. Beyond it she glimpsed a pale grey building, a shady courtyard. The driver slowed and jerked his head towards the grey building: 'Sri Aurobindo Ashram, madam, very famous.'

'I know,' she said curtly. He looked dashed. As they reached the end of the road she saw that it was called rue de la Marine. She heard Judith's voice in her head: 'Don't be fooled, darling. The street names may be French but it's India. Just remember that.'

The driver was clearly lost, turning left then right, calling out repeatedly for directions. It was Charlotte who saw the house on the corner of the rue Laval, with its big gates and wrought-iron sign: 'Etabli 1884'. 'There it is!' she said loudly, 'Grand Hotel de France!'

Weeds pushed through the thin gravel of the drive; wild columbines clustered round the house, reflecting their blue on to the flaky white stucco walls. A broken fountain housed a bird's nest.

That night she wrote to Judith, 'All well. My reservation noted. The hotel is very French . . .'

As was the owner.

'Madame de l'Esprit?' Charlotte began, tentatively.

'*C'est moi.* Oriane de l'Esprit.'

Like the garden, its owner had changed. The slender pearl-tipped fingers had become claws, the hands scattered with liver-spots like the speckled surface of a soufflé; the swan-like neck had grown scrawny and was veiled these days by scarves of gauzy cloth.

When Charlotte exclaimed 'Oriane! What a lovely name!' she said, 'Like Proust's *duchesse*, you know.' Adding, as she always did, 'But of course you do not. Young people can't read Proust any more. The television has rotted their minds.'

The sparse white hair was dragged back in a punishing bun. Her small, pale ears, fragile as snail shells, lay exposed. She shifted irritably in the reclining chair on the verandah and seemed to have lost interest in the new arrival.

Charlotte looked around for a member of the staff. Then *la patronne* beckoned her closer.

'Why have you come to Pondi?' she asked, frowning. 'Why not the so-called golden triangle. New Delhi. Maharaja hotels. Your lost empire. All that nostalgia for the British Raj.'

'I'm not a British Raj person,' Charlotte said.

'Why then have you come?' The French accent was overlaid with the slight singsong of those who have spent their lives in the subcontinent. 'Are you one of those westerners who is drawn to the Ashram, in search of . . . spiritual uplift?' There was a slight but unmistakable tinge of scorn; verbal quotation marks framed the last two words.

Why had she come? Charlotte said, her voice sharp, 'I plan to go to Auroville.'

'Auroville?'

'Yes.' She had no intention of explaining her reasons to strangers. 'I'm told the architecture is interesting.'

There was a pause. Blue eyes milky with cataracts studied Charlotte. Then Oriane twitched a shoulder impatiently: 'For people who like a mish-mash of south-Indian style with bits and pieces of European modernism it might do. For myself I have other preferences – do you know the *Maison carrée* at Nimes?'

Charlotte opened her mouth but Oriane was ahead of her. Architecture was not what it had been, *hélas*. She had quite a lot to say about the châteaux of the Loire and Richelieu's mansion . . . what Mansart did with Versailles and the Place Vendôme –'though even he at times could be *un peu vulgaire.*' The Gabriels were preferable –'*architectes du roi* . . . Le Petit Trianon, charming . . . that was with Le Nôtre of course, a good gardener, that one.'

In an attempt to stem the flow, Charlotte slipped in, 'Didn't Le Nôtre design Kensington Gardens and Green Park?' adding provocatively, 'In London?' She received a milky blue glare of irritation. 'I dare say,' said Oriane, 'if they are any good.' She moved on rapidly to Viollet-le-Duc, 'and Perret's little pupil who did clever things with concrete, Charles-Edouard Jeanneret. Partly Swiss, but you would hardly have known. Now that was an architect! *Formidable*! You may recall he laid out the town plan for Chandigarh, up north, in the Punjab. Quite brilliant.'

She paused, to allow the English girl to reveal her ignorance of this part-Swiss genius. Charlotte said, sensing it would annoy, 'Jeanneret? Oh, Le Corbusier, you mean. Yes, brilliant,' and was rewarded with an ill-concealed scowl of irritation: Madame de l'Esprit had planned to leave her floundering. There was a feeling of fifteen-all about the exchange.

Oriane gripped her stick and attempted to rise from the

reclining chair. Gravity defeated her, but she decided to ignore the set-back and went on, as though answering a question.

'Yes. In any case we managed very well, here in Pondi. You have seen the canal? Before Merger, when the French were in charge, the canal was an object of beauty, it ran through the centre of town, cool, clean, the *quais* on either side shaded with trees. Now, the filthy drain that remains they plan to cover with cement. Soon it will be completely hidden from view, like an old buried secret, and only those who were here before will remember its existence. You should not waste your time here. There are better things to see elsewhere.'

She sounded exhausted, and leaned back, eyes closed. Then she banged violently on the tiled floor with her stick and called, 'Guruvappa!'

He came out from the shadowy hall to her side and helped her out of the chair. As he assisted Oriane out of the room he gave Charlotte a quick, kindly glance and an apologetic smile. They vanished through the bead-curtained doorway, Oriane's voice floating back: 'Dinner is served at 7.30.' As communication, it verged on the peremptory. Charlotte felt she should snap to attention and salute.

In the corridor Oriane paused and looked back through the shifting, clicking beads at the girl, who was now turning over the pages of a guide to the town.

'Is she expected, do you suppose?' she said, frowning. 'Should Auroville be warned?' Then she shrugged. 'Not my affair.'

Later, Guru, riding past the gates of the Ashram in a rickshaw, saw the English girl standing outside on the pavement, staring at the building. She glanced about her, undecided. White-clad figures came and went and there was a glimpse of a flowery courtyard, a drift of incense on the warm air. Bicycles were parked several rows deep beside the pavements, leaning neatly, one against the next. A beggar hovered further off and a cycle-rickshaw man tinkled his bell and called, 'Madame? Here madame!' There was the sound of a bell from within, the wooden gate closed and there was silence. The girl turned away.

Guru's rickshaw turned the corner and emerged on to the Promenade. Charlotte followed the same route, walking slowly, checking street-names in her guidebook. The wind was blowing from the sea; it blew through the wide gateway of the white municipality building still called the Hotel de Ville, and blew the leaves off the sea-front trees into the compound of the Customs House – still marked *Douanes* – but now grown shabby and neglected. A statue of Gandhi, much larger than life, towering improbably above the Promenade, turned its back on the bay, framed by an onion-domed open structure like an outsize gazebo, ringed with eight slender, ornately carved pillars of yellow stone. Before Merger, another statue had stared down at the passers-by; a bulkier figure, his wig falling to his shoulders, eighteenth-century garb, thigh boots – Governor Dupleix. Now the governor languished in the consulate garden not far away, his heavy features streaked by the droppings of seagulls.

There was a sense of ease; people strolled along the Promenade as the sky drained from blue to mother-of-pearl. The sun, about to disappear behind the trees of government park, stared Gandhi full in the face, and painted the sea-wall pale gold. Charlotte, map in hand, leaned on the wall and found the parapet still, unexpectedly, hot to the touch, though the air had cooled. Birds swooped, silhouettes against the copper sunset. Women and children lingered on the sand below Gandhi, their feet in the surf, the hems of the women's saris soaked by sudden small waves. The children hopped back and forth, shrieking happily, their sandals neatly lined up on a rock behind them, keeping dry, while on a higher rock men sat, smoking, chattering. These were the ones who could afford to enjoy leisure. For others, work went on; small boys and old men sold snacks: yellow chickpeas, crisp, spiced potato balls. Birds circled the old lighthouse, and settled fleetingly on the weathervane, setting it moving like a sluggish carousel.

In the space of a few moments dusk had darkened the sky and veiled the bright scene , blotting out colour, turning the landscape to indigo and ink and smoky grey. The light thickened. The breeze had dropped and a stillness in the air intensified all sounds. There was a sense of quickening, the rooks settling noisily in the trees of the little public park, people on bicycles filling the streets, bells ringing loudly, the whole town on the move as the light died.

Chapter 21

In the dining room of the Grand Hotel de France tables were laid for four or for two. Charlotte, seated alone, felt incomplete; she spoiled the symmetry. Through the open archway Guru regarded the girl: she sat very upright at the table, pale-skinned, dark hair, untidy curls. Her eyes were the colour of amber beads, though concealed at the moment by small, steel-rimmed glasses. He thought she looked young and vulnerable. He bore her no ill-will but he wished she had not come. Like a pebble dropped into a stagnant pool she was already creating ripples.

Charlotte had a sense of being watched and grew nervous, the frown-mark between the dark brows more pronounced. She rubbed the back of her neck for a moment, trying to ease the steady throb of pain. She made a show of studying her guidebook, sipped her glass of iced water, glanced about irritably.

No one else had yet appeared, though it was now 7.35. Overhead the fans turned lazily, lost in the gloom of the high ceilings, their whirring loud in the silence. Oriane, clad in a floating gown of pale turquoise, stalked the dining room, slowly, like a ghostly warden, her stick tapping sharply on the tiled floor. A strong whiff of garlic floated from the direction of the kitchen. Encouraged by this, Charlotte asked one of the servants if she could order some wine. He signalled across the room with a movement of his head and Guru came over to the table. Charlotte repeated her question. He said gently, 'Only beer or mineral water, I fear.'

She caught Oriane's glance from across the room, eyebrows raised enquiringly.

'I thought you would have had wine, Madame de l'Esprit.' A mistake. The opal eyes flashed.

'You could have wine, if you have no palate. In the old days wine was made here, Golconda wine, not bad, acceptable. But once the French were no longer in charge . . .' She shrugged. 'There is imported wine I believe, but at those prices I refuse to purchase. Take the beer.'

Gradually others arrived: a family of four, pale-haired parents, children seemingly made of silver and alabaster, probably Swedish . . . a young American couple who murmured intimately and inaudibly . . . a quartet of French, noisy, irreverent, assured of Madame's approval.

A servant appeared with the first course. Charlotte heard Oriane telling the French table that it was *'aspic de poisson'*, going into what seemed fairly revolting detail about how aspic was made. The texture was extraordinary and the overwhelming flavour was of garlic. Charlotte laid down her fork in defeat, dreading the arrival of Madame de l'Esprit at her table with raised eyebrows, questions, a contemptuous twitch of her shoulder.

Maintaining her distance, Oriane surveyed the guests, eyes narrowed, aware that the pale family had problems: the younger of the marble-skinned girls had refused to touch her food. This was something that clearly deserved to be ignored. Charlotte refused the coffee and sipped her bottled beer.

At about the same moment, though five hours earlier by the clock, Judith went into the kitchen to make herself a mug of tea. Through the basement window she watched occasional lower limbs hurrying by, en route to chilly bedsits or tastefully renovated Victorian terrace houses.

From her observation of lower limbs Judith could mark the turn of the seasons. As bare legs gave way to tights, then woolly leggings she could draw conclusions about their owners and what they were engaged in, speculate about their state of mind. Some sauntered by in groups, drifting from wine-bar or club; others scissored past, tense and anxious to be home. There were pairs locked thigh to thigh, sensuously close, and others, separated by carrier bags and by more than that, walking together yet apart. Moods could be gauged from the stride or hesitation of a person's legs. Fashion was only partially on view: she saw the rise and fall of hemlines and of heels, though not the expanding and shrinking of shoulder pads. Flares were back, she noted with surprise. How very odd and ugly they looked now, and how beautiful she had felt wearing her loons, the first time around. She had loved it all, the beads and flowers, the freedom. The last year of a magical decade, one that was to be the defining period of her life. 1969. *We all knew things would change. And we, too, would change.* But those last months, like someone straddling a see-saw, keeping the delicate balance, she had dreamed it might last for ever, the loving and the dreaming and the hope. Then the year turned and the earth quaked underfoot and Judith was changed. But not obviously: two nights before Charlotte was born Judith had gone to a party off the King's Road wearing denim flares and a gold lace top and no one had even noticed the bulge.

Judith remembered the party because that was the night she had finally decided not to go back. Everyone encouraged her: 'not fair on the child, not fair on you.' She didn't blame them. Nor did she blame herself. And yet regret surfaced, in moments that arrived without warning, the blues that come in the early hours, lowering the spirits, tugging wisps of remorse from dark corners, whispering 'What if. . . ?'

With paradise lost (or common sense reasserted?) she worked for a while as a graphic designer for a provincial television company, creating flashy credit-titles to persuade viewers the programme would be worth watching. Later she did drawings round the edges of features in a pop magazine and realised one day that she had been literally marginalised.

Judith had discouraged this trip into the past; she thought it was a mistake. But she would never have expressed that view to her daughter. She had merely pointed out that Charlotte was investing too much hope in this pathetic odyssey. That she would be disappointed. Neither of them was capable of using the stronger words that hovered unspoken. Long ago, Judith had made a decision renouncing turmoil. She had settled with some relief for the middle ground; she held back from intimate personal revelation. So she offered a warning, but with restraint. Eschewing the dramatic, she said merely that she feared Charlotte would be disappointed.

The nearest she came to revealing how she felt was just before Charlotte left. They hugged, in the boisterous, slightly impersonal way that had become the routine, and Judith said cheerfully, 'Be careful, won't you. Don't fall under the spell.' But her eyes were anxious.

Chapter 22

The Sri Aurobindo library was quiet in its way: no one shouted or threw furniture about, but there was a constant exchange of murmured question and answer, occasional exclamations of annoyance or surprise, a thudding of books on tables, a pulling out of chairs and shuffling of feet.

Charlotte was leafing through the thin volume she had requested when a small, sad-eyed man carrying a briefcase paused by the table. Charlotte looked up.

'Good morning.' He hesitated. 'And you are from?'

'England.'

'Ah.' He nodded, glancing at the book. 'You are perhaps yourself an architect?'

'No.'

Did that sound unnecessarily brusque? She added, reluctantly, 'I work in local government.'

'Ah!' He nodded again, impressed. 'Local government. Sphere of influence. Decision-taking and so forth.'

Charlotte thought about decision-taking. Her sphere of influence, she could have told him, was limited: extensions, conversions, renewals and refurbishments. Back-yard swimming pools in pine chalets. Neo-Georgian garages in conservation areas. Protected trees. Overshadowing. Hazardous materials. Smells . . . The local council planning department was a long way from Whitehall.

There was a silence.

'Did you want this book?' she asked. 'Are you waiting for it?'

He looked stricken. 'Oh, on the contrary. I wondered merely whether I could assist . . .'

He picked up the book, gazing at it with what looked like reverence.

'Auroville,' he murmured, 'most interesting! An experience not to be missed.'

'Yes, I plan to go –'

'But I could take you – I have a trusty moped.'

'Oh no, really, that's most kind, but I can manage.' Her tone was definite.

He said, 'Well. If you need help at all . . . Without wheels it can be difficult.'

His suit was threadbare, the briefcase so shabby that its once smooth leather surface had acquired the rubbed bloom of suede.

'I know it well. I have lived and worked there – on a farm you know – for many years.'

She looked at him with sharpening interest. 'Many years?'

'Indeed. More than twenty.'

'Then you must be one of the pioneers.'

'You could say so.'

'How fascinating.'

'It is hard at times.' He paused. 'Allow me to introduce myself: A.D. Chetty. Will you have a cup of tea?'

It soon became clear to Charlotte that inviting people for cups of tea was not a normal event in Mr Chetty's life. He led her round one street after another, pausing unhappily before busy tea-stalls, kiosks and run-down eating rooms and a corner-shop offering *Fromage de Ferme*.

'No, no. This will not do at all.' He stood, thinking, then raised a finger in triumph. 'There is one place on the beach.'

Le Petit Bistro stood on the Promenade, jutting out over the sea. Tables and chairs were set out on a balcony that ran round the three sides so that the waves foamed beneath it. Sitting on the balcony was like being on the prow of a ship. Once, Charlotte thought, it must have had a certain elegance, waiters smart in black and white serving *croque-monsieur*, French wine, coffee in tiny, gold-rimmed cups. Now it was self-service, and customers paid in advance, then lined up at a hatch to the kitchen and exchanged tickets for cardboard plates of puri and alu. Some ordered flabby, English-looking sandwiches, with a dollop of tomato ketchup on the side. Mr Chetty urged her to take something to eat, and ordered their tea.

They carried their small plastic beakers to a table on the balcony, and he enquired whereabouts in London she lived.

'Kentish Town,' Mr Chetty repeated, savouring the name through a mouthful of tea. 'I am not personally acquainted with the neighbourhood. Southall was my neck of the woods. Quite a busy centre of commerce, it was then.'

He had been kept busy all right; a perplexed youth sent for by imperious uncles who used him as a messenger between shop and market. He shared a room with five others, all nephews or cousins, and had no time off – '*Off*? What is this "off"?' his uncle shouted when he tentatively raised the matter. 'Do *I* have time off?'

He had stayed a year and only once, greatly daring, had he purchased a bus ticket and explored London – a dizzy day of Buckingham Palace, Horseguards Parade, Trafalgar Square ... 'The National Gallery,' he said to Charlotte, 'a most inspiring institution.' (And would have been even more so had he been able to admire the inside as well as the outside.) The uncles had not been pleased. There were no further outings.

Charlotte and Mr Chetty were alone on the balcony. Around them the surf thundered and the wind blew warm, giving them a curious privacy. Other customers preferred to sit sheltered, indoors.

'Auroville,' he said, 'has been my life.' It was important for him to be there. For others like him.

'There is a danger, you see, that it could be perceived as a neo-colonial development. Foreigners telling us what to do and so forth. The Indian involvement is hence essential. Especially from the South.' He waved his arms helplessly. 'The idea of Auroville is divine. It must survive. It must.' He sounded despairing. 'At the beginning it was different. We required little. We had an idealistic view of things – why not?'

It was, he said, a spartan time. 'The Mother was our guiding spirit. She said, somewhere there must be a place where people could live with truth and harmony. "First the bulldozers," she said, "Then the poets." Of course this was very metaphorical stuff: we had no bulldozers. Just our bare hands, at the beginning . . . And her inspiration.'

Judith had spoken of the Mother, an ambiguous, enigmatic figure, Aurobindo's acolyte; to some, sharing Aurobindo's divinity, to others, a manipulative power behind the throne. Mr Chetty had no doubts. 'Without the Mother there would be no Auroville.'

He looked at her thoughtfully and Charlotte sensed that questions of a personal nature were about to be put. She pre-empted them. 'I must go,' she said. He looked hurt and she added 'Hotel lunch is served at 12.30 –'

'Of course, of course! I too must partake of something. Well. Let me know if you would care for a lift. I would be delighted to transport you.'

The rather grand phrase hardly conveyed an accurate picture of his battered moped, parked at the railings near the library. 'Possibly we shall meet again.'

She waved as they parted, and turned to watch the small figure as he crossed the road, shoulders slightly hunched, hurrying back to his trusty pair of wheels, his divine work.

It was indeed almost time for lunch. The smell of garlic

rose from the kitchen and invaded Charlotte's room, clinging to the mosquito net, washing over her as she stood under the modest gush of the cold-water shower. Garlic curled into her nostrils, filling her mouth. Garlic suds squelched in her armpits and foamed between her toes.

She descended cautiously to the dining room and took her seat. The record player was going full blast: 'César Franck,' Oriane called, from the reclining rattan chair on the verandah; 'Belgian, *hélas*, but he had talent. Those fools at the *conservatoire*! He is the one they should have celebrated. This is where the French symphonic school began. With him! You hear the pain in that minor key? An old man, but listen to him express that pain.'

She was dressed today from head to foot in white – dress, scarf, silken bandeau round her head, white stockings, and on the small feet, sticking out from her hem, a pair of white gym shoes, scuffed and practical.

'I dress in white because I am in mourning,' she announced loudly, above the music.

'Oh, I'm sorry . . .' Charlotte began, but Oriane was twitching her shoulders in irritation.

'Boff! It is not *personal* loss I speak of, but national. On this day, long ago, Pondicherry surrendered to –' a pause and venomous emphasis, 'the *British*. One can only remember and mourn.'

She banged her stick. 'Guru!'

He appeared from the shadows where as always he seemed to have been waiting for her call. She thrust out an arm and he raised her bodily from the reclining chair. As soon as she was upright she shook off his helping hand –'See to the kitchen! They are busy ruining things.' She turned back. 'These days even cauliflowers are brought in from Bangalore, but we grew everything right here, *petits pois, asperges*, the town was beautiful, the people elegant –' She shrugged and stomped off ahead, into her private territory.

Through the bead curtain she turned and looked back again at the girl. Deplorable dress sense, the droopy frock was unfortunate. Still, she had her mother's slim body and Raymond's curly hair –

The bracket clock on the wall struck the hour and Charlotte looked up: the light caught her eyes. Oriane's eyesight provided no specific details, but she knew that they were amber, dark-lashed. Who would have thought, after so long ... She tried to dredge up significant conversations, actions, but her mind flittered, bat-like, from one moment to another, wearying her. It was too long ago and she refused to feel guilty or responsible. As she recalled it she had neither encouraged nor discouraged. Her behaviour had been correct – *impeccable*. She shook her head as though shaking off troublesome flies, or unwanted thoughts.

Chapter 23

Charlotte's first visit to the Ashram began badly. The Ashramites, calm, poised north Indians for the most part, wore white and had an aura of confident sanctity that she found daunting. No one stopped her at the gate yet she felt a trespasser. She looked around, getting her bearings. Steps led up to a verandah where aged Ashramites sat on wicker chairs and fanned themselves in a leisurely way.

There was a quiet calm about the place that she found a soothing contrast to the normal Indian background of uproar and confusion. The leafy shade, the sense of serenity should have soothed her. Instead, she found herself taken aback by the remote expressions on the faces around her. No one returned her tentative smile, indeed, some readjusted their features fractionally to hint at a reproving frown. Smiling, one step away from chattering, was clearly seen as a sign of unwelcome levity. These were the inheritors of Aurobindo's yoga and they knew it. But no one barred her way or questioned her, and perhaps she was being unreasonable to expect a welcome – just another curious visitor among so many passing through.

Standing, undecided, on the point of leaving, she saw that one of the ancients was leaning towards her, finger raised.

'Shoes off!' he instructed, a little wearily. 'Shoes off!'

She hastily removed her sandals and wandered towards the

shady courtyard, feeling the warmth of the stone slabs on her bare feet.

The scent of the flowers covering the grey granite of the double tomb of Aurobindo and the Mother filled the courtyard; the incense curled lazily into the air. Around her, visitors arrived, sat quietly, meditating, praying, reading from small books with tiny print. Among them Charlotte was pleasantly surprised to see Mr Chetty seated nearby, his briefcase by his side.

He caught her eye and nodded approvingly. When Charlotte got up, he too rose, and accompanied her.

'A fortunate encounter!' he murmured, ducking his head cheerfully. A thin woman in a plain white sari stood by the steps. Dark shadows lay beneath her eyes and her face was cross-hatched with fine lines. Her features could have seemed severe, but she was smiling.

Mr Chetty beamed. 'This is an old friend, a very old friend, Gita. And a new friend.' He paused.

'Charlotte,' she said reluctantly.

'You look hot,' the woman said, 'we'll go to my room and you'll have some lime juice and ginger. Good for you.' She spoke with the authority that seemed to distinguish the Ashramites, and led the way round the corner to a small concrete block.

Gita's room was stark: a narrow cot, a bed-roll, a tin trunk. Battered books, many of them medical. The only touch of decoration a photograph of Aurobindo and the Mother with marigolds in a small brass bowl. The window looked over tree-tops towards the sea and a cool breeze blew through the room. She gave them fresh lime juice spiked with ginger and they sat sipping.

'What's the matter with your neck? I notice you rubbing it.'

Charlotte hastily dropped her hand. 'Maybe I pulled a muscle. Nothing serious.'

'If it's hurting you, it needs attention. Go to the Ashram physiotherapy department. Arjuna will show you where it is.'

She saw Charlotte hesitate and added drily, 'Don't worry, you won't get any mystical healing or incantations but they may give you a spot of ultrasound if they think you need it. And you don't pay anything.'

Mr Chetty said anxiously, 'I hope you were not late for your lunch.' He turned to Gita: 'The hotel seems rather strict . . .'

Gita's features dissolved into sudden amusement. 'Hotel de France? So I believe. Bit of a tartar, hmm?'

Oriane was wearing dark blue this evening, with a shimmering gold silk scarf wound round her head like a turban. Here and there, haphazardly, she had pinned brooches that glittered in the lamp-light. With her weightless frailty supporting all this splendour she looked like a small scarecrow wrapped in Christmas decorations.

'You're celebrating something?' Charlotte ventured, and was rewarded by a gracious smile. 'February 1747. When Governor Dupleix received a visit from one of the Indian princes he wore – *apart* his formal attire, a silk turban bedecked with pearls and precious stones.' She touched her own turban as though to reassure herself it was still there. 'He went on foot to greet the Nawab, shaded with white silk umbrellas, and cooled with fans of peacock feathers . . .' The pale blue eyes seemed to be looking into the past she described, a procession of torch-bearers, palanquins and soldiers whose muskets glittered as they caught the light from the flambeaux. She sighed and shrugged away the splendour.

'And are you exploring Pondi?' she enquired. 'The museum –'

'I spent some time at the Ashram this morning. In the

192

courtyard, you know. The flowers, the silence, it had a serenity –'

But mention of the Ashram had been unwise. Oriane's face turned quite dark with rage and she stomped up and down the verandah, pausing to wave her stick about with a force that imperilled her balance.

'Serenity? The Ashram has become a farce, a business – all those Guest Houses, dozens of them, and showrooms selling scarves and hand-made paper – where is the mysticism that was its inspiration? But of course,' she added malevolently, 'What can you expect of Indians? Their absurd idolatries, this ... *folie*, this idiotic business of protecting cows, their failure to grow mushrooms –'

'Mushrooms?' Charlotte was confused. What had mushrooms to do with it? Perhaps Oriane meant magic mushrooms? Mystical mushrooms? But no. She meant ordinary mushrooms – *champignons*.

'*Bien sûr*. Oh, I encouraged them, it would have been an investment. I alone would have purchased large amounts for the kitchen. And no doubt that man at the other hotel –'

'What other hotel?' Charlotte asked. No other European hotel had been mentioned to her. 'One of the Indian hotels?'

'No, no!' Oriane waved an impatient hand. She certainly had no intention of discussing a rival establishment. The hotelier in question, an elegant Frenchman who in his younger days had played *boules* with visiting Europeans, had apparently said to someone, long ago, that Oriane saw herself as the Madame Récamier of Pondi. She had turned the gibe on its head and agreed maliciously that she might have been – if a salon could ever have been assembled in such unpromising circumstances.

She changed the subject: 'I hear you are not to take lunch with us tomorrow. A trip to Auroville.'

'Yes.'

'Have a good breakfast then. You will starve out there.'

She was about to say more but she caught sight of something through the arch to the kitchen and her eyes flashed.

'Subra! Serve the guests!'

Once again Charlotte sat alone, marooned, while the servants criss-crossed the dining room, tacking from table to table, offering glittering rafts of fish, silver sauce boats, salad bowls from which the garlic rose, hovering like a sea mist.

'Madame?' The dessert tray appeared beneath her nose. 'Crème caramel? *C'est très bon.*'

Her stomach was behaving oddly, clenching itself spasmodically into a tight ball. She was conscious of a sour, stale taste. Her tongue, monstrously thickened, seemed to fill her dried-out mouth. Her teeth were chattering and she felt curiously off-balance. The floor beneath her feet tilted like the deck of a ship.

From far off she heard a voice suggesting coffee, madame, and knew she had to reach her room without delay.

Chapter 24

It was Guru who told Charlotte how to get to Auroville. She would need a taxi, there was always one down by the canal, 'though bicycles are often used.'

'Bicycles! But it's so far!'

'There's no need to go all through the town. You can take the old sea road, through the plantations. It's about seven kilometres. A pleasant drive.'

He found the girl touching in her perplexity, her lack of poise. A daughter, a granddaughter might have given him a similar pleasure, had things gone differently.

She in turn found him comforting to talk to, this elderly Indian with his exquisite manners and kindness, and she made the mistake of saying so to Oriane.

Ah oui, the manners, the *politesse,* Oriane said, silkily vicious. 'They learn it at St Paul's, you know. And that place on the Thames, near Windsor Castle. We had some of them here in the English Foreign Service.' He had come in while she was speaking and she added, 'Yes, he has *le style anglais.* Am I not right, Guru?'

He refused to rise to her bait and in any case Oriane had tapped her way out of the room by then, a sure way of having the last word. Her voice floated back from the terrace: 'He's a Brahmin, you know. They think they are better than anyone else.'

Charlotte was confused: major-domo in a fading provincial hotel seemed an odd occupation for a high-born Hindu educated at a British Public School. Perhaps the family fortunes had declined. But she was grateful for his benign presence.

'I was a bit thrown by the Ashram. Some of them seemed almost . . . unfriendly.'

'Well, like the Jesuits, the Ashramites prefer to shape the clay, start with the child; unless an outsider is serious about studying Aurobindo's yoga they don't really encourage more than the routine visit. An organised tour of the workshops, a meditation in the courtyard, and of course the bookshop, to purchase recommended reading and picture postcards . . .' He added, with a fastidious grimace, 'I should avoid the postcards.'

When, three days before, she had disgraced herself, vomiting strenuously before quite reaching the bathroom, Guru had taken charge, seeing her to her room, calling one of the Tamil cleaning girls to undress and wash her. For the last two days he had sent up plain rice, curds, tea without milk, and called in at regular intervals to see if she needed anything.

Oriane declared herself perplexed. 'Clearly it was something you consumed in Madras. Those city kitchens . . . Never have we experienced such a thing in the hotel!' It was clear that she found it inconsiderate, to arrive and fall sick with such lack of moderation. But she had sent for her own doctor, and was firm that no charge would be made to the visitor.

'I know you young people, *les jeunes* today. Doubtless you have failed to make adequate provision . . .'

Being in the presence of ill-health made her uneasy and climbing the stairs was hard for her –'Guru can look after you, *c'est son métier*,' she said, holding herself aloof, hovering in the bedroom doorway. 'Subra in the kitchen has been saying prayers for your recovery but I suppose that will

196

do you no harm. Remember, Pascal too, hedged his bets as you people say.'

Oriane banged her stick on the tiles and squawked 'Guru! Attend to the child!' and drifted towards the terrace steps, pausing regally to allow two servant girls to assist her to the ground floor.

It was hotter today, and Oriane wore a loose shift of pale green cotton. From the doorway like an echo of her presence, a refreshing perfume wafted over Charlotte. She sniffed enquiringly.

'Vetiver and lemon,' Guruvappa said. 'Madame de l'Esprit wears it on appropriate days.'

'What makes a day appropriate?'

'Largely the temperature. The mood can also be a factor. It's an old custom, to scent garments after laundering, with fragrances that suit the weather. Madame took to the idea at some point. Today she's wearing green, you may have noticed; lemon with vetiver complements the colour. She occasionally wears sandalwood when in a cheerful frame of mind, and in the cool season, attar of roses or patchouli with a crimson gown.' He smiled with what in a less sweet-natured person Charlotte would have described as malicious amusement. 'I believe she read that the wife of Governor Dupleix is said to have matched her perfume to her gowns. I'm not sure Madame remembers that this is a native custom.'

'She speaks good English,' Charlotte remarked. 'Considering everyone must have spoken French here, when she was young.'

'Ah,' he said, his thin face rearranging itself into a mocking smile, the eyebrows rising like the wings of small dark birds. 'But then it's not such a difficult language, is it? Speaking for myself, getting to grips with English literature never presented much of a problem compared with Tamil and Sanskrit.'

He picked up her empty water carafe. 'I'll send up some fresh water for you.' He added, 'You speak rather good French.'

'I went to the French Lycée in London for a while.' Until Judith's mother died and her step-father decided grandparental assistance with school fees was no longer on offer. 'Find a Sixth Form college,' he advised. The change had proved disastrous: where Charlotte had achieved excellence she was now lost. At home in French culture, she was ignorant of the names and faces, even the sounds of her generation's icons, her interests too literary and too foreign. Accustomed to gossiping in French she had a good grasp of *argot*, but her new classmates found her English too formal, almost stilted. They found her odd. She sensed that people were ill-at-ease with her. She was first ingratiating, then supercilious. Neither helped. Attempting to shed oddity Charlotte stopped concentrating; she was late for classes, she became assimilated. She became average.

The sound of a symphony floated up from the record player on the verandah below, and through it came the sound of Oriane in full flood: 'César Franck, *he* is the one they should have honoured . . . !'

That night, waking hot and thirsty, Charlotte saw that the water carafe had not been replaced. She pulled on a dressing-gown and went to the door. The hotel was in darkness, the other guests presumably asleep. Moonlight filtering through the windows gleamed on the stairs and she felt her way down cautiously. She knew the kitchen was through the archway from the dining room.

As she reached the turn in the stairs she heard faint sounds from the ground floor, sounds that seemed to be coming from Oriane's private quarters at the back of the house. Voices, speaking low, overlapping. In the darkness the voices drifted, other-worldly, like ghostly echoes of past conversations. A man's voice, a woman's, murmured exchanges and then – ringing out – a high-pitched cry, like a lamentation.

Suddenly it became impossible to intrude. Licking dry lips, Charlotte turned back to her room.

Chapter 25

The taxi bumped past the post office still blazoned with a sign that read *Services des Postes et Telegraphes Indiens* and turned left on to the north boulevard, plunging into noise, dirt, colour; shabby buses sounding their horns, lorries strung with tinsel and holy figurines. The bells of painted cycle-rickshaws tinkled incessantly, bicycles three-deep, wobbled precariously between the battered, rusty cars, bullock-carts rolled steadily through the traffic, the creamy oxen nodding their heads.

The 'Frenchness' of the town was soon left behind. By the roadside little markets were crowded, people bought vegetables, filled pots at pumps. *Filmi* music blared from loudspeakers, lurid posters for action movies covered crumbling houses. They were heading north on the old Madras road, with wooden shacks and bazaar stalls edging the crumbling tarmac. Ahead, weirdly, the road seemed to end in a wall of palm trees, the palms rising up like a screen, into which the traffic vanished. But imperceptibly the road was curving, leading them deep into a shady green landscape that could have been Indonesia, a world away from boulevards and public parks. Village life reasserted itself: scrawny men wrapped in brief loincloths, women in washed-out saris walked between thatched huts walled with mud or woven palm, beneath neem trees and tall coconut palms. By the roadside weavers worked in the shade, lengths of cotton slung like elongated hammocks over wooden loom supports.

The taxi driver waved at the tall palms growing by the roadside. Many were marked with a mysterious whitewash hieroglyph, the three-letter symbol glimmering palely on the dark trunks.

'EGR. East Grand Road,' he announced, glancing back at her. 'Forthcoming development. Good for business.' So the white splashes were the plague marks, these were doomed trees, destined for the chop, for scheduled redevelopment. This would cease to be the old Madras road, rural, leisurely, running through the coconut plantations, the sea glimpsed through the trees. It would become another commercial route, lorries thundering past two abreast, sending dust swirling high to the tops of the surviving palms. There would be an end to the weavers working on the verges. This sleepy, rural road, shaded by banyans, the palm trees leaning benignly towards one another like attenuated guardian angels, would become just another motorway.

The car hit a heap of rubble, shuddered and ploughed on. No maintenance was being carried out, why should it, with a new road to be built in due course? The tarmac was now so damaged, in places so thinned and fragile that it lay like black lace over the dark red earth beneath it. The taxi juddered over another bump and Charlotte's head snapped back with an agonising wrench. Maybe, she reflected, there was, after all, something to be said for progress.

The driver swivelled his head to beam at her, gesturing towards the palm plantations. 'Coconut trees, madame, a blessing from the gods –'

'Watch the road!' she shrieked, as a bus came straight for them. He swung the wheel and taxi and bus missed by inches, both leaning heavily on their horns. He threw her a triumphant smile.

'Nothing will be wasted. The leaves the villagers are using

for roof, the trunk for the fishing boats, the covering of the nut will become rope, and the inside, delicious for eating and oil for the hair. And the milk to drink! Would you like some coco-water, fresh from shell –'

'Watch the *road*!' she implored.

Then, almost beneath the wheels of an overloaded bus, the taxi suddenly swung left across the traffic and turned down a sandy, red earth track through parched looking, deserted fields. The driver glanced back at her. 'Auroville,' he said.

The beaten earth track was bumpy and rutted, edged with scrubland, the raw red earth occasionally relieved by a grove of coconut palms. The taxi jounced on, swerving to avoid the bigger pot-holes, plunging into the shallower ones. Around them, tall trees reached towards the sky.

As they wound their way through the dirt roads, here and there she saw unfinished buildings with rusting metal rods sprouting from roofless walls. On some, creeper had begun to spread and flower, like Sleeping Beauty houses, frozen in mid-construction, waiting to be released from a spell. Where are the streets? Charlotte wondered. Where are the people? Where is the city?

Uncertainly, she asked aloud, 'But where is Auroville?' and he threw her a grin, accustomed to this reaction. 'All around, madam. Is here.' And drove on. Sheltered among clumps of trees or behind rioting hedges of bougainvillaea were communities. She caught sight of simple wooden signposts as they drove past turnings: *Protection* . . . *Fraternity* . . . *Utility* . . . *Vérité* . . . *Certitude* . . .

Another signpost cautioned: Drive Slow – *Revelation*. An arrow pointed to *Aspiration*. ('And there is also *Perspiration*,' the driver said. He laughed, this was obviously a joke regularly enjoyed by visitors.) Down a turning lay *Bliss* and beyond that, *Harmony*. Some had wire fencing, a gate. Others lay at the end of curving lanes. These were the settlements, the names resonant with hope and faith.

It was oppressively deserted. Clutching her painful neck Charlotte glanced left and right, trying to see some sign of activity. The driver hesitated at a fork in the track, then turned right and almost at once jammed on his brakes and waved at a small, faded signpost pointing the way to a settlement: *Arcadie*. She had reached Arcadia.

Chapter 26

The taxi drove off in a cloud of dust which slowly settled over the track, the bushes and the settlement. The landscape was monotonously red and green: red rocks, red earth, red dust; the green dull beneath the prevailing layer of rust. It was a world seemingly without moisture: the paths cracked and hard, the untilled land gaping in fissures, the soil dried out, friable. Even the undergrowth looked dry: metallic stalks, leaves thick and hard as leather. No sign of human life. She realised that what she had taken for silence was ringing with a sound that came at her from all around: the rustling of the crickets.

She had always known about Auroville, dreamed about it. Dissatisfied with Judith's bald description, she had invented a fairy-tale version of it in her mind. There it had flourished, a shining place where you cast off conflict and greed at the city gates like B-movie cowboys checking their guns at the saloon entrance. Like all the best fairy-tales it had contained an ogre, but she had been prepared for that too. What took her by surprise was the place itself. Now that she was within the city she felt lost, dismayed by the emptiness. Guru had tried to warn her about this: 'Auroville can be difficult for strangers. It requires an imaginative leap. Remember that it was founded on hope. It was a new approach, another go at Utopia. For some, the hope survives, but Utopias have a bad track record, you know . . .'

Auroville was impossible to pin down: it existed as an idea, potently; it also existed as a place, but less convincingly. There was no tarmac, no traffic, there were no shops. Apparently there were no people. Just the harsh red earth, its emptiness broken only by trees and sharp-edged bushes.

Slowly she walked past the open gate, up a winding drive towards a cluster of low buildings, one of them the *Arcadie* Guest House with its communal dining hall. She felt edgy: this was an alien environment, ungiving, harsh. Already she missed the bustle and charm of Pondi, the paved streets, the white houses, the breeze off the sea, the flowers and fountains, the charms of a faded hotel on the corner of the rue Laval.

She heard Judith's voice in her head: 'It won't be what you imagine. Be prepared for disappointment.' She had brushed off the advice, cool: the trouble with mothers was that they were forever trying to fit you up with armour they had fashioned out of their pain, to shield you with their experience. They could never see that things had changed since their day, and however lovingly they shaped and hammered and polished, the protection never fitted the occasion. So she had heard without listening, 'be prepared for disappointment', and now she was in Arcadia, at a loss, filled with apprehension and suddenly wishing herself elsewhere.

The settlement was grouped around a clearing in the trees, small houses, uncompromising cubes set at odds to one another, looking rather like dice thrown down in the dust. There had been attempts at gardens of a sort and shrubs grew stubbornly in the dry soil; one compound was ringed with banana trees, another was shaded by a tall acacia. But it was a settlement surrounded by parched land that stretched to the horizon. Without wheels, as Mr Chetty had warned her, she could go nowhere.

Nothing was as she had expected: she had thought to

wander around, unobserved, collect evidence, do some discreet spying and then announce her presence. But where, here, could she wander? So she waited.

Slowly, people were trickling back for lunch, on cycles, mopeds, powerful motorbikes. They smiled vaguely at Charlotte as they went by and one muscular woman in dungarees murmured, 'Eating *chez nous*, are you?' and passed on without waiting for an answer. After a while, when most tables were occupied, a man with yellow hair tied in a pony-tail beckoned her over and suggested she should seat herself. Without formality, people introduced themselves. First names sufficed. It was a polyglot gathering, their common tongue a fluid mixture of English and French, the locution oddly skewed, so that no one sounded quite right, even speaking their own language. When the food arrived they helped themselves without finesse, leaning across, shovelling on large helpings. 'Take some lunch,' a neighbour urged. 'But watch out, it's beaucoup spicy.'

She had her mouth full of brinjal curry when someone asked her why she was there: was she planning to stay a long time? Was she there to work? Teach? Or was it a holiday? She took a moment, chewing, swallowing. She had come, she replied, to see Auroville. And to meet – she swallowed again – she was hoping to meet an Aurovillian architect, a Frenchman called Raymond –

'Raymond? Well there he is, with some visitors. You can meet him right now.'

He was at a table across the room, talking to two Italian women while he ate, picking abstractedly at his food. He wore a dhoti and kurta, and with his dark colouring and thick, curly hair greying attractively, he could have passed for a north Indian. Their faces alight with interest, the two women were clearly under his spell. Charlotte registered the good looks: the glowing brown eyes, the thin, bearded, deeply lined face, a smile that suggested intimacy. Her food forgotten, she watched him, caught an occasional phrase through the hubbub. The women projected understanding and sympathy. They leaned towards him listening, nodding. Charlotte sensed that women might often find themselves in this position, the consoling, comforting role, the logical conclusion to their generous impulse and his charm.

Then, to her embarrassment, her neighbour called across, made known Charlotte's presence: 'Someone to see you, Raymond,' and he was waving her over, pulling out a chair for her to join them.

He said something but the roaring in her ears drowned out the sound. Smiling, nodding encouragingly, he waited for her to speak. She thought at first her voice had died on her, that she was mouthing silently, then she heard herself say, 'I'm Charlotte.'

What did she expect? A Victorian melodrama reaction: the villain rearing back, eyes staring, arms flung up to fend off the avenging angel? Another disappointment. He got to his feet, smiling. 'Charlotte! My dear. Welcome to Auroville,' and kissed her on both cheeks.

'So –'

One of the Italian women broke in, 'And what brings you here, Charlotte?'

She hesitated, and he said, smiling, 'A quest, *n'est-ce pas*?' And added, 'Isn't that what brings everyone to Auroville?'

'I –'

'– Raymond has built many beautiful things here,' one of the Italians said, with an expansive wave of her arms.

'Will you show me some?'

A rueful grimace. 'My best work is in France, you know. Here we are always short of money –'

'But the house!' exclaimed one of the women. 'Your *bella casa*! The so-original courtyard!'

'– it remains unfinished,' he protested.

The woman patted Charlotte's arm: 'But you must see the

house! And we will come with you. He will, perhaps, build us also a house.' He shrugged and gave in and smiled at Charlotte. 'We will talk, later, yes?'

Auroville discouraged motorised vehicles, but the house was difficult to get to, a jeep a necessary evil. It was parked beyond the gate, in the shade of an acacia tree, alarmingly battered; scratched and dented on every exterior surface. Raymond bowed gracefully and waved them aboard.

They bounced off down the track, past signposts to the various settlements: *Transition ... Transformation ... Fertile Windmill... Aurogreen...* At one they stopped, to see a house Raymond had designed years before: a ziggurat in concrete and glass; at another there was a message to be passed on. The landscape was changing, becoming more open, there were fewer trees; palms reared tall into the sky with small, inadequate sprouts of leaves at the top, like a frayed and worn-out paint brush.

The track became sandier, more uneven, the jeep zigzagging across the deeply worn tracks. They passed huts and palm-roofed structures and workers in the fields, and at last they came out on to a ridge where Raymond's half-constructed house stood.

They climbed down and stood looking at '*la bella casa*', now being photographed from every angle by the Italians. 'It is made from local, unfired brick,' one of them called to Charlotte, 'constructed by Raymond and his workmen, using this red earth that lies around us ...' Charlotte began to think of them as the Vestals, serving at the sacred altar.

Wide arches led from room to room, the ceilings vaulted. At the heart of the structure lay an open central courtyard, and from the bay a constant cool breeze blew through the house. He took her up to the flat roof and she looked across the tops of the low cashew trees that surrounded them to where the sea was just visible, a sliver of bright blue above the red horizon.

'I chose this spot for the sea-breeze to cool the house – and for the cashew trees. You can smell the blossom for miles around,' he murmured. 'For me, when I have been away and come back, that is the smell of Auroville.'

He went ahead of them down the brick steps. One of the Vestals murmured sympathetically that he had begun the house long ago, 'for someone who went away and did not return. This is why it remains unfinished.'

And Charlotte saw, looking more closely, that what she had taken for work in progress was actually an abandoned structure: the half-built house had stood so long unfinished that its exposed reinforcement rods had rusted into furry red fingers, its bricks had acquired a patina from the monsoon rains and the sun.

'Someone who went away and did not return.' Was this to have been their family home? Would she have played here, had Judith stayed on, slept in a room cooled by the sea-breeze and perfumed with the scent of cashews?

When they came down the steps, a Tamil woman had spread mats for them and was laying out stainless steel beakers. She moved gracefully, squatting her way across the tiles as she arranged the beakers. Thin, frail-boned, ageless, she held the edge of her sari betweeen her teeth so that her face was partially hidden. She did not look up and her movements had an anonymity that rendered her invisible. No one thought to thank her. 'Coffee,' Raymond said, and subsided with cat-like fluidity on to a mat. Stiff-kneed, Charlotte followed. With the Italians she completed a little circle round the master. The Tamil woman poured pale milky coffee into the beakers and silently retreated, vanishing into the undergrowth. Somewhere in the distance Charlotte heard the sound of a powerful motorbike approaching. Raymond was posing for a photograph with one of the Vestals when a young Tamil girl strode round the side of the house. She wore bleached-out shorts and shirt and sturdy canvas boots; her glossy black hair was cut short. She had the classic, Tamil rounded features and large eyes, but there was no smile to spare for the group, although Raymond greeted her with a wave. She said with a trace of irritation, 'I thought I'd find you here.'

'Some coffee –'

'No thanks. Are you aware of the time?'

'Well –'

'You were supposed to be doing something this afternoon. People were expecting you.' Her voice was flat, weary.

'I sent a message. I said I would be late.'

'As usual.'

He grimaced. 'When we begin to run our lives on bureaucratic punctuality and make no allowances for the unexpected, Auroville will be finished. Here is someone who has come all the way from London to see me. She deserves special attention.'

The Vestals had tactfully moved away. For a moment the three were alone: Charlotte, the girl and Raymond. He leaned towards Charlotte, the brown eyes bright but hooded. In a conversational tone he asked, 'How is your mother these days, Charlotte? How is Yoodeet?'

Yoodeet? Charlotte repeated to herself. Of course. It was his French way of saying Judith. Smiling, eyes screwed up against the sun, he looked up at the girl in shorts standing next to them and lightly clasped her dark, slender ankle. 'Dolly,' he said, 'meet Charlotte. Meet your sister.'

Judith, in the Great North London Health Food Bazaar, hand poised between the silken tofu and the alfalfa sprouts, finds herself dreaming about the past. Understandable, in view of Charlotte's journey there.

Guru, in his bare, cell-like room in the Hotel de France, is reading. The old habits are never entirely shaken off: the great Sanskrit volumes sit on his shelves but there are still times when he reaches for the newer fellows, for Auden or MacNeice; when their thoughts chime with his. Today is one of those times. *You cannot cage the minute/within its nets of gold . . .* He finds his thoughts looping back to a time filled with pain, a time grown mercifully dim in memory. Dreaming is an old man's consolation, but it can reawaken unwelcome turbulence. He feels a twinge of anxiety.

From Oriane's bedroom at the far end of the passage comes a familiar squawk: 'Guru! The kitchen is silent! Those devils are asleep! If dinner is late they are out on their ear. No one cares about standards any more. *Plus de discipline . . .'*

Above her head the fan turns slowly. A large insect, buzzing loudly, tries to fly in through the window, thwarted by the fine netting. Clumsily it bangs against the screen. She lifts the mosquito net and throws a shoe at the window as a discouragement.

Judith reaches for a pack of aduki beans, some misu sauce and a bag of raw cashew nuts. The man at the check-out is busy, serving a young girl. He takes his time, laughing with her over her purchases. There is eye contact, awareness. Judith knows that when her turn comes she will be dealt with briskly. She recalls with wry amusement that all her good points had originally been remarked on in French and had deteriorated into English: where once she had been *petite* she was now dumpy; what had been a *retroussé* nose had become merely snub, and the *mignonne* slenderness that Raymond had wrapped in his shawl, in his arms, had thickened, waist merging undramatically with widening hips. (This is all lies. Self-pity. She can still, with some difficulty, get into her original Levi's, the torn and patched pair she had never thrown away. Labourers on building sites still whistled, and she – with shameful political incorrectness – was pleased, worse: she was grateful.)

Waiting at the check-out while the young couple laugh

and banter, she samples her purchases, nibbling, tasting. She unloads her basket and he keys in the purchases on the till.

'The cashew nuts are stale,' she says.

'They came in fresh on Thursday.' The tone is definite.

'I don't care when they came in, they're stale.'

'I assure you –'

'I know about cashew nuts,' she says. (They should be milky white and break with a little snap, releasing a subtle fragrance into your mouth, sweet yet with a spicy under-tone –)

'They're stale,' she says.

She sees him catch the eye of a colleague and give an almost imperceptible shrug. There's always one, a nutter causing trouble.

'D'you want a refund?'

Oh yes, please. A refund of my life. A credit note against mistakes made. Another chance at the game, a fresh start –

'Thank you.' She returns the nuts and accepts her change. As she walks away he shouts angrily, 'I'm not accepting any liability. It's a goodwill gesture.'

Beneath her mosquito net, Oriane shifts restlessly, picking at the scab of memory. The past hurts. Another insect is buzzing, trying to reach the sunlight beyond the mesh of the window. One of the disadvantages – one of the many disadvantages of age, she reflects, is that sweet, easy sleep is no longer to be casually enjoyed, taken for granted. Brooding on this unfairness she falls into a dreamless siesta.

Chapter 27

The jeep went bumping past peanut fields, through the coconut palms and the cashew plantations, the wheels grinding in the sandy lane, lurching dangerously and occasionally stalling. Young boys, farmers' children, grinning and calling to Raymond by name, pulled up bunches of peanuts and thrust them into the stationary jeep. He would give them his potently charming smile and wave as the jeep coughed into life again.

When the taxi came, Charlotte said goodbye, *au revoir*, yes she would come again next day. 'Why not stay?' Dolly suggested. 'All this coming and going in taxis, so expensive. You could rent a moped.' But unexpectedly, Charlotte's room, her link with Pondi, suddenly felt like a lifeline. It was too soon to let go.

'Dolly, meet your sister,' he had said casually, only the smallest of gleams in his eyes revealing that he was aware of the enormity of what he was doing. Stupefied, unprepared, Charlotte had stared up at the young girl, at the smooth dark skin, the eyes that perhaps had something of Raymond, the cheeks round as a peach. The mouth which surely could curve in a wide, white smile was severe, her expression one of unsurprised appraisal. Dolly had the advantage. She, at least, had been aware she had a sister.

This was to have been a day of confrontation; the culmination of years of waiting, a settlement of accounts.

213

You have taken away my peace of mind, she had cried silently, anticipating the event. You have created a void where comfort should be. What is your excuse? How do you plead?

Instead there had been the banality of polite conversation, of – unbelievably – a social encounter.

Dolly, meet your sister. Was accuracy important? Half-sister. Charlotte's mother had not warned her about Dolly. Did Judith even know about her?

In *Arcadie*, waiting for the taxi, Charlotte said brusquely to her father, 'If your best work is in Europe, that means you must have left here sometimes. Travelled.'

'But of course.'

So he had made visits to France – maybe even to England – without feeling the need to see his child. She searched for words, her throat constricted, and he touched her arm lightly and said, 'Charlotte, we are strangers. I did not know how to break into your life without causing you pain. It would not have been a kindness.'

Dolly, yards away, not even looking at them, tilted her head like a cat and picked up the words. Without turning, still studying the horizon, she said sharply, 'Raymond is always kind. He can't bear to see anyone unhappy, you know. He wants to make us all feel good. It's his greatest quality.'

'Ah Dolly,' he said, 'you are so hard on me.'

What did it mean, this fencing between father and daughter? Dolly had said only that he liked to make people happy. Her own charge was quite different: you made me cry, Daddy, wondering where you were and why. What's your excuse, Daddy? Why did you never write, call, arrive on the doorstep with your sun-sallow skin and an armful of brightly wrapped presents? Why did you make me feel unwanted?

But of course when he asked, 'Will you be so hard on me

214

also, Lottie?' she smiled, tightly, and shifted in a movement between a shrug and a shrink and said nothing.

'Do you have a picture of your mother?' Dolly asked. 'I'd like to see what she looks like.'

'No.' Charlotte felt defensive. 'Do you?' she asked, 'have a picture of yours?'

Dolly raised her eyebrows, amused. 'Hardly. I see her every day. You've met her. She served the coffee.' The silent Tamil woman, squatting on the beaten earth floor, moving among them unregarded, threading through the group like a cat, unacknowledged.

Shocked, Charlotte could find no words. Dolly saw, and smiled unkindly. 'Don't worry. Not your problem.'

Raymond's house in *Arcadie* stood slightly away from the main settlement, set among trees. It grew out of the ground like a sturdy mushroom, its solid white concrete walls curving beneath its domed cap of a roof. Like Corbusier's church at Ronchamp, it ignored conventional geometry and straight lines. It was in reality two houses, the upper story open-plan, full of light and airy space, where he lived, and beneath it the squat column of the 'stalk'; close to the earth with the windowless look of a village hut. Here he lived with, yet not with, Dolly's mother.

'Does she speak English or French?' Charlotte asked.

'Neither. God, she hardly speaks Tamil. It all went wrong, you see. Raymond meant well. He wanted to help her. The trouble is ... maybe we should be more careful about offering kindness to strangers. Let well alone.'

The gleaming dark eyes appraised Charlotte coolly. 'I drew a picture of you once. It had one of everything – one leg, one arm, one eye. I called it Half Sister. There was no mouth because you couldn't talk to me. It's very strange, finally seeing you in the flesh. After all the years I spent hoping to meet this Half Sister. I wrote you long letters –'

'But I never got any letters!' Charlotte exclaimed, anguished.

'Oh, but I never sent them.'

They had remained, written but unposted, messages in a bottle that had never been launched.

As the taxi pulled away in a cloud of red dust, Raymond waved, turned to greet a friend and with an arm round his shoulders, drifted back towards the central *Arcadie* building, already deep in conversation. Dolly, dark and gleaming, poised like an ancient statue dressed incongruously in washed-out shorts and shirt and practical boots, raised an arm in a salute of farewell.

The taxi drove past the dried-out fields, colour fading from the sky as the sun dropped behind the trees. The road was choked with local traffic: ox-carts nodding their way home, cyclists laden with shopping, three-wheelers chugging, heavily charged with over-weight matrons. It was the cow-dust hour, the swirling air still pink from the dying sun. Lurching and bouncing they wove through oncoming mopeds, buses and cycle-rickshaws, Charlotte holding her neck, attempting to rise and fall in the rhythm of the pot-holes like a rider on a trotting horse.

They left the sea, the coconut palms and the villages shadowed by the banyans, and came in by the north boulevard to the cosy familiarity of the town. The dust of Auroville grated between her teeth. It had lodged in her eyelashes and scraped her eyes when she blinked; she felt itchy and on edge all over, her thoughts a turmoil. Above all she felt frustrated: Raymond was like wind or water, he offered no purchase to the explorer, he slipped out of reach, a charmer in a dhoti who seemed to run his life like an informal seminar. 'When can we talk?' she had muttered when they said goodbye. He opened his arms welcomingly.

'I am always here.'

'Tomorrow then?'

'Tomorrow, *bien sûr.*'

Oriane was centre stage, on the verandah, magnificent in a floor-length red silk gown threaded with gold when Charlotte came up the steps.

'A red dress!' Charlotte said. 'Like Proust's Oriane.'

'Ah, no longer. But we have much in common, she and I; when I was younger I too wore stars in my hair and shoes that matched my gown –'

'But I hope that for you, a friend's call for help would have taken priority over the matter of changing your shoes –'

Oriane frowned ominously. 'As to that, *à mon avis,* Proust was somewhat hard on the poor woman. *Figurez-vous,* you are ready, about to step into your coach when someone –'

'Swann was a friend, an old friend –'

'– he arrives and wishes to detain you with a problem, a conversation that will clearly cause you to be late for dinner.'

'He was dying.'

'But not that very evening! In any case, he could have been wrong, he could have been exaggerating. Anyway, it was her husband who told her to change her shoes and then there was no time to talk.' She added, 'There was no need for her to feel guilty.'

She glanced with distaste at Charlotte, at the dust covering her skin like the bloom on a fruit, clogging her hair. 'Evidently you have been to Auroville.'

'Yes,' said Charlotte, testing the words, trying out the phrase, 'I went to see my father.'

'*Ah, oui,*' Oriane said with composure, 'Raymond. I thought I detected a resemblance.'

For a moment Charlotte felt her jaw had actually dropped: did everyone know everything, while only she stumbled in the dark?

Charlotte would have questioned her – 'So you knew my

mother –' she began, but Oriane turned away and headed off towards the kitchen, stick clicking sharply on the tiles. Some words floated back along the corridor. 'We were acquainted. But it was long ago, all that.'

Charlotte stood under the shower, eyes closed. Bloody liquid ran from her head and traced a scarlet map down her body, swirled across the concrete floor and gurgled darkly down the drain. She washed away the red dust, but fear was creeping into her like an infection; she had been shocked by the harshness of the landscape, the spiky red plants like bits of rusting metal, the unfinished house that stood like a reproach on its plateau overlooking the sea. She felt herself defenceless against a bland charmer who refused to play his part in the tragedy she had constructed. And then Dolly . . . The water ran red, then paler, as though she were bleeding into transparency.

It was late. Dinner had been cleared away and the other tables were empty, but Charlotte still had half of her beer to finish. Oriane put a record on: something special was required tonight, she said and chose Ravel: 'It is like a formal French garden, his music, the cool perfection . . . but then, underneath, it is not at all *formel*; there is something . . . unsettling.' She listened for a moment or two, her hand moving in time with the music.

'Madame de l'Esprit,' Charlotte said tentatively, but Oriane raised an imperious hand, head tilted towards the record player. When the music came to an end she turned away towards the curtained archway to her private quarters.

Charlotte hesitated, then followed her. How did one announce oneself at an archway? No door to knock on. Rattle the curtain? She coughed and called tentatively, 'Madame de l'Esprit . . .'

'*Entrez.*'

Charlotte drew aside the curtain and stepped into the dimly-lit drawing room. Oriane leaned on her stick, peering closely at a large map on one of the walls. She turned her head and glanced over her shoulder without any change of expression. Then she beckoned Charlotte in.

'I thought you might be able to tell me –'

Oriane pointed her stick at the map.

'There,' she announced. 'See.' The map was very old; it picked out the five French territories in India. 'Once, French schoolchildren used to chant the names: Yanam, Mahé, Karikal, Chandernagore, Pondicherry.' The original trading posts which the Company had transformed first with factories, then forts and churches, and fine houses for their administrators – 'they knew how to live, those men!' Oriane exclaimed. 'Twenty-one-gun salutes! Elephants in silver armour! Velvet palanquins. Drums and trumpets! When Dupleix's wife dressed for a banquet, her jewels were the equal of anything at Versailles.' She paused and muttered, *'un peu vulgaire, après tout...'* She fastened a claw on Charlotte's arm and drew her to a long side table covered with leather-bound books. 'The documents are worthy of consideration. See how it was, *un petit village* ... Look here.'

Charlotte knew when she was beaten.

A huddle of fishermen's huts on the Coromandel coast, near the border of the hostile kingdom of Golconda, well placed to offer assistance to the beleaguered garrison at St Thome in 1673 – 'but we were there long before that!' Oriane exclaimed, 'long before Louis XIV. Study this chart. Look: 1600. *Le petit village,* it lay on the estuary, just a native encampment. But it was the beginning. The ruler of Bijapur gave it to us – you might ask, why should he do that?'

She put her hand to a small portrait, like a pilgrim touching an icon. 'My ancestor. He went to Sher Khan, to ask for food, for supplies for the the men, and he did it so well – you will not find this in the history books, in the books it is Bellanger de Lespinay who has the glory, but in fact, it was one of his young officers, de l'Esprit –' she scrabbled among the old books, turning pages, poring myopically over the faded brown ink, nose almost touching the paper. 'He wrote in his letters, I have the volume here somewhere, that they called it New Town – Puducheri in Tamil.'

She waved at another engraving.

'*Le jeune aventurier* de l'Esprit – a fine swordsman, but he lacked stature, which impeded his career. He sailed from Rouen in 1527 bound for the Malabar coast. Ah, they were brave, the young men, *ils étaient courageux!* They went to Sumatra, the Nicobars, but this was the place they came back to. They were splendid, those men of ours! I know what Richelieu said about the hasty temper of the French, that they wish the accomplishment of their desires in the moment of their conception, and therefore long voyages are not proper for them, well *nous voilà*! A clever man, Richelieu, but he got things wrong sometimes.'

For a precarious moment she took her weight off her stick and waved it about, at the sepia portraits dominating the walls. 'Despite the long voyages, they did not do too badly, eh? François Martin, Dumas, the great Dupleix! And always, we were there, *capitaine* de l'Esprit who sailed with Decaen, *lieutenant* de l'Esprit who stormed the fort at Madras with Bussy . . . We could have had it all! India could have been our jewel. But the king was too busy admiring the nipples of his latest whore, the court lining its own pockets. Dupleix was betrayed, *le pauvre*. But we had our little empire. You should have seen this place! We had art and music; poets and philosophers came from France. I can remember when my parents –'

She paused. 'At least they did not have the pain of being here for Merger – Pondi still flew the tricolor when they last walked on the Esplanade.' She shrugged. 'Well, those were the old days, things were done differently.' A twitch of the shoulders. '*C'est fini,* all that.' With a twinge of pity Charlotte gave thanks that Madame was unaware that things were 'done differently' now even at the Grand Hotel de France; that she had lost the battle. The *cuisine française* was not quite that, the garlic too strong for European tastes, the occasional attempt at a local dish hampered by the prejudices of the *patronne*, the cultures failing to meld.

The pale, wrinkled face was stony, filled with bitter regret for a time that could never return.

'This house is ancient. It has been the scene of great events, though not always public ones. I could tell you stories . . .' She peered at a small, framed picture above the bureau. Charlotte saw that it was a watercolour of the hotel – or rather, the house, for no wrought-iron name stood over the gates. This was the house in an earlier manifestation, a family residence, the walls stuccoed a faded saffron, a tree shading the path where no tree now stood. The artist had captured the graceful appeal of the building, the deep, shadowy verandah, the terrace from which, at that time, swags of some bright creeper hung down. The gleaming fountain. The path appeared to be of fine white gravel.

Oriane stared at it, her eyes narrowed to slits. 'My great-grandfather painted that picture, or so the story goes . . . In his journal he writes of it, and of other matters . . . Bonaparte could have been Emperor of India. They betrayed him, *les cons.* Those pygmies running the Revolution – *les petits cornichons.*'

She tapped her way round the walls, peering at the bewigged and frozen faces. So many young men, so many dreams.

She herself of course, had always dreamed of seeing France but, somehow it never happened. There were . . . complications. So here she remained. 'Surrounded by barbarity. One keeps the tricolor flying. And then, one hears France, too, has changed . . . Is it true that in the Champs Elysées one can find people eating pizza – in the street? And that *pommes frites* are described as French fries?'

'I think that is possible.'

She sighed. '*Après tout . . .*'

Without turning her head and with no change of tone she said, 'Guru thinks I should rest now.' Charlotte had heard no sound of footsteps, but looking round she saw that he was waiting silently by the curtained entrance.

Oriane frowned. 'I am not tired. What do old men know about it? Go away Guru.'

She stared at a framed Royal charter, her eyes watering with the effort of focusing on the faded print. 'The family name was threaded through the history of this place, fighting battles, signing treaties, intriguing. It was in our blood . . .' She put up a hand to straighten a portrait of General de Gaulle, framed in carved wood.

Charlotte said, 'You knew my parents –'

But Oriane seemed to have lost interest in the past. She wandered out through the door, past the silent, waiting man, down the corridor towards her bedroom.

Guru smiled a little wearily at Charlotte. 'She has seen things change, you see; watched people come and go, history in the making. What she recalls is the way things were, *la douceur de vivre*. But unlike Talleyrand, what she looks back at is life not before the Revolution but before 1954. Before Merger. How else could she survive here, outliving her dreams?'

And Charlotte, knowing only what she had been told, saw how it might have been. In her version of an alternative life Oriane should have married splendidly and taken her place in a society that she knew only from books – a Paris where etiquette really mattered, where precedence at the dinner table was still a matter for analytical discussion. But that Paris no longer existed. And what would she have made of McDonalds and suburban *hypermarchés*, EuroDisney and a

TV channel devoted to soft and hard porn? *Après tout*, Pondi was what she knew best – was all she knew. Pondi and its past.

Chapter 28

The street-life slid past: bazaar stalls, a potter at work, the weavers at the roadside, a man painting his oxen's ears in brilliant rings of colour – for some religious festival, Charlotte supposed. The taxi driver called out, 'Cows will be advert for local political party – horns are now party colours.' They hit a pot-hole and bounced on.

'Come to *Arcadie*,' he said, 'I am always there.' She had rehearsed questions, prepared answers, a lifetime of curiosity to be satisfied. But when the taxi got to *Arcadie*, Raymond was not there. Dolly, tinkering with her motorbike, was left to explain: someone had needed his help. He had gone to Madras for building materials.

Charlotte stood, lost, upset, anger building up. She remembered now that Judith had warned her. Without dramatising, she had spoken of 'disappointment'. But this was worse than disappointment.

Dolly said, 'I have to see my mother for a minute. You want to come? After all, you have a connection.'

As Dolly told it – the story of the Samaritan – the Tamil woman and the doomed child were part of Raymond's all-embracing, indiscriminate kindness. She pronounced the word with heavy irony. 'His kindness. He didn't think it through. And then of course, the relationship that followed was destructive all round. Félicité – Raymond's little joke, he named her after a woman in some story who was house-keeper to a great writer for years and never understood a word of what he wrote – Félicité was cut off from her roots. Exiled. Half an hour from her village and she might as well have been a thousand miles away. The damn child died anyway, so the gesture had all been for nothing.'

When Charlotte was led into the room by Dolly she thought at first that it was empty. Then she made out the shape of Dolly's mother, her washed-out sari blending with the pale interior walls.

Dolly sank gracefully to a squat and Charlotte did her best to follow. She wobbled, precariously balanced. Around the walls Félicité had pinned up brightly coloured pictures cut from magazines, old calendars and a plastic flower in a transparent wrapper. A bed-roll was neatly tucked into one corner, and pots, terracotta and steel, were stacked next to the small brick stove. They sat in silence for a moment or two.

'She used to cook for him,' Dolly murmured, 'but there was no way they could sit and eat together, she was stuck with the old tradition, she waited till he was finished, and he couldn't stand that. So now he eats in one of the communal dining rooms. It's simpler.' She launched into rapid Tamil, the syllables flowing in a continuous stream. Félicité murmured something brief.

Dolly said, 'She wants to know if you're thirsty.'

Charlotte shook her head. 'What does she think about someone turning up like this from the outside world, me, I mean, after all these years?'

'She doesn't think about things like that. The concept doesn't arise. She is. We are. You arrive. Then you depart.'

'Is there no way I can get through to her?' Charlotte wanted to seize the woman's shoulders, shake her into some response. 'Tell her I'm glad we met.'

'I've done that,' Dolly said. 'Let's go, this room gives me the creeps.'

She ducked out of the low doorway. Charlotte rose to follow her – and her legs buckled. Cramp seized her muscles as she attempted to move. She gave a yelp of pain, and found Félicité squatting beside her, rubbing skilfully at the knotted, painful muscles. She massaged rapidly, smoothing away the stabbing pins and needles. Charlotte watched the thin fingers, the stick-like arms. She felt tears prick her eyelids and took Félicité's hands, feeling the roughness of the fingers. She lifted one dark hand and held it briefly against her cheek.

She rose cautiously, and they moved off, Charlotte hurrying, stumbling, blinded by unshed tears. What was it about this place that undid her? She who never wept at home. 'It's all right,' she heard Dolly call from behind her, amusement in her voice. 'You can cry if you want to. It's not against the rules.' But Charlotte blinked rapidly, swallowing, and saved her dignity.

As they bounced away down the path on Dolly's motor-bike, the vast honeycomb sphere of the Matrimandir came into view, hovering above the treetops, a mass of rusting iron and concrete, a crane and scaffolding now seemingly part of its structure as though welded into permanent attachment. In its very incompleteness, its rawness, it achieved a force that compelled attention.

'We keep running out of money,' Dolly shouted above the engine roar. 'One of my earliest memories was seeing this half-built thing and hearing Raymond say it would soon be completed. Maybe next year. But at least the meditation chamber's ready.'

The Matrimandir sat on its foundation pillars, towering over a shallow amphitheatre with a stone lotus urn standing like a sentinel at the outer rim. An occasional Aurovillian slowly climbed the ramp that circled the shell, dwarfed by its bulk. The sun hovered just above the horizon, a crimson beacon glimmering through the trees, and the earth glowed darkly, as though stoked by a furnace below the surface.

'Outsiders aren't supposed to be allowed in, at this time of day,' Dolly said, 'but we'll slide you in – you're not really an outsider, are you?' They climbed the ramp, circling the inner core of the latticed sphere, mounting higher.

The ramp ended at a heavy curtain. They removed their shoes, drew aside the curtain and went into the chamber.

Writing to Judith that night Charlotte was unable to describe what followed. She wanted to hold the experience inside herself, unexamined, and certainly undescribed, for a while. And she was aware of a sad irony, that it should be for her to be feeling all this; to be in a position to tell her mother about the Matrimandir experience: Judith who had been part of the dream, never knew the reality. She had left before the building existed.

And how could Charlotte put down on a postcard all there was to say?

Like a dreamer surrendering to the pull of a phantom world, she had stepped into the chamber, half-blinded for a moment, not by brilliance but its opposite: the hazy, almost smoky air shimmering with a pearly light. The twelve-sided room was vast, its floors and walls of white marble, with twelve slender white pillars standing like sentinels round the enormous crystal cradled in golden struts that glowed softly at the centre of the chamber. The ceiling was so far off that the tops of the columns soaring to meet it were lost in gloom, veiled in shadow. A profound calm enfolded her, dispelling further thought and she sank to the ground, her legs for once folding themselves obediently beneath her. Her eyes rested tranquilly on the crystal which held within it glimmers of shifting light – shafts of gold and milky gleams of opal. Reflected sunlight beamed from some high source enveloped the surface of the sphere. The crystal grew and shrank, filling her line of vision like a vast shining planet, then receding to a glittering point. Time passed.

When they came out it was dusk. Walking away, Charlotte looked back and saw the concrete bulk glowing like a honeycomb, softly lit from within, radiating an extraordinary sense of peace and protection.

Chapter 29

The taxi-driver had assumed the moped would get out of his way. There was a slamming of brakes and a faint but heartfelt wail of protest. Mr Chetty wobbled slowly into a prickly hedge. Charlotte leaped out of the taxi. It was quite dark now, but he recognised her in the glare from the headlamps and his frown of dismay vanished.

'Are you hurt at all? My apologies –'

He invited her to have a cool drink, she would be so welcome, and directed the taxi driver to the settlement.

He brought her water in a steel beaker –'I had hoped to provide some fresh fruit juice, but . . .' He gave a resigned shrug. He carried another beaker to the taxi driver, then returned. He smiled tenderly. 'So you have come to Auroville. And have you found what you were looking for?'

To her horror she found herself, as she began briskly to deal with the question, suddenly unable to continue. She stopped abruptly, gulped at the water, scrubbed her face with her hand, the paprika coloured dust mingling with tears to form an orange paste which she smeared across her cheeks, all the while crying as she had not cried for years.

He waited, refilling the beaker, making small sounds of distress, waving his hands as though conducting the outpouring before him. She was unable to explain that these were not tears of unhappiness, because she would then have had to explain what they were – and she was unsure of that herself.

She left, finally, explaining that she would be returning, would be staying for a while at the *Arcadie* Guest House. That was when he too mentioned hiring a moped, 'For independence. You should consult Motor Cycle Centre,' he suggested diffidently. 'It is quite centrally located in Pondi. Look in tomorrow if you have time.'

The Motor Cycle Centre was a shed at the back of a beaten-earth yard filled with machines in various stages of decrepitude. There were ferocious looking motorbikes with pipe organs growing from their core, the metal scorched and blackened. There were tiny Japanese mopeds, little more than toys. Charlotte paused by the smallest, the least impressive of all the mopeds. 'This one?' she suggested tentatively.

Jamal, who ran the hire part of the business, was picking his teeth with some thoroughness. He nodded.

'How does it work? Could I have a lesson?'

He stared at her pityingly. 'We don't have time for that sort of thing. You'll just pick it up, you know. As you go. Not difficult. Key. Turn on – so. Kick-start – so. This is speed. This is petrol. Handlebars. Twist like so for acceleration. Squeeze for braking.'

As she was wheeling the moped away, Mr Chetty appeared at the gates and called out cheerfully, 'Ah! Good morning! You have taken my advice then. Excellent.'

'Well . . . I still have to learn how –'

From the yard Jamal called out loudly, 'He knows the way to Auroville, he could take it for you.'

Mr Chetty murmured, 'I would be happy –'

Jamal cut in brutally, 'Just give him a couple of rupees.' He had seen through the precarious social façade to the threadbare reality. Charlotte saw Mr Chetty's face go deep red with shame. He clutched his briefcase tightly and stood very straight, staring down at the moped, and continued his sentence: 'I would be happy to do this for you as a *favour*, of course.' She heard the emphasis. 'If it would save you trouble.'

Save her also the terror of careering trucks, the buses, the weaving cyclists, the ox-carts creaking dreamily up the centre of the road, the pot-holes and the dust.

'I'm most grateful,' Charlotte said. Jamal was still keeping an eye on them. She raised her voice: 'Would you be my guest at lunch?'

She saw with some satisfaction that Jamal looked surprised. Mr Chetty too.

'At the hotel?' he asked.

'Well, yes.'

His face became quite expressionless so that she was uncertain whether he was thrilled or possibly offended. Then he said, 'That is most kind of you.'

He repeated, frequently, how kind of her it was as they walked to the rue Laval. Asked if the Ashram physiotherapy was helping her neck. But once at the hotel, Mr Chetty was ill at ease. He sat down quickly at Charlotte's table before the servant could pull out a chair for him. He refused beer and gulped a large glass of water, but had no appetite. His normal flow of words had quite dried up and he sat unhappily staring down at the tablecloth, from time to time dabbing at his lips with his napkin. Charlotte felt she had done the wrong thing: she had wanted to make a gesture on his behalf, to snub Jamal. And she had wanted to offer him a treat, a good meal. Now she felt ashamed of what could be construed as a patronising attitude.

Charlotte decided her guest should be presented without delay, to avoid possible embarrassment. There was no sign of Guruvappa who could have proved a tactful intermediary, and *la patronne* had an unpredictable attitude to strangers.

'May I introduce –' she began as Oriane came towards them, but Mr Chetty got to his feet and broke in diffidently: 'Madame de l'Esprit and I are previously acquainted.'

Oriane halted, moved closer. She stared at him, catlike, head jutting, unblinking. One of the servants approached her with a query, but she waved him away, silently studying the small, nervous man.

'Arjuna?' she said.

He nodded, smiling.

Whether he or she stretched out a hand first, Charlotte was uncertain, but all at once they were shaking hands, formally, in the French way. Oriane's face wavered, the sharply etched lines and furrows dissolving as though smoothed out by an unseen hand. Her eyes were swimming. Then she flung back her head and gave a croak of laughter, and hugged the small man, kissing him on both cheeks as her stick fell, clattering, to the floor. She rubbed her mouth and her eyes with the palm of her hand while he retrieved the stick, handing it back.

'Well! Sit down, sit down.' She studied him, shaking her head disbelievingly.

'It has been many years,' he murmured.

'You look as thin as ever.'

He nodded apologetically. 'I fear it is a question of metabolism. I remain . . .' he smiled again, 'lacking substance.'

'You will eat properly today at least.'

She swivelled her eyes to Charlotte. 'We are becoming involved with Auroville I see. Well. You have chosen a good time. The end of February. Anniversary celebrations, all kinds of –'

She came to a sudden stop, turned and walked unsteadily away, her stick tapping sharply on the tiles. Beyond the bead curtain Oriane hesitated, lost for a moment. She called, panic-stricken, 'Guru!'

In the dining room Charlotte heard the familiar, peremptory squawk.

'So you know each other.'

'Oh yes,' he nodded. 'Early days. Everyone knew everyone.'

'You must have known my mother then, Judith. She and Raymond were . . . together.'

Arjuna Chetty scanned his memory and vaguely recalled a slender girl who sometimes cycled into Pondi to visit the library.

'Yes,' he said, 'of course. She was here for a while, but then she went back – to continue her studies I imagine.'

'Was she happy here?'

'Happy? She was happy, I think. We were all happy then.'

When the taxi dropped Charlotte at Auroville, *Arcadie* slumbered in a mid-afternoon torpor. The guest house kitchen was silent, the whole place deserted. She put down her bags and walked around for a few minutes, hoping to see some sign of life, then gave up and sat on the steps, in the shade thrown by the building. She drifted into an uneasy doze and woke with a start, to find Mr Chetty hovering, a few feet away, apparently examining the tree-tops, too polite to disturb her.

She scrambled to her feet –'Mr Chetty! I'm so sorry –'

'No, no! I arrived more quickly than anticipated!'

The moped stood nearby, dusty and battered and reassuringly small, leaning on its stand. He must have wheeled it the last few yards in order not to wake her.

'Now you are mobile!' he exclaimed. 'Able to come and go as you please.'

Only now did it occur to her that he must have abandoned his trusty pair of wheels in Pondi to bring the moped to Arcadia. She began to apologise but he waved away the words and hurried off down the path with his odd, hobbling gait.

She set out on a journey of exploration, wobbling, stalling, falling into a ditch. Bumping her way down a side track she saw the dome of the Matrimandir skimming the tree-tops and turned off, drawn back towards it. But everything was different in the afternoon. Taxis and a minibus had pulled up and tourists on a day-trip descended, squabbling among themselves the way hot, tired holiday-makers tend to, the silk-clad women holding their saris close as they picked their way over the rough, muddy ground in their dainty sandals, the men glancing at their Rolexes and frowning. There were arguments about who had precedence in the queue, whose tickets carried more weight. Less affluent visitors in plainer saris and cheaper sandals were elbowed aside. Since only limited numbers were admitted, there was a nervous aware-ness that not everyone might get in.

Cool young Aurovillians, in shorts and sandals, some with pony-tails, broke off their building work and began to check the visitors' passes. Bi-lingual bluster, moving rapidly between Hindi and English, proved valueless. Fair play was impassively maintained and at four o'clock the untidy queue began the winding climb up the ramp to the chamber entrance.

The afternoon heat was at its most intense and Charlotte was looking forward to the illusion of coolness that the moped would bring her – the breeze created by motion. But when she attempted the kick-start, the engine coughed and subsided into silence. The machine remained dead. Auroville lay around her in a trance of heat, no one to be seen.

She was attempting another kick-start when in the distance she saw a cloud of red dust, out of which emerged the jeep with Raymond at the wheel, the back filled with building materials – pipes and a jumble of metal bits and pieces. He embraced her cheerfully, looked over the moped, did something mysterious to its entrails and it started at once. Charlotte was mortified: how helpless and foolish she must seem to these self-reliant people.

He reached into the jeep for a bottle of water. 'You should drink more. Easy to become dehydrated.'

The water was warm, stale-tasting, but she gulped it eagerly, surprised to find how thirsty she was.

He squatted down beside her and she thought how right he looked in his kurta and dhoti, and tried to imagine him in Paris or London, buttoned into a shirt and modish suit, the bare brown feet imprisoned in leather.

He had checked the moped again and tightened a loose nut. Now he rested, tranquil, his fingers curled lightly about her ankle.

This was something Charlotte found difficult: this being silent with someone. In London a silence in company could only mean lack of communion. People met and talked. A pause was acceptable: a thoughtful pause if a serious discussion required it, a sensuous pause if passion were involved. But extended silence spelt social failure. Here, people could sit together simply without talking. It must be an oriental thing and she lacked the knack. There was, too, the physical thing: feeling his hand on her foot she was aware of her muscles stiffening, her posture becoming awkward: she could not accept this casual intimacy, and after a moment or two she found a reason for shifting, for moving her leg, brushing away an imagined mosquito.

There was a question she could have asked, but she was constrained by tact. He sensed her hesitation.

'What?'

She was embarrassed. 'It's just . . .' She shook her head and allowed the silence to grow. At last she said, 'I feel so . . . lost here, in this dry, dead place.'

He looked astonished. 'Dry? Dead? But *ma chère*, this is paradise. We live here in peace. The – what you call, market force does not drive us. We make things, create. People paint or write, make pottery, jewellery, design clothes. We work with the villagers, teach their children. There are Hindus here and Muslims, Christians, atheists, but we are not divided. This place was founded on an ideal. To look for the truth of things and live by it. And to keep a hold on the spiritual element in life. We are imperfect creatures, *ma chère*, but we try. Look at the newspapers: more explosions, killings, riots, Hindu against Muslim. Caste against caste. Aurobindo warned the country that this would happen if they could not live together in harmony, as Gandhi had warned before him. And elsewhere, are things any better? In your part of the world? Civil war, slaughter. In Auroville we are untouched by all that.'

'Can you remain untouched?'

He shrugged ruefully. 'I hope. At any rate we must live as though that possibility is certain. I am sure you have read Camus: we must behave as though life had meaning.'

He insisted that she drink some more of the warm water from the plastic bottle. 'We will talk, soon. But now I must deliver the materials. People are expecting me.'

At the *Arcadie* Guest House she lay under the overhead fan, took a cold shower with the aid of a bucket and tin mug, and joined the others for supper.

'How's the moped?' Dolly asked.

'I had a problem but Raymond put it right.'

'Oh excellent. So he was able to help you. He must have been pleased.'

The tone was weary.

'Dolly –'

'I have to see someone.'

She strode out to her motorbike and roared away, fast, a turmoil of pale dust surrounded by darkness. Then Raymond arrived, a chair was pulled out for him, and he was at once the centre of things as he laughed and greeted them them all. 'Ah, Lottie!' – radiating warmth.

People here were not to be counted on, it seemed. They moved disconcertingly in and out of the roles assigned to them.

'We were all acquainted,' Oriane had said. But it was long ago.

Chapter 30

For days they had been building the bonfire; children dragging fallen branches, bringing unwanted bits of timber for the young men to put in position, creating a huge cone like a wigwam in the centre of the shallow saucer of the amphitheatre. Nearby stood the lotus-bud urn of stone, and beyond the amphitheatre, on one side, towered the great banyan tree that had seen the drought years and now the greening of the plateau. On the other side stood the architectural contradiction of the Matrimandir – a concrete mass that floated light as a bubble on its supporting pillars, watching over them all like a totem.

It was the twenty-fourth anniversary of Auroville. The ritual pre-dawn bonfire blazed and in the darkness the voice of the Mother echoed eerily across the plateau –

'*Auroville belongs to nobody in particular. Auroville belongs to humanity as a whole . . .*'

Not a supernatural manifestation but a recording – the amphitheatre filled with Aurovillians and Ashramites, the cool air perfumed with woodsmoke and the scent of cashew blossom.

The darkness was criss-crossed with headlamps, hundreds of mopeds and motorbikes converging on the Matrimandir, the noise of their engines echoing like gunfire. Golden sparks flew upwards from the bonfire, erupting from a centre that burned like a crucible, sending its heat out across the amphitheatre. The shallow-stepped saucer was filled with seated figures, Raymond among them, sitting cross-legged, back straight, a pale blanket draped round his shoulders. He saw Charlotte and beckoned her over.

She wore a sweater, a scarf round her head. Raymond sensed that she was always prepared, she had foresight. Judith had never planned ahead, never thought about chill night winds, threats of any sort. He had wrapped the warm cloth round her frail body that dawn, while they were still friends, before they became lovers, before they became enemies. 'You are cold, Yoodeet . . . ' And she had grown colder, before she left, her tears rebuking him.

'. . . *a place of unending education, of constant progress . . .*'

Children danced round the flames like small demons, and over a loudspeaker, from across the fields boomed the sonorous, quavering voice of the Mother, repeating, as every year, the charter of the City of Dawn.

As her voiced faded, music took over: drifting, other-worldly sonorities, the sort of sound metallic leaves might make, moving in a breeze. The fire crackled, and gradually the sky in the east brightened. At six, the music died away and people got stiffly to their feet and drifted towards the Matrimandir. Old differences were forgotten and Ashram-ites and Aurovillians embraced and greeted one another as though meeting after a long journey.

Raymond, as always, was the centre of a group. He drew Charlotte in, an arm round her shoulders, smiling.

Venerable Ashramites drifted towards the Matrimandir, nodding genially to left and right. All around, people hugged and laughed without reason as is the way at reunions.

Every year they gathered, celebrated, reminisced. And this was an anniversary with a difference: for the first time the crystal was in place in the meditation chamber.

Picking up the threads of the story, interweaving and

239

recollecting like old story-tellers, they retraced the trail, recalling the disappointments and the quest.

... Glass slippers have been worn to royal palaces, carriages fashioned out of pumpkins, flax spun into gold, but the flawless crystal was for the everyday world, it must be durable ...

Could such a crystal be made? They recalled now the disheartening responses, the regrets, the factories who thought perhaps – and then changed their minds, the glassworks who did not reply at all. The time that passed. Then, from West Germany, from Schott, in Mainz, the answer: 'Why not? We can do the casting, Zeiss in Oberkochen will do the polish.'

The testing began. The special optical glass Schott were using had a science fiction sound to it – Borkrun 7. Men in white coats laboured like sorcerers' apprentices for months, studying the effect of light penetrating matter ... the influence of temperature on a vast globe – what would be the effect of uneven heating, of reflected sun hitting the top of the sphere? Would it crack? Shatter? The mirrors of the revolving heliostat on the top of Matrimandir must be woven into the spell, everything had to be taken into the calculation.

The original casting measured more than 80cms in diameter and weighed 1100 kilos. It took the white-coated wizards fifteen hours to cast it – pouring the molten glass into a mould of refractory brick imprisoned in metal bands and fixed to an iron and steel brassplate. They watched over the monstrous crystal, held the temperature constant, and baked it for five weeks in an oven to draw out every trace of strain.

Roughly rounded, polished and checked for striations, bubbles, streaks, warps, grooves, flecks and foreign bodies, it was still a lump of glass, until the final cutting process – the turning and grinding to the last fraction of a millimetre. Then the polishers lowered it into a wooden case and sent it on its way.

'When we opened the case, we could hardly believe our eyes: it sat there in its wrapping, beautiful, glowing, perfect.'

And they placed it at the centre of Matrimandir, resting on a cradle of gilded struts. The biggest crystal in the world.

The bonfire was dying down, its lurid flames paling in the first rays of the sun. The amphitheatre was emptying.

'It was so different,' Raymond said, 'that first year.'

Twenty-four years before, the bonfire had blazed – a huge cone, crackling and spitting like a self-contained volcano, smoke rising, pale against the dark sky, the fiery rain streaming upwards, the children's faces red with reflected flames. There had been dignitaries who shook hands with the architects and wished everyone well with great heartiness. The President of India was there, and young people from more than a hundred countries and the twenty-two states of India, each bringing a handful of soil to throw into the empty lotus-bud urn. There had been celebrations; an epidemic of speeches. Euphoria. Raymond and Oriane had danced together, the sort of wild, spontaneous waltz that goes with Bastille Day, or the dawn of a new Utopia, a dance that needs no music. They had whirled until Oriane, breathless, cried 'Enough, enough!' collapsing into laughter and exhaustion, her arms round his neck, her head on his shoulder. He had wondered whether Judith might be upset, but she had smiled and applauded. The more surprising that later, she broke into stormy tears and left, huddled under her backpack. Oriane, he recalled now, had been remarkably unconcerned about her departure, when he had hoped for sympathy, looked for guidance. 'You are an artist, Raymond,' she said briskly, 'artists should not be distracted by domestic arrangements.'

When Charlotte asked him now, about those early days, how it had been, he found it hard to separate the strands of the different stories that added up to a life. The disappointments, the clashes, the moments of achievement or loss of confidence, the unrelenting work, the laughter. And the people who had passed in and out of his orbit. But of course it was Judith that Charlotte wanted to hear about.

'Ah, Yoodeet,' he said, trying to pin down the images that had blurred with time. 'She worked so hard, you know.' He thought back and saw her, the fair English skin burning in the harsh sun, her fingers calloused. But she had not complained, and in the soft pre-dawn, when the sky lightened to a misty lavender that defined the window of their palm-thatched hut, he had kissed her small breasts and her roughened fingers and bruised feet and folded his arms round the slender body that lay so lightly on his.

'Did you love her?' Charlotte asked abruptly, breaking into his thoughts.

He looked at the peaked face, unevenly browned by the sun, the small frown-mark visible behind the round, steel-rimmed glasses. She had inherited Judith's uncertain look when asking difficult questions.

'But of course,' he said, telling her what she wanted to hear. And in any case it was the truth: why should he not have loved Judith? He loved them all.

'Now, Lottie,' he said, 'we go to breakfast,' and led the way on his motorbike, Félicité perched side-saddle behind him, her sari wrapped close, Dolly following.

Félicité made coffee for everyone, and there were rolls from the Auroville bakery. Charlotte leaned her back against the curving cement wall of Raymond's house and floated on a cloud of goodwill, half listening to the voices around her, and the more distant sounds of mopeds and greetings being called, and the repeated crowing of irate roosters, upstaged by early risers.

The day before, an outsider, a baffled visitor, had asked her, 'but where is the city?' Seeing her dusty moped and scratched sandals he had assumed she was a resident and Charlotte was suddenly reluctant to disabuse him of the error. The local council office, the grey London streets, the supermarket and wine-bar now seemed the foreign country; Auroville felt dangerously like home.

Mr Chetty's room, the door standing open, was easily identified: the rubbed, yellowish briefcase leaned against the wall. The room was bare, without ornament except for the usual picture of Aurobindo and the Mother. Two clean shirts and a towel occupied a narrow rail. Beneath the bed she glimpsed a tin box which presumably held what other clothes he possessed. Hanging from a flimsy picture-hook on the wall next to the bed was a photograph: a cheaply framed snapshot of a young girl, her smooth oval face dark against the bleached-out white of her sari, the head slightly tilted as though awaiting the answer to a question.

'Charlotte! Welcome, welcome!' Mr Chetty had appeared noiselessly behind her and stood, smiling and waving his hands nervously as though conducting an orchestra. He looked chagrined.

'Once again I am to be found wanting in the hospitality stakes – dear me, I invited you to breakfast and it seems breakfast is no longer to be had –'

'It's my fault, I'm late.'

'Well, water is the wine of the gods, shall we partake of nature's nectar?'

While he poured water into steel beakers Charlotte glanced again at the photograph above his bed. The snapshot was yellowing, faded.

'You can see she has changed somewhat,' he said. 'Who has not? But I feel . . . a good likeness, wouldn't you say?'

Charlotte frowned, peering closely, and he came to her rescue. 'You have met – we drank lime juice and ginger together. But Gita was only sixteen when the snapshot was taken.' To Charlotte's horror his eyes filled with tears.

'I'm sorry –' she felt responsible.

'Do not distress yourself. Anniversary days are always somewhat emotional.'

Arjuna Chetty had known Gita since they were children. Her small figure, clad in the blue and white school uniform, her shiny satchel and smoothly braided hair with a spray of jasmine tucked neatly to one side, were part of the daily scenery. At festival times they celebrated together, at *Diwali* they helped to light the tiny oil lamps that glimmered on every ledge, sharing jokes and secrets at the temple, watching the older boys fly kites on windy days. Being with her was as natural as breathing.

When he was sent off to London, to the uncles in Southall, they wrote regularly, and when he returned in disgrace, a failure at the cut-and-thrust of business life, their private conversations included plans for the future – plans which neither family considered relevant.

Arjuna's father had a low opinion of his son's talents, but at least the boy could help along the family exchequer by bringing in a substantial dowry. Gita's family had no money and her father – unusually – was disinclined to land himself in deep debt to marry off his daughter.

'A sad time,' Mr Chetty observed, smiling gently. 'I thought I would surely die. But people do not die of sorrow. Gita also was sorrowful, but she won a scholarship, she was what we called clever-clever. She became a doctor, gynaecologist. Much needed.'

He gazed out at the hard white sunlight.

'Unfortunately, the place she was needed was in the North. She gained considerable success. We lost touch. Such is life.' He shrugged and said briskly, 'Will you be attending the children's concert? It is almost time.'

The children sang lustily, Tamil, German, Italian, American . . . twenty nationalities fused into an Aurovillian stream of sound. Charlotte found she was sitting behind a contingent from the Ashram, Gita among them. The Ashramites, so clean, white-clad, their stillness setting them apart, had a dignity and poise sharply at odds with the cheerful untidiness of the Aurovillians. As they filed out after the concert, Charlotte said to Gita, 'I've been hearing about your glittering career.'

'Oh, please. This is Arjuna's nonsense. I was a good doctor you know. But promotion meant one spent more time on filling in forms and public speaking than examining patients. Not quite the aim.'

One day, she said, attending a medical conference in Madras, she was taken by friends to visit the Ashram. She met the Mother.

'I left Delhi, brought everything I possessed and handed it over to the Ashram. I began to read Aurobindo. I saw that what had gone before had been just a preparation . . .'

Charlotte said tentatively, 'Your scientific background . . . didn't that rather get in the way of the Supramental and all the rest of it?'

'Only if you approach it on a very literal, limited level.' The words sounded like a rebuke but the tone was kindly.

Children rushed past and Aurovillians called to one another in their Frenglish patois. Up ahead the Ashramites were waiting for the car to take them back to Pondi. One of them beckoned to Gita. She waved reassuringly, and turned back to Charlotte.

'I'm sure you've heard the story of Aurobindo meeting a French physicist one day, and they talked about the nature of the universe, matter and energy and so forth. They were discussing Einstein's search for a theory that would link the smallest, sub-atomic particle to the grand cosmic pattern, the equation that would show we are all made of the same substance. This was in the twenties and Einstein was a young man. He never did solve the problem, but he knew the answer was there. So did Aurobindo. That day, talking to the physicist he quoted some lines from the Swetaswatara Upanishad, *"Thou art man and woman, boy and girl, old and worn thou walkest bent over a staff; thou art the blue bird and the green and the scarlet-eyed."* The world is made of a single substance. Just another way of putting it. Science can be a matter of language.'

The car had arrived and the Ashramites were climbing in, beckoning to Gita. Charlotte glanced at Mr Chetty. 'But how did you two meet again?'

'It was February, and like today, some of us from the Ashram came to Auroville for the birthday celebration.' And there in the amphitheatre, supervising the children at the bonfire, Gita saw Arjuna Chetty again.

'My dear old friend. So wonderful to think we have been reunited after all those years, hmm?'

He smiled, shaking his head. 'Divine pattern.'

Oriane, at midnight, finds she cannot sleep. She takes refuge, as she does so often, in the distant past. It comforts her to slow the wheel of time, to live the long journey of a letter from Paris to Pondi; to follow the laborious course between an order and its execution. To study her father's portrait taken with a visiting prince. To read a report from a botanical journal on a new variety of lily, *Lilium Oriane*, fragrant and hardy, of unusual colouring: ivory marked with blue. She finds it amusing that Thierry, who had moved in high circles and enjoyed moments of glory, had achieved immortality in a small blue flower, while she might be remembered as a striped lily she had never cared for.

This, then, is her archive. There was much more, once, but she cast what she designated as clutter into the flames. Leather-bound books and things in frames had survived. She wanders like a wraith, placing her stick with care so that no tapping disturbs the silence.

The bracket clock in the dining room chimes the hour. One o'clock. February is always a bad time for her: too many memories. Too many echoes. She goes back to bed. In that halfway-country where dreams and reality meet she sees her life in moments, a series of possibilities slipping out of reach as the clock ticks.

The night is warm and she switches on the overhead fan. It squeaks in protest as always, and as always she remembers it should be seen to.

Chapter 31

'Special day tomorrow for the Ashram,' Mr Chetty had said. 'Golden day, 29th Feb. Not to be missed.' Charlotte was there by eight o'clock. She was not among the first – some had arrived before dawn, determined to occupy a privileged position for the mass meditation.

The courtyard was half-full, people – most clad in white – sitting in neat rows, cross-legged, quiet. Beneath the neem tree a vast awning of blue cloth stretched from one side to the other to shelter the pilgrims from the sun that was already visible above the rooftops. As time passed the courtyard filled up, people were moved closer together, the air grew warm, then thick with heat. Charlotte felt her pores expand; her hair grew lank with sweat, between her bare toes the skin was damp and slippery.

Behind her, a Bengali family whispered to one another: 'Already we have one thousand people in courtyard, altogether five thousand overflow in street. Uncle is late, he will be placed elsewhere, no doubt in the street.'

'Impossible! You must fetch him in.'

'Out of question! There is no room!'

Supervising Ashramites attempted to winkle out under fourteens ('not allowed in courtyard,' muttered the Bengali source of information). Next to them were two very small boys. 'How old?' the Ashramite demanded, pointing to the fiirst. 'Fourteen! Fourteen!' cried the father vehemently, and closed his eyes.

Charlotte glanced at her watch: 8.25. She sat, trying to empty her mind, to rise above her bodily sensations. She counted backwards, silently repeated '*Om*'. After what seemed hours she looked at her watch again: 8.29. An old woman two rows in front had fallen asleep and was snoring steadily. A man nearby broke wind. A well-fleshed matron energetically fanned herself.

Slowly the clock inched forward. Outside the walls rickshaw bells, the sounds of children's voices, calls, mingled and blurred. Within, murmurs, and soft padding of bare feet on the ground. At last an ancient Ashramite appeared on a rooftop. A silent countdown to zero-hour, then he banged a cymbal with a soft hammer three times.

Now true silence descended. Stillness. Even the birds were silenced. The world hung unmoving. Charlotte waited for the great peace to descend on her also, but she remained dispiritingly earthbound. Too many people, too close: she sensed their breathing, the tiny movements of their muscles, felt the heartbeat all around her, their blood pumping, the cells multiplying and dying: the pullulation of atoms which they all shared: *man and woman, boy and girl, Thou art the blue bird and the green and the scarlet-eyed* ... they were indeed all of the same substance, the place was swarming like an anthill.

The courtyard had filled to bursting point and even beneath the blue awning the heat was oven-like. She longed for a cooling breeze; the sea-breeze that blew in off the bay on to the Promenade. Concentration could achieve anything, they said. She concentrated. She held the sea-breeze in her thoughts, imprisoned it. In her mind she stood on the shore, stretching out her hands over the ocean, her arms melting, becoming sea and sky and wind. She skimmed the foam like a bird, surged with the waves, and then she drew back, drawing the wind, pulling it towards her, pulling – and into the courtyard came a breath of air, wafting across the open space, touching her face with cool fingers washing over her like water. She raised her face to the sky, drained of energy, as though after an enormous physical effort. She felt refreshed, renewed – as if some unadmitted pain within her had been eased.

Chapter 32

The beach lay on a long, curving bay, the sand stretching pale gold from the wall of palm trees down to the water-line, with an occasional catamaran hauled up, drying out in the sun while its owner mended his nets. But this was no paddling seaside place, this was the Bay of Bengal and the breakers came rolling in, taller than a man, curling, curving, exploding on to the sand with a force that sent spray yards into the air. The sea roared softly in its throat like a brooding lion, and Charlotte hovered nervously at its edge. Raymond stood beside her, a dark brown, hard-muscled figure, a scrap of black cloth at the groin the only cover to his nakedness. His curly grey hair and beard sparkling with sea-spray, he looked like a sea god, poised to plunge. Together they waited till a wave paused, quieter, as though drawing breath between the big surges. 'Now,' he said, and they dived through the breaker to the water beyond. He vanished beneath the surface and brought up a shell, dived again, supple as a dolphin, while she hung suspended, weightless, rising and falling in the swell, carried like a cockleshell on the blue-green back of the ocean. Nearby, Dolly and Kwesi, a young Ghanaian, kicked and splashed, laughing.

One or two couples and families were still dotted about on the sand, but the beach was almost empty now, a landscape striped in blue and green and pale yellow. Earlier the breeze had been strong, whipping the palm leaves so that they seemed to be waving and beckoning from across the sand. Gradually the sea grew calmer, and Charlotte wandered out into water milky as jade, and wallowed, as she had seen buffaloes doing, letting the gentle rollers break against her legs and wash over her.

She turned and watched them, Raymond and Dolly throwing a ball to each other, bodies graceful and relaxed. Freeze-frame, Charlotte instructed, and imagined them stilled, held in some emblematic pose. Judith could have worked on the picture, giving them highlights and haloes as befitted their status. Wet from the sea, Dolly's body glittered like a jet bead, her hair sculpted to her head. Raymond was all bronze and gold. I wonder, Charlotte reflected, if Raymond finds me dull? I am, of course, rather a dull person. Not everyone can be a star. She rubbed the smooth whorl of the shell he had brought up from the sand and handed to her. 'Does it have a name?' she had asked, and he said, yes indeed, *Architectonica Perspectiva* – truly. Very common around here!' and roared with laughter. The others waved to her from the beach and she waded up to join them.

February slipped into March and the temperature rose day by day. Charlotte was left much to herself, that was the way here. No one had time to play tour-guide, and she was grateful for that. She did T'ai Chi under the trees, slipped into the Ashram physiotherapy department for an occasional treatment. As she got to know Auroville better, she relished the many signs of life reclaimed, the sheltering trees, the foaming bougainvillaea, orange, purple, white; the brave attempts at lawns, hedges, flower beds, the fruit trees and blossom. Everywhere growing things pushed their way through the rosy soil, and she heard Guru's voice reciting the line that Oriane protested she would never be able to pronounce correctly – 'Annihilating all that's made to a green thought in a green shade' ... She found the place increasingly beautiful, and said so in her postcards home.

Judith spread out the scribbled pasteboard rectangles and studied the neatly written notes with a surge of resentment. Motherhood had a lot to answer for, cutting you off from risk, spontaneity, egotism, as you use up your energy on behalf of someone else. You postpone the daring and the dangerous, fulfil your responsibilities. But one day you find excitement is no longer on offer. You have taken a different road.

And now her daughter was sending postcards home from a place Judith recalled as a burnt, bleak desert, and describing a sort of Eden. Looking back was a waste of time, she always told herself, but today she was incapable of taking her own advice. Auroville hung in her mind like a mirage, the real, remembered Auroville blending weirdly with the place that came alive on these all too vivid postcards. It was a place where things grew. But also where things could be destroyed.

Chapter 33

They took the old sea road to Madras. Badly pot-holed,
longer than the inland route, it retained a tinge of romance, it
looked the way an Indian road should, following the curve of
the land, tree-shaded, drawn into the life of the villages it ran
through, the frail tarmac strewn with sheaves of corn so that
the wheels of passing vehicles could act as a form of threshing
machine, the village women and children unhurriedly gathering up the loose grain in the pause between cars.

Raymond, driving the jeep, was faithful to it: 'Who wants
to go the soulless way? Why? To save a few kilometres?'
They bumped and bucketed their way along, Charlotte
protected by human cushioning: Dolly on her left, Arjuna
Chetty on her right, murmuring an apology every time he
swayed against her. He occupied less than his fair share of the
seat, and even so, Charlotte had the impression he was
squeezing his buttocks tight in order to take up less room.
Next to Raymond sat one of the Vestals. They were hoping
that Raymond would build them a *'bella casa'* and enable
them to withdraw from the turmoil of life in Milan. The
young Ghanaian architect, Kwesi, talked intensely of quan-
tity surveys, water drilling and electricity cables.

Though this stretch of the road was new to Charlotte,
everything seemed familiar – the small bazaars, the families
living in drains or on the bare earth, the pumps where people
washed and filled their pots, the roadside weavers with the

taut hammock of cotton that lengthened beneath their shuttles.

The feathery trees cast shadows; not the dark, cool shade she knew at home, more a dimming of brilliance within the glare of the encircling sun so that the shadows themselves were filled with reflected light, casting a glow into the faces of villagers resting on the wooden beds they had dragged outdoors.

Raymond pointed to a tall tree and called back over his shoulder, 'Did you see the birds of Paradise, Lottie? The females are discreet, but the males! Such colours! Hundreds of years ago, in New Guinea, the natives sold the birds with the so-brilliant feathers to traders after they had dried them over the fire. But for convenience of storage they cut the feet off the corpses. And one day a respectable scientist announced that he had concluded from a study of the birds of many colours that they had no legs and flew continuously in the skies, existing only on ambrosia, the food of Paradise . . .' He laughed. 'Legends can be built on a foundation of misconception. We can never be sure of understanding the past. *N'est-ce pas* Lottie?'

She gave him a quick look but he was gazing serenely ahead. Without any perceptible change of tone, he shifted gear and added, conversationally, 'So you know, when things go wrong between nations – or between people – it is not easy, later, to explain why. Because things happen in the present but are explained in terms of how we recall the past.'

This was his way, this eliptical style. Surrounded by people he could throw out clues, juggle with situations he seemed incapable of facing head-on. She felt uncomfortable, wondering what the others might be making of the conversation, but each of them drew conclusions of their own, chiming with their own preoccupations. The Vestal drew Raymond's attention to an outcrop of stone by the shore that might have been a prehistoric monolith, but which he assured her was the remains of a Pallava temple; Dolly suggested sharply that Raymond would do better to concentrate on the road, now that they were approaching Madras; and Arjuna Chetty, deep in thought, possibly lost in his own rereadings of the past, said nothing.

They drove through the city, the bustle of crowded pavements spilling into the street, worsening the traffic jams. Drivers shouted abuse, trucks blared *fiilmi* music, cars hooted, cyclists and rickshaws pinged their bells. The jeep was held up at a big roundabout by a march, a demonstration with people waving placards, others carrying banners. Raymond swung off and threaded his way through quieter side-streets till he found a place to park. He had building equipment to pick up, Dolly had a list of artists' materials needed by the Auroville architectural office, Mr Chetty had come – he said – to visit an agricultural research centre, but Charlotte suspected that his real purpose for the journey was to act as her guide to the museum: 'Unsurpassed collection of bronze Natarajas, and a most curious Christ standing on a lotus blossom in the cathedral. I would say unique.'

As they reached the main road they had once more to skirt the marchers – there were now two, or possibly three, demonstrations in progress because the banners seemed to cancel each other out, 'Tamil Nadu – Yes!' 'Hindu India with BJP', 'Urdu Speakers Shout Back!' (sadly, depending on English for its impact). A crimson banner demanded equality for *Dalits*, Untouchables, more militant now, once more trying to escape from the bonds of caste. Chanting and some scuffling broke out and the crowd surged, separating Charlotte from her companions. There were angry voices all around her but she felt unafraid. These people were expressing their anger or their frustration at official attitudes; she was not endangered by the violence of their feelings. She caught sight of Mr Chetty wriggling his way back to her side through the crowd and waved at him.

'You will be needing something to drink after the long drive,' he said with unexpected firmness. Charlotte began to disagree, but it was hard to make herself heard above the noise.

'Here is a place,' he said. 'Please go in and order some *lassi*, cool yoghourt, I must find Dolly.' He was sucked back into the throng.

The explosion shattered the windows of the little tea-room. The blast of hot air slammed her against the wall, then the panic-stricken flight of the other customers took her with it, so that she was carried out of the door and down the street, like a swimmer caught up in the powerful surge of breakers in the Bay. Like an undertow, the pull of the crowd sucked her off her feet and she struggled frantically to keep her head above the tide of bodies, scrabbling for a grip on the ground. The dust from the explosion filled the air and she too panicked. She realised that her last glimpse of Dolly had been on the pavement quite near the explosion. To have found someone, only to have them obliterated seemed too cruel a joke to be possible. She screamed out Dolly's name, but her voice was drowned in the cacophony around her.

She found herself thrust against the wall of a building and bracing herself against it, kicked off to fight her way back through the crowd, deafened by screams and shouted exhortations. Then she was through, held back only by a sparse line of *lathi* wielding police. Several people had been cut by flying glass; they squatted, some crying, picking fragments of glass from their skin and clothing, fingers bleeding, one – a small child – wailing in fear, searching for his mother.

One person had caught the full force of the blast. Lying sprawled, huddled into the angle between the pavement and a shattered shop-front as though hurled by an angry hand, was Mr Chetty, his body looking small and unprotected in his threadbare suit, usually so neat, now torn and thick with dust. Someone had thrown a thin coat over him and a dark stain was seeping through the cloth. Charlotte struggled past a policeman, crying out, 'I know him, he's a friend!' The jostling and whistle-blowing and noise filled the air above her head as she knelt by his side.

'Ambulance is needed!' someone called frantically, adding, in a sort of groan, 'Those bloody fanatics!' Arjuna Chetty seemed boneless, flattened into the pavement, his face twisted, in pain or fear, she was unsure which, his eyes closed tightly. A voice called 'Not to be touched! Injuries are very bad.' Beneath the light coat Mr Chetty's modest supply of blood flowed from him, soaking the pavement, darkening the greyish mud to vermilion. His eyelids twitched and his eyes opened, cautiously. He looked bewildered, frightened, his gaze blank. Then he focused on Charlotte's face, close beside him, and tried to speak.

She looked up at the ring of faces clustered round them, and the moaning, weeping people nearby, at a policeman: 'Where's the *ambulance*, for God's sake!'

'Ambulance?' Mr Chetty muttered. 'For me?'

'Yes.'

'Oh dear.' He seemed to have no spare breath, and lay gasping for a moment. 'What has occurred?'

'I think it was a bomb, Mr Chetty.'

'Are many people injured?'

'No. Just . . .'

'Just myself?' He breathed with difficulty. 'Quite a small bomb then.'

His face seemed to grow smaller as his eyes closed again.

The ambulance could be heard before it arrived, siren screaming, the crowd scattering before it. There was a crash of metal doors, high-pitched voices shouting questions in competition with one another. 'Oh God,' exclaimed the shopkeeper with resignation, 'it's the usual bloody muddle and panic.' Charlotte was still kneeling beside Mr Chetty when the ambulance men pushed aside the onlookers and reached the pavement. She became aware that sharp grit had pressed deep into her knees – it was like kneeling on drawing pins.

She got to her feet, stumbling, reaching for the wall to save herself from falling on to Mr Chetty, but she saw that he was no longer with them, had quietly gone on his way leaving his outworn body to be lifted joltingly on to a stretcher and shoved into the ambulance, to be disposed of.

They had left his briefcase behind and Charlotte picked it up, brushing off the dust, hugging it close. The briefcase, blood-stained and lacerated by the explosion, was now beyond use, its flap wrenched away from the stitched seams.

She caught sight of Raymond through the crowd, hurrying towards her, pulling Dolly with him. The dark red dust where Mr Chetty had lain was already beginning to dry out, the stain losing its intensity. A stray dog, sidling through the crowd, paused, sniffed the dust and lifted his leg. The stream of urine hit the wall and cascaded in a spray across the pavement, so that the blood came up fresh. The shopkeeper caught sight of the stray and aimed a kick at it. 'Bloody pi-dogs! No respect!' He spat on to the now patchily stained pavement and began to attend to his broken window.

At the house on the corner of the rue Laval Oriane studied a Madras newspaper account of a political demonstration. 'BOMB BLASTS CITY STREET. ONE FATALITY'. It was a brief account, mentioning the name of the victim, the circumstances of the explosion. Political unrest was cited, sectarian violence.

'Guru,' she called. Then she remembered that he was not there.

Chapter 34

The post office in Pondi was moderately busy. From every side came a hubbub of voices; people jostled, frustrated customers called out peremptorily or waited, cowed, depending on their perceived status. Paperwork was completed in triplicate with minute attention to every detail. Clerks sat gazing at forms as though facing complicated algebraic equations. At last Charlotte reached the crucial position at the head of the undisciplined crowd at the counter, caught the appropriate eye and pushed forward her scrap of paper. The clerk glanced at the scrawled number –

'International? Next counter.'

When the telephone trilled and the clerk gestured towards an empty booth, Charlotte had almost given up the idea of reaching Judith. She closed the door of the booth and picked up the phone.

'Hullo? Ma?'

'Aah . . . mmm.'

Judith's voice was muffled by the poor line. The words themselves sounded hampered.

'Ma? Are you all right?'

Blurred phrases clustered by her ear, bees hovering at the mouth of a flower, trying to get in but somehow missing the way.

Buzz-buzz-mmm–mmm-

Through a lull in the static, a few words slid across the seas and the hours that divided them.

'How's Auroville?'

'Well I was thinking of staying on, for a bit.'

A pause.

'Won't that be a problem? The office . . .'

'I might chuck it in.' A joke seemed called for: 'I could learn to love my amoebic infestation just like everyone else.'

In the watery light of the basement Judith experiences a sinking of the heart. It was all she had feared. Charlotte had fallen under the spell. She would be reclaimed by the demon father with his amber eyes and his beautiful hands and vanish for ever into the faery kingdom –

'So what d'you think?'

'Um . . .'

'Ma?'

'I'm here.'

'Are you okay? You sound funny.'

'Oh, well, I slipped on the area steps coming back from a dinner party, bounced all the way down on my bum, wrenched my shoulder, but I'm fine.'

'Listen, it was just a thought. Not really serious. I'll come home –'

'You mustn't change your plans for me –'

'Why not? I'll come home.' Pause. 'If you'd like me to. If you need me.'

This was cruel, putting Judith on the spot. Forcing her to admit to something that was foreign to her. She might be incapable of it. And then again –

This is a turning point, Charlotte thought, suddenly breathless, as though a cold hand squeezed her lungs. What shall it be? Speak, Judith. I'm holding the balance, we don't weigh a heart against a feather like the ancient Egyptians on the day of judgment, but I could put both our lives in one basket and weigh them against a word that says –

'Well I could use a little help fastening my bra . . .'

This was the old escape route of flippancy, the stylised duet that passed for confessional without ever baring breast or soul. She skewered her mother with the question direct: 'Do you need me? Do you want me to come home?'

Sweat trickled down Charlotte's neck. Outside the smeared glass walls of the booth people waited, staring in at her without embarrassment. She stared back, used now to the Indian way. A small child pressed his nose to the glass, eyes round and interested. She pulled a funny face and grinned down at him. His mouth curved in pleasure. On the cement floor were old scraps of paper, torn and grubby, the remaining evidence of once-urgent links forged, severed and forgotten.

In her basement Judith shifts gingerly, her sacroiliac sending jabbing messages of pain. The day long past when she and Raymond had spoken for the last time, the same question had hovered, like the echo of a cry, between them. She had written, asking him to get in touch, specifying a time. In the droopy sweater and long skirt she wore all that winter, she stood, telephone cradled in one hand, infant in the other, and told Raymond she was not coming back. Say you need me, she had willed him to admit, say you want me to come back, give me some reason to change my mind. But Raymond had said only that he would miss her and maybe she would return when she was stronger.

She had grown stronger, strong enough to cope alone, but never strong enough to go back. Say you need me, she had wanted to scream down the crackling wire, but she had not and he had not. Always she had replayed that scene as Raymond not saying he needed her, but now she remembered also that she had not asked him. And now Charlotte was waiting for her to speak. Did she want Charlotte to come home?

'Yes,' Judith said, and began to cry.

Dusk deepened and the lights blinked on along the Promenade. The soft darkness blurred the details so that passers-by could no longer see the palm-thatch hut nestling in the courtyard of a once-elegant French house, nor its cracked façade, broken balustrading and flaking stucco. In the blue of the night flaws were hidden and what remained were pale, graceful buildings overlooking the sea, palm trees dark against their pallor.

Earlier Charlotte had said goodbye to Gita, in her cramped cell. Arjuna Chetty was with them in spirit – and in substance, because Charlotte had brought his briefcase.

'I thought you might like to have it.'

'The awful briefcase. He hated it, you know. That ghastly mother of his foisted it on him. She was a complete snob; I think she felt that with the briefcase he at least looked like the professional man she had hoped he would be. That's why he always wore the suit. He carted this object about everywhere, it was utterly impractical, he had nothing to put in it most of the time, it weighed a ton, but he'd promised her he would keep it and so he did. Thank you. Yes, I'd like it. Poor Arjuna, he had a perhaps disproportionate sense of duty to his parents. Refusing to bring in a dowry was his one rebellion.' There was a pause. She added, 'And Auroville, of course.'

'I know someone,' Charlotte said, 'who holds the view that Utopias never work. He said Auroville, like all the other attempts, will wind down through loss of energy.'

'You've been talking to old Guruvappa,' Gita said, 'he's always banging on about entropy. No, what I fear more is that it will change its nature, become too . . . popular. One doesn't want it becoming a sort of Club Meditation holiday centre, people popping in to taste the idealism *en passant* and "time permitting" as the brochures put it, take a quick look at the crystal before moving on. We can only hope the spirit survives, hmm?'

It was time for Charlotte to leave. 'Farewell dinner with my father and sister at the Alliance Française.' She looked across the little cement-walled room to the portraits of Aurobindo and the Mother flanked by the marigold garland. 'Gita, don't you find all this rather ... odd? The iconography, the mystical mumbo-jumbo?'

'Dear Charlotte. *Iconography*? Every Catholic church a Marian shrine, every altar a crucifixion! Mystical mumbo-jumbo? You can accept a Virgin birth, resurrection after three days, water into wine, the whole Son-of-Godness stuff, and then you balk at the mere suggestion of divinity here. Isn't that a bit like swallowing a camel and straining at a gnat, to quote one of your chaps? Shall we agree to be tolerant in our mutual scepticisms?'

Charlotte was walking away from her when she called out, 'Incidentally. How's your neck?'

Charlotte rotated her head cautiously. 'Better! Fantastic physiotherapy.'

'A rose by any other name,' Gita said drily, and turned back, into the house.

The lights in their frosted globes defined the curve of the Promenade. Gandhi's statue stared over the trees and houses to the faint glimmer of pink that lingered in the western sky. Behind him the sea was inky, quiet tonight, with just a soothing rush and swirl from the rocks below.

Inland from the sea-front the street-dwellers were preparing briskly for the night, setting up cooking pots on the cracked pavement, laying out mats or sheets for sleeping. The children, lustrous eyed, their hair a curly tangle, watched the passers-by incuriously, bare feet dusty, a snail-track gleam trickling from nostril to upper lip. No one begged.

The Alliance Française, like the Ashram, lay behind high walls, but there the resemblance ended: at the Alliance there were lights in the trees and the sounds of voices, laughter and music. There was bustle and – floating in the air from thirty yards away – that quintessentially French smell, the combination of sizzling butter, fresh-baked bread and garlic; the subtle fragrance that went with *escargots* or mussels, the wine-rich scent of *coq-au-vin*. Here France still set the standard; Merger might never have happened.

It was a lively, noisy dinner party, Raymond had brought half Auroville with him. 'Were you expecting a crowd?' Dolly murmured. 'Well you got one.' She wore a dress tonight, an Auroville creation, full-skirted, in blue-green cotton delicate as silk.

'Will you write to me?' Charlotte asked.

'Why not?'

'And post the letters?'

Shall we meet again? She wanted to ask, but hesitated to presume. '*Bien sûr*,' Dolly said. And added, 'We may even meet. Miracles can happen.'

They were on the roof-terrace with the scent of jasmine drifting in the air, mingling with the smell of grilling meat from the barbecue. The stars hung above them and the lights in the trees below were like reflections on dark water. Understanding the past is always hard, Raymond had said that day in the jeep. He was wearing jeans and a faded blue shirt tonight, the only time she had seen him out of Indian clothes. He looked younger, unexpectedly glamorous, and she felt, for the first time, something of the physical pull he must have exerted over Judith, all those years ago.

He shook her arm gently, 'Lottie, you are dreaming. Come, I will show you something.' He led her inside, through the dining room and opened the door to a small chamber with paintings on the walls. One of them – a tiny sketch – was, he said, by Braque. It showed the entrance to a Parisian house; at the bottom was scribbled, in French, 'Anticipated Memories'.

'There is a nice story,' Raymond said. 'One day when both

men were young, Braque paid a visit to Picasso in Mont-martre, but Picasso was out, so Braque left a little message for him – a card on which he scribbled the words 'Anticipated Memories'. It is an interesting idea, don't you think, the memories we cling to of events that did not take place. It goes in the archives of our minds with the monuments cities are famous for, but which no longer exist ... the Pharos at Alexandria, the Colossus of Rhodes, the labyrinth at Knossos – though that may never have existed, as such. I think of meetings in the same way, meetings which never took place, *tu comprends*, but which we remember as if they had. One can imagine what they would have covered or uncovered, in an ideal world. But sometimes we can anticipate too much, reality cannot match the expectation, my dear.' The smile lit up his face, offering warmth, intimacy. But she saw now that the smile, like a *trompe-l'oeil* doorway painted on a stone wall, led nowhere. He put an arm round her shoulders and hugged her gently, 'Disappointment is part of the pattern, *ma chère*.'

She remembered Judith using almost the same words, when they had talked of Charlotte's quest, tracking down the absent father. Raymond added, 'But you know, disappointment is entirely subjective. It doesn't change the event or person that caused it. They remain exactly what they always were.'

'And you never feel guilty.'

He shook his head. 'Not any more. Long ago I faced the reality about myself. How other people feel about me depends on whether they can accept that reality. I am not concerned with trying to live up to other people's ideas of what I ought to be. I am. I do what I do. You have the same freedom.'

Knowing she sounded naive, even petulant, Charlotte said, 'I can't work out whether you're a good man or a bad one.'

'Why should you, when I can be both. Isn't that more interesting?'

'Maybe,' she said, 'but I wouldn't want to live with you.'

He laughed, delighted, 'Ah! You are learning,' and led her back to the roof-terrace.

Chapter 35

She had intended to call in at the Hotel de France on several occasions, but either she had been short of time or she had simply forgotten. It came to the last day and she knew she could not leave Pondi without saying goodbye.

When the taxi pulled up at the wrought-iron gate, Charlotte saw with shock that some cataclysm had struck: a bomb – bigger this time – had devastated the hotel. Then she realised that the chaos was of a different nature: building work was in progress. Walls had been knocked down, others were being constructed; the house was changing its shape. A labourer thoughtfully balanced a brick in his hand, another was studying a half-demolished wall. 'Under new ownership' announced a colourful board at the gate.

At the far end of the drive she saw a familiar figure, waving his arms impatiently at a worker, giving orders. It was Jamal from the Motor Cycle Centre. She went towards him and he looked round, frowning irritably. Then he recognised her.

'No more mopeds! I'm now in hotel business.'

She looked about for signs of Oriane or Guru.

'Where is the owner –'

'Owning group is LHC – Lovely Hotel Consortium. You are thinking possibly of *former* owner, Mr Guruvappa –'

'Mr Guruvappa owned the hotel?'

'Indubitably.'

'Since when?'

'Since – oh, many years.'

Of course. So much made sense now: Guru's long-suffering, amused patience; Oriane's overdone tantrums. Other people's designs for living that can seem so mysterious, are simple when read correctly.

'And is Mr Guruvappa here?'

'No longer.' He had, it seemed, suddenly sold up and retired to his country property. 'Address not known to me personally.'

'And where is Madame de l'Esprit?' she asked. He looked blank. Charlotte felt a momentary shock. Do we vanish so fast? Leave so little trace?

'The French lady who ran the hotel.'

Jamal shrugged. 'Evidently she too has retired.'

The deep verandah where Oriane had played César Franck and Fauré was to be the coffee-shop. Of garlic there was not a trace. The name too had vanished. No more Grand Hotel de France. Even the setting was transformed, no longer the rue Laval. The Pondi Beach Resort, Laval Street, Jamal told her, flourishing a bunch of leaflets, would be open for reservations next season.

'Was it necessary to rename the street?'

'Not my doing personally, of course. Government decision. Logical. About time.'

The annexe, he said would triple their bed capacity. 'Every room with air con.' Next door's compound was under negotiation. 'Package tours will be catered for and coach trips to surrounding temple towns. In due course, swimming pool. Plans are underfoot.'

Pre-packed Pondi for the mass tourism market? Top Ten Temple videos on sale in the hotel shop? Was that to be its fate?

The broken fountain had gone, the garden drowned in a sea of rubble. The *hotel particulier* that had stood on this spot for centuries would be subsumed by its latest avatar. The

Hotel de France would be engulfed by its annexe. Just as the fountain had replaced the impractical ornamental pond with its vulnerable goldfish, so the fountain had in turn outlived its usefulness. No one wanted to trail their fingers in the rippling water. Now sun-bronzed bodies would splash and dive in the bright blue, chlorinated fun-pool.

Jamal was proud of the new premises. Walk around, he suggested, make yourself at home. 'Extension will be modern,' he said, 'with roof garden. Terrace. Guests can see the ocean.'

Yes, Charlotte thought, a good idea, and they will feel the wind that blows from the sea. But will any of them, on a hot, airless day, be able to stretch out their arms and melt into the sea and sky, draw the wind from across the waves, bathe in its cool, refreshing current . . . ?

Jamal began to explain to her about building an inner courtyard linking the two buildings, a living space, a room open to the sky, and suddenly a familiar phrase hit Charlotte and she realised that she was hearing Raymond's words quoted, that it was Raymond who was in charge of the reconstruction. Somehow it seemed the perfect irony that he should be the one to obliterate the house in the rue Laval – though he would put it differently of course: he was safeguarding its next metamorphosis, assisting at its rebirth – that was appropriate, surely?

Charlotte wandered down the corridor towards the kitchens, stepping over bits of broken brick, avoiding the electric cables snaking across the floors. 'In due course,' Jamal called, 'telephone will be installed.'

At the end of the corridor she paused at a half-open door: this had been Guru's room, the quiet cell he retired to, with his books. The room was stripped of its furniture, but a built-in cupboard remained, doors half-wrenched off their hinges by some impatient worker. Charlotte saw scraps of paper, a folded sheet of newsprint carrying a report of some momentous event, now forgotten. She peered more closely and noticed a pale square of card trapped by a nail at the back. She reached in and slid it free.

It was a photograph, a snapshot, that showed the two of them, Oriane and Guru, taken by the gates of the hotel on some long-gone day of celebration.

Charlotte slipped the photograph into her handbag and went back down the drive. Coming towards her she saw another familiar figure: Subra. He too looked different, his clothes more stylish, an air about him of responsibility, quite the elder statesman. He greeted her, smiling. 'Good day madame. What you think?'

'I think it looks very impressive.'

'I think so also. And I shall be manager here, with my son.'

'Congratulations!' She paused, abandoned discretion and plunged. 'Subra: Madame de l'Esprit and Mr Guruvappa, where have they gone?'

Behind them there was the crack of breaking glass and a window crashed noisily to the ground. Dusty air swirled from the gaping window frame as though freed from an imprisoning space.

'It is a shady place with many trees,' Subra said. 'Very peaceful.'

The little pavilion had been restored. Its frontage shaded by high-spreading branches, it was cool and airy. Below it, surrounded by neem trees, the lake glowed like a vast crystal at the centre of the hollow. On the other bank, the columbines that Thierry had dug up and taken to the rue Laval wavered like bright blue flames licking the ruined temple walls. Oriane sat on the steps, as she had done on her first visit, her feet stirring fallen leaves.

'Something of us goes into the trees we live among,'

Raymond had said once, as he dug and planted. 'And something of the trees enters us – if we allow.'

Oriane narrowed her opal eyes and glanced up at the branches, moving above her in a light breeze. 'Shall we wear leaves and put down roots here, Guru? Shall we become a part of the place, grow into a couple of small, unimpressive trees?'

'A pagan thought,' Guru said, 'but why not? You always did hedge your bets.'

'All I have to lose is my doubt,' she mocked him.

And, playing the old game, he said, 'Quite so. Remember Browning.'

'I *refuse* to remember an Englishman at the end of my life!' she croaked, adding with a ghost of her old malice, 'But *après tout*, Browning was *very* un-English.'

'And *après tout*, you aren't quite at the end of your life.'

She twitched a shoulder. 'Boff,' she said.

The driver had gone for a drink of water and Charlotte sat in the car alone for a moment. She glanced at the wrought-iron gates, one slightly damaged now. Down the drive, rising from rubble as Pondi had risen in the past, the house on the corner of the rue Laval was renewing itself again. The glassed-in verandah caught the sunlight, blinding her so that for a moment she seemed to see two figures standing there by the gate. Then the driver jumped in, slamming the door, and she saw that two turbanned workmen were loping towards the house, burdened with bricks.

'Madras airport?' he checked. 'Okay to go?'

As the car headed into the traffic she took out the photograph and looked at it again.

Oriane wore a print frock, the thin cotton material wrapped tight against her by a breeze, revealing a body whose slenderness of hip and shoulder was edging into angularity. Her hair, shoulder-length and unruly, was whipped by the breeze, blown across her face. Behind the dark strands her eyes gleam, as if through a silken mask. She has just raised her hand to brush back the hair, free her mouth, and she is laughing in surprised delight.

Guru, in white cotton kurta-pyjamas is at her side, standing slightly behind her. Amused by something or someone unseen, he bends forward to catch her eye, leaning towards her, his head half-turned, as she glances sideways at him, both of them caught in a moment of complicity, sharing an eternal joke.

Across the years Charlotte could hear their laughter.

ACKNOWLEDGEMENTS

Auroville and the Sri Aurobindo Ashram in Pondicherry are real places. The Grand Hotel de France exists, alas, only inside my head and on the page. There are real people who come and go in the book – Aurobindo himself, the Mother, Paul Richard, Governor Dupleix, his wife Jeanne, Napoleon, General Decaen and Ananda Ranga Pillai, whose extraordinary diary provided me with a wealth of detail about life in eighteenth-century Pondicherry. Historical personages apart, the people whose stories are told in this book are fictitious, and no resemblance to persons living or dead is intended.

I have tried to the best of my ability to give an accurate picture of historical events. However, where fictional characters are introduced, I have felt free to embroider the bald facts.

I have had the privilege of visiting the Ashram on several occasions, and have stayed in Auroville – though not in *Arcadie*, which I invented. I am grateful to my friends in Auroville for welcoming me into the community on the plateau, which struggles on against such odds, though now financially assisted by the Indian Government, and to Ashramite friends for their kindness on my visits.

The Private Diary of Ananda Ranga Pillai, written between 1736–1761, translated from the Tamil, and printed by the Madras Government Press in 1928 in 12 volumes, stayed with me, thanks to the benign lending policy of the London Library, through much of the writing of this book. I also read many of Aurobindo's works, as well as books about him by others, notably *Sri Aurobindo or the Adventure of Consciousness* by Satprem, published by the Institute for Evolutionary Research, New York, and a biography, *Sri Aurobindo*, by Jesse Roarke, published and printed by the Sri Aurobindo Ashram Press, Pondicherry.